TALES FROM THE DARK LANDS

By the same author

A Quiver of Ghosts
Tales from the Other Side
Tales from Beyond
Tales of Darkness
The Partaker
The Fantastic World of Kamtellar
The Brats
The Cradle Demon

TALES FROM THE DARK LANDS

R. Chetwynd-Hayes

WILLIAM KIMBER · LONDON

First published in 1984 by
WILLIAM KIMBER & CO. LIMITED
100 Jermyn Street, London SW1Y 6EE

ISBN 0 7183 0535 3

Photoset in North Wales by
Derek Doyle & Associates Mold, Clwyd
and printed in Great Britain by
Biddles Limited, Guildford, Surrey

Contents

Author's Note

'Something Comes In From The Garden' and 'The Man Who Stayed Behind' were first published in my collection *Night Ghouls* published by Fontana Books in 1975.

R.C-H.

I

Mayfield

Of course the car broke down miles from anywhere and Miles Hamilton, who had not the slightest idea of what lay under the bonnet, swore, kicked one unoffending tyre, then surveyed the surrounding countryside. Flat fields divided by low hedges, a small wood some way to the left and cloud-capped hills in the distance. He looked back the way he had come – more or less the same, minus the hills. The last town he had passed through must be at least twenty miles away and he could not remember seeing a garage anywhere along the route.

Bearing in mind the excellent adage: Never go back – advance, he took the first step that tradition has it, is the beginning of a thousand mile journey.

He had walked for the best part of an hour when he came to the side road which was distinguished by a signpost; a single post affair with a tapered arm on the top that bore the inscription: 'Mayfield House'.

Three symbolic images flashed across Miles Hamilton's brain. A comfortable armchair, a teapot with attendant cup and saucer and a telephone. He turned left and trudged up an unpaved road, his eyes alert for Mayfield House, wondering if it would be manor, farm or merely an overgrown cottage.

In fact it turned out to be a not over-large structure, with six windows up and four down, with a massive porch dividing the frontage neatly in half, standing in the midst of an unkempt garden. Miles opened a gate, walked up a dandelion-flanked path and entered the porch, where – after some hesitation – he jerked an old-fashioned bell-pull. It had an iron skeleton handle attached to a length of black chain. Far away a bell clanged.

The door seemed to open with great reluctance; a moaning of oil-starved hinges, a shuddering of wooden panels, as though it had not been required to perform this service for a long time. A middle-aged man attired in a black cut-away jacket, matching trousers and a white cravat, cleared his throat and said:

'Miss Mayfield's residence, sir. Permit me in her name to welcome you to Mayfield House.'

This – together with the fellow's get-up – was so unexpected, Miles could only stammer: 'I've ... I've ... had a breakdown and ... '

The butler – what else could he be? – stood to one side. 'If you will kindly enter, sir, I will acquaint Miss Mayfield of your arrival.'

'Thank ... thank you very much.'

He entered a hall that had oak-panelled walls, was lit by stained-glass windows and looked not unlike a deserted church. The butler – indeed he must be – opened a door and bowed the visitor into a room that seemed to have an over-abundance of tables, with well-padded chairs chasing themselves round them for right of place. The personage performed another bow.

'If you will be so good as to wait here, sir.'

He shut the door and left Miles alone, deciding he must be causing a lot of trouble, merely for the use of a telephone and maybe a cup of tea thrown in. Chairs had been provided, with plenty to spare.

The room had a musty smell as though a fire had not been lit in the giant fireplace for many a long year; there were cobwebs festooning the ceiling and fluttering down over the numerous pictures that all but covered the four walls, depicting gentlemen in periwigs, bell-bottomed coats and flowing cloaks; ladies with exposed bosoms, bared shoulders and round simpering faces. All were inclined to be on the plump side, each bearing a remarkable resemblance to all the others, but Miles came to the conclusion he did not fancy any of them. He spoke aloud.

'Could do with a good clean out. Wonder why fancy pants doesn't get cracking with a feather duster and mop?'

The door opened and the personage reappeared.

'Miss Mayfield will receive you now, sir. If you would be so good as to follow me.'

Miles said: 'Right. Yes, thank you very much.'

He followed the plump, upright figure back into the hall, along a wide corridor, then stopped when they reached a solid-looking mahogany door with a cut-glass handle. The butler tapped gently on one panel, turned the glass handle and caused the door to slide back. His sonorous voice made utterance.

'The visitor, Miss Mayfield.'

This room had been most certainly well looked after, for the beautiful old carpet positively glistened, chairs and small tables did not harbour so much as a speck of dust and the ceiling resembled a snow-filled sky. An old lady who reclined on a chaise longue looked up as the visitor entered.

She could have been in her late sixties or early seventies; had white hair piled high on top of her narrow head and was attired in a long black dress. A pair of shrewd blue eyes surveyed Miles, while a harsh, cultivated voice spoke.

'Please forgive me for not rising, but I am forced to reserve my strength these days. But it is such a rare pleasure for us to receive a visitor, I do most warmly welcome you, sir.'

Miles was at a loss how to answer such a fulsome welcome, but he advanced with a bright smile and grabbed the raised wrinkled hand. He sensed this was being tendered for kissing, not shaking, so brushed his lips over the outstretched fingers.

'I only ... ' he began, but was not allowed to proceed further.

'Pray be seated. This chair near me, for advancing years has robbed me of that keen hearing which – I may now boast – was the pride of my youth.'

Miles sank into a chair that threatened to engulf him.

'Actually my car broke down and I wondered if you would be so kind as to allow me the use of your phone.'

The old lady screwed her face up into a grimace and banged one ear with a clenched fist. 'Great balls of fire! Worse than I thought. Every word you utter sounds like so much gibberish. But you young people have a language of your own nowadays. To say nothing of your clothes. But am I to assume that your carriage has gone off the road and you'd like some assistance in getting it to rights again? Clearly you have no servant in attendance.'

Miles thought – the old thing is round the bend – and decided to remain silent until inspiration supplied him with a suitable answer. Miss Mayfield frowned. 'You have neglected to inform me whom I have the honour of entertaining.'

'Sorry – Miles Hamilton.'

'Ah! Related to the Dorset Hamiltons, no doubt. I am Sarah Mayfield. Alas the last of the line. My niece, who will be here shortly, is my sister's child and bears the plebeian name of Benson. Her father was in trade. You will grant us the pleasure of your company for dinner?'

'You are very kind ... '

'That's settled then. If you would be so kind as to pull the bell cord, I'll give Meadows instructions.'

Finding the bell pull was a bit of a problem, until Miss Mayfield tut-tutted and pointed to a length of brocade complete with a blue tassle that hung by the fireplace. Meadows – the personage – appeared almost at once and received his instructions with something akin to disapproval.

'This gentleman will be staying for dinner,' Miss Mayfield stated. 'See that another place is laid.'

'Very good, ma'am.'

'And tell Miss Claudia I wish to see her at once. At once.'

'I will do so directly, ma'am.'

When the door had been closed she addressed Miles.

'Gals these days walk through life half-asleep. At once means an hour hence. When I was Claudia's age at once meant I came on the run, or my dear papa would want to know why.'

Miles wondered how his deserted car was faring, then remembered he had left the door unlocked and the keys in the ignition. If someone came along who knew more about engines than he did, it might be fifty miles away by now. But he was hungry and this bizarre situation did not lack entertainment value, so he sat still and assumed an attentive expression. Miss Mayfield made another tut-tut sound, followed by: 'Where on earth is that gal?' when the door opened and a vision walked into the room.

Glossy auburn hair framed a pale oval face, full red lips were slightly parted to reveal perfect teeth. A slender, but mature figure was draped in a long, blue velvet dress. But the lovely, large blue eyes were marred by a glaze that might have been due to boredom or a sullen disposition. Miles was in no mood to be critical; he rose and waited for Miss Mayfield to make an introduction.

'This,' the old lady stated, 'is my wayward, spoilt and generally speaking, ill-tempered niece, Claudia. Claudia – Mr Miles Hamilton – of the Dorset Hamiltons – who has had the misfortune to suffer a mishap with his carriage.'

Claudia sank into a little curtsey and said in a clear, low voice. 'I am honoured, sir.'

Without being completely certain as to what he was doing or saying, Miles bowed and said: 'Your humble servant, Miss Claudia.'

'Well, sit down, girl,' Miss Mayfield ordered. 'Do you want to keep the poor man on his feet all night?'

Claudia sank into a chair and looked so lovely and bored, Miles – a shy young man where beautiful women were concerned – found himself incapable of speech. Miss Mayfield suffered from no such impediment.

'How have you been occupying yourself, child? Wasting your time no doubt. Moon-struck. Staring out of the window, looking for the Prince Charming who never comes.'

To Miles' great joy the wayward beauty was looking at him with some interest. She spoke again in that low fascinating voice.

'I saw this young gentleman arrive. Why is he wearing those strange clothes?'

Miss Mayfield expelled her breath as a deep sigh. 'If I've told you once, I've told you a million times, do not make personal remarks. No doubt Mr Hamilton's costume is all the rage in London now.'

Miles looked down at his tweed sports jacket and grey trousers and wondered what was so extraordinary about them. 'Most men of my age are wearing them,' he admitted. 'But, if I may say so, your dress is something out of this world, Miss Claudia.'

'There,' Miss Mayfield said, 'you have had a compliment paid you, which is certainly more than you deserve. What have you to say?'

The girl smiled and a dimple appeared on either cheek.

'Thank you kindly, sir.'

'And that's the best you can expect,' Miss Mayfield remarked caustically. 'Now, when will that dinner be ready?'

As though in answer to her question the door opened to

admit Meadows, who after another inclination of the head, announced: 'Dinner is served, ma'am.'

'About time, too. Mr Hamilton, you will take my niece in. I will lead the way.'

With a lovely hand resting on his arm, following an old woman that might have escaped from a Dickens novel, Miles pondered on the possibility that all three – including Meadows – were deriving amusement from involving a complete stranger in some kind of charade.

The dining-room looked like a film set left over from a gothic horror movie, for the three tall candles that stood at regular intervals on the long table, sent dancing shadows over walls and ceiling, partly revealing an immense sideboard that appeared to be covered with grotesque carvings – mainly cats' heads so far as Miles could see – and an array of swords that glittered ominously in the dim light. Miss Mayfield pointed to a seat on her right.

'You will sit there, Mr Hamilton – Claudia opposite. That means I can keep a hospitable eye on my guest and a wary one on my niece. Meadows ... ' – the butler advanced from the shadows – ' ... you may serve the soup.'

Miles had to concede that if this was a weird charade, at least it would not be a hungry one. Course followed course, each brought into the room by a tall maid attired in a neck to ankle black dress, relieved by a white cap and apron. The door groaned every time she opened it and this was the only audible evidence of her presence. Also Miles only caught the occasional glimpse of her, as though she slid silently from one shadow to the next, while walking on tip-toe.

The conversation lacked credibility.

'I assume you are a shining ornament in London society, Mr Hamilton,' Miss Mayfield stated, conveying a portion of grilled fish to her mouth with a two-prong fork.

Miles who was feeling a trifle bemused after three glasses of wine, waved his fork airily and replied: 'Oh, I get around.'

The old lady leaned forward and assumed a faint leering expression.

'What is the latest scandal from the palace?'

Miles stared at her with wide-eyed amazement.

'I haven't heard any scandal.'

She rapped her fork on the table. 'Come, come, the entire nation is talking of HRH's escapades. Can he have grown more circumspect? It is said he married Mrs Fitzherbert back in '83.'

"I'm sorry – who is Mrs Fitzherbert?'

The old lady appeared to regard this question as the epitome of wit. She emitted a series of crackling chuckles, banged her fork four times on the table, then delivered an opinion.

'A droll fellow! Great balls of fire, you've got my niece laughing, although the unaccustomed exercise will probably crack her face. Who's Mrs Fitzherbert! That's rich!'

And indeed the lovely face opposite had been transformed into one vast dimpled smile, although Miles was at a loss to know how he could have supplied the cause. Miss Mayfield began to enlighten him.

'But come, sir, being one of the *ton*, you must have heard a little more than we who are buried in this out of the way place. Will parliament pay Prinny's debts?'

Miles swallowed a small fish bone and could not speak until the fit of coughing had subsided. 'Prinny! You're talking about the Prince Regent!'

Miss Mayfield looked as if she too were on the verge of choking. 'Don't tell us they've given him the regency! Has His Majesty gone completely mad? This is blood-stirring news.'

'Well, I'm not all that hot on history, but I do know George III went mad sometime or the other and the Prince of Wales became regent.'

Miss Mayfield raised a shaking forefinger and pointed it within an inch of the young man's nose. 'You'll be the death of me! History! Not good at ... '

Miles found his glass had been refilled and decided he might as well play along with this mad game, particularly if it gave pleasure to the beautiful creature opposite.

'Now you come to mention it, I do remember the Prince Regent married Mrs Fitzherbert and they had a son. Called George after his father.'

Smiles slowly died to be replaced by expression of joyful amazement. Claudia asked in a loud whisper:

'Are you certain, sir? We hear so little and it would be a mercy if you would take pity on our ignorance. When was the son born?'

Miles wrinkled his brow. 'You have me there. Soon after the marriage, I suppose.'

Miss Mayfield did some calculating on her fingers. 'That means he must be twenty-seven now. And it has taken all this time for us to learn of the event. We are very indebted to you, Mr Hamilton.'

'Not at all,' Miles said with becoming modesty, 'but I'm not at all certain when the son was born. I mean, he might be younger.'

It was then that he became aware of another matter that claimed his full attention. A slender foot was gently investigating his left ankle. And Claudia was looking at him with an unblinking stare that more than suggested she found both him and his fund of royal scandal intensely interesting. Playing footsie was an enthralling occupation, but not so heart-stopping as the prospect it promised – always supposing he could somehow separate beauty from the dragon.

Both of course were as nutty as a fruit cake, but so far as Claudia was concerned he would scrape the barrel of faulty memory, or invent juicy tit-bits purporting to originate in early nineteenth Whitehall, until the cows came home. Then he remembered a nursery rhyme that was generally supposed to be based on an incident involving the future George IV. He assumed a lecherous leer.

'Have you heard this one?

> 'Georgie Porgy, pudding and pie,
> 'Kissed the girls and made them cry.
> 'When the boys came out to play'
> 'Georgie Porgy ran away.'

'Yes!' Miss Mayfield gasped. 'And?'

'Well – Prinny went after two sisters ... '

'Wanted to bed them down.'

'Yes, yes indeed. Then their two brothers turned up with horsewhips and Prinny escaped through a back window.'

'Who were the sisters?' Claudia asked, pushing her stocking covered leg up Miles's left trouser leg.

He said the first name that came to mind. 'Cavendish.'

Miss Mayfield's eyes looked as if they might leave her head at any moment. 'Not related to the Hampshire Cavendishes?'

Miles felt like a man in a dark passage who is not certain where to tread next. 'Yes – I believe so.'

This surfeit of titillating gossip appeared to be too much for Miss Mayfield, for she wiped her brow on an off-white lace handkerchief, then pushed her chair back. 'I do think it's about time I had a little rest. Claudia, take our guest to the portrait gallery and let him feast his eyes on our immediate forebears. Although none of our gals have had to repel the advances of a prince of the blood, we are well connected.'

Miles rose, helped the old lady to rise, then beat Meadows to the door. He bowed as she went out, thereby meriting the remark:

'Blood will always tell.'

He went back to Claudia who had not stirred from her chair, but sat looking at him with unnaturally bright eyes. Miles shuffled his feet, then asked:

'Well, am I to be permitted a glimpse of your forebears?'

She shrugged. 'If that's what you want.'

'Unless,' he added quickly, 'you have something of greater interest to show me.'

She got up and came round the table, then poked him in the ribs.

'You are over-bold, sir, but I am not greatly displeased.'

For the first time Miles became aware of a faint feeling of repulsion, something that could not be defined, for the girl was lovely, her remark one that a normal young man would more than welcome and in keeping with this ridiculous charade.

'Perhaps, sir,' she said coyly, 'you will be pleased to follow me.'

He did. Out into the hall, up a broad staircase and on to a landing, where his guide opened one door and entered a sumptuously appointed bedroom. Miles looked at the giant four-poster bed and nodded.

'One could get lost in that,' he said thoughtfully.

During the course of a not uneventful life, Miles had noted that once the barriers were down, women had no sense of decency. Claudia gave a passable imitation of a nymphomaniac who finds clothes an unbearable encumbrance. And she had an awful lot of them. She ripped the blue velvet dress in her haste to get rid of it, then followed chemise, innumerable petticoats, plus garments that Miles was not aware existed. When she had reached the stage of revealing white rounded shoulders and peerless breasts, she gave him a slightly irritated look.

'You are tardy, sir. It is not proper that a lady should be disrobed, while the gentleman remains in a state of full dress.'

Miles exclaimed: 'What! Sorry,' and removed his sports jacket. The action was becoming too fast and he could be likened to a runner who hoped to make first place, but now finds the tape receding in front of him. And the room did not look right. All very grand, very period and most certainly the glorious creature who now lay on the bed naked as Eve before the discovery of apples, left nothing to be desired, but Miles experienced an overwhelming urge to be back in his motor car waiting for a good Samaritan to give him a tow.

He approached the bed, unbuckled his belt, then paused. Claudia viewed this reluctance with growing displeasure.

'When a lady is prepared, sir, it is very like an insult when he does not at least show some enthusiasm.'

From below stairs came the sound of a raucous voice.

'Damned mutton stew again. No wonder me digestion is all to pot.'

'Who was that?' Miles demanded.

The vision on the bed made answer. 'The maid complaining. She does nothing else. Pray, sir, remove that obnoxious clothing, for I have not known a man since Michaelmas and my blood is near boiling point.'

Miles could be no less than shocked at such candour, which although in keeping with a young lady who could strip with such expertise, damped rather than stoked the fires of passion. He looked at the discarded clothing that lay like closely connected islands across the floor, then at the girl that lay on the bed. Could it be she was not quite so beautiful as he had thought, that there was in fact a hint of fullness of features that merited the appellation of bloated? Rising panic made him say:

'If you will excuse me for a moment. I'll be back in a jiffy.'

The creature on the bed screamed at him. 'If you leave now, you will never come back.'

He ran from the room, stumbled down the stairs, dimly

aware that something strange was happening all around him. Elaborate wallpaper was being transformed into faded blue emulsion paint, thick carpet to well-worn linoleum, a metamorphosis that became complete when he came down into the hall. It now looked like the foyer of a sixth-rate hotel, having a semi-circular counter in one corner, a potted palm that needed pruning and an assortment of sagging armchairs. An elderly woman attired in a wrinkled pink dress was regarding him with some disfavour.

'Mr Hamilton, Melford's have telephoned to say they have found your car and it should be ready by tomorrow morning.'

Miles clamped a shaking hand to his forehead. 'Please, I don't understand. Where am I?'

The woman's voice acquired a deeper coating of ice. 'This is the Mayfield Residential Hotel, a *respectable* establishment. When you arrived earlier this evening, your car having broken down, I agreed you should spend the night here, although it is not my practice to accommodate occasional guests. I assumed you were a gentleman, Mr Hamilton.'

Miles waved an impatient hand. 'Just a minute. Where is Miss Mayfield and her niece Claudia?'

The woman narrowed her eyes. 'I trust you have not been drinking. There has not been a Mayfield in this house for at least a hundred years.'

'Then there must be someone who pretends ... ' He stopped and looked round the hall. Before it had been neglected; now it was simply squalid, but still retained a vestige of grandeur.

'You were saying, Mr Hamilton?'

'I was going to say there must be someone who is pretending to be a Miss Mayfield, to say nothing of her niece. But ... How long have I been here?'

The woman – he felt no need to know her name – glanced at a wall clock. 'I fail to follow your line of enquiry, but you arrived just after five and it is now nine-fifteen.'

'And did I eat a meal?'

'You did ample justice to dinner, before ascending to the – upper regions – with that brazen hussy who is *my* niece. She leaves tomorrow morning.'

'I would like to see the dining-room.'

'It is through the first door on the left as you very well know.

Needless to say I would appreciate your early departure in the morning. And do not leave your room during the night – or admit anyone at all.'

Miles was half way across the hall when he spoke over one shoulder. 'I'm not all that keen to spend a night in it myself.'

The dining-room presented an appearance that might be expected from a run-down residential hotel. A long table covered by a not over-clean cloth, used plates still cluttered a cheap sideboard; the only picture on the walls was a fly-spotted portrait of the royal family.

However the room was not unoccupied. A grey-haired man who bore some slight resemblance to Meadows, sat half way down the table sipping white wine from a tall glass. He looked up and creased his face into a wry grin.

'Ah! The erring stranger. The disturber of muddy waters. I almost enjoyed the damned stewed mutton. Oh, for the impetuosity of youth.'

Miles pulled out a chair and sat down, facing the grey-haired man with some trepidation.

'You saw what happened this evening. Can you help me? What did I do?'

'Pie-eyed, were you? Often get that way myself. By the way, my name is Armstrong. Major Armstrong.'

'And I'm Miles Hamilton.'

They gravely shook hands over the table, before the major took a deep swig from his glass.

'Would you care ... ? No? Sure? Well now, as I recollect you chatted up our worthy hostess and her buxom niece. Didn't take any notice of the rest of us. In fact none at all. When I asked you to pass the salt, I was ignored. Still if you'd had a drop too much, that's understandable. Then after the chocolate pudding, you took the wench upstairs. Don't blame you, although she's a bit much for my taste. Too obvious, if you get my meaning.'

Miles hastened to ask his next question.

'Do you know anything about the history of this place? Who owned it at the beginning of the last century?'

The major nodded slowly and refilled his glass. 'That I do. Grew up in these parts, played in this house when I was knee-high to a grasshopper. The place being almost empty.

Had a bit of a reputation – spooks and so forth, although I never saw anything myself. But then I wouldn't. As much imagination as a doorpost. But all of us kids had heard of the infamous Sarah Mayfield and her gorgeous niece Claudia.'

Miles felt his pulse quicken. 'What can you tell me about them?'

'It would appear the old girl and her niece lived all alone here, save for a butler called Meadows and a sinister-looking maid. You must understand that in those days this was the only house for miles around and any traveller who found himself stranded, had no option but come here for shelter. Miss Mayfield always obliged. But if the traveller was alone, he never came out of the house again.'

'What!'

Major Armstrong chuckled. 'Thought that would shake you. The old girl gave him a good dinner, then the beautiful Claudia lured him upstairs, and when he was fully occupied, Meadows came in, bashed him over the head, carried him down to the cellar, where he was finished off and the contents of his purse taken up to Miss Mayfield on a silver tray.'

Miles ejaculated: 'Oh, my God!' thereby causing Major Armstrong to express some concern.

'Say, you all right, old boy? You've gone a bit green round the gills. It's only a story, you know. Although it must be mainly true as the facts came out at the trial.'

'Trial!'

'Yes. They finally slipped up. Some lord came here alone, but neglected to inform his hostess that a servant had been sent to Marchester with information where he would be. When a relative turned up he refused to believe that his lordship had gone for a walk and not come back. Do you know they found over thirty bodies in the cellar?'

'What happened to them?'

'Reburied in the churchyard, I suppose. Oh! You mean the Mayfield lot. Hanged. Sarah, Claudia and the butler. The maid was never found. Must have bolted. Claudia put on quite a show. Was turned off in a red satin dress.'

After a pause Miles said weakly: 'If you don't mind, I would like a glass of that stuff. In fact – if you can spare them – two.'

Major Armstrong flinched. 'Please – don't call the best madeira stuff.'

Miles did spend a sleepless night at the Mayfield Residential Hotel, in a bed with a groaning mattress. Next morning, just before continuing his journey, he caught a glimpse of the girl who had been Miss Mayfield's 'stand-in'. Plump, blowzy, bottle-blonde; she bore no resemblance to that glorious creature. Later when speeding along a motorway, he tried to find some explanation for his experience.

The only theory that he could come up with did little to comfort a disturbed mind. Two ghosts – he accepted the word with reluctance – had superimposed their former likenesses on two living people, while that ridiculous conversation must have taken place in his head. That had to be the answer. Mental chit-chat while his tongue exchanged small talk with that awful landlady and her over-blown niece.

But what about Meadows and the dimly seen maid? Had Major Armstrong stood in for the butler?

He drove into Marchester and succeeded – for a while – in dismissing the entire business from his mind.

But not for long.

He found the old gibbet was still standing.

II

Something Comes In From The Garden

'The house will suit me down to the ground,' Robert Erwin stated, then instantly regretted his too apparent enthusiasm. 'I mean of course if we can come to some agreement regarding price.'

The house agent smiled one of those enigmatic smiles that are peculiar to his kind. 'I am sure we can reach a satisfactory agreement, Mr Erwin. However, there is just one piece of information that I have been instructed to pass on to any prospective buyer. The house is haunted.'

There was a short silence while Robert looked out of the window, then back at the agent again. Presently he said: 'You mean that?'

The man nodded. 'I have reason to believe my client fully believes what she says. You of course are at liberty to draw your own conclusions.'

'What ... ' Robert coughed, then went bravely on, ' ... what form does the alleged haunting take?'

'I have no further information. My client has stipulated that the prospective buyer spends a probationary month in the house before signing the contract. I find this to be ethical, if not very business-like. I would of course ask for a deposit as a sign of your good faith, on the understanding that it be refunded, should you decide to vacate the premises at the end of the stated period.'

'I'll think it over,' Robert promised.

*

He moved into Ennerdale House on the first of October. Edna and the children liked the house, the garden – an expanse of green lawn, surrounded on three sides by tall yew trees – the neighbourhood, the air, and everything about it. He knew this was the enthusiasm that comes with change and that familiarity would dull its keenness. But he was content. The ghost he had dismissed as a shadow phantom created by a senile or disturbed mind. He himself had decided that he would believe only what he saw. Disregarding the probationary period, they moved all their furniture in, and gave the house a new coat of paint so that soon it smiled happily out across the moors. Robert ran a motor-mower back and forth across the lawn until it resembled a smooth green carpet, while Richard who was twelve, and Joan, ten, did things with spades and forks in the borders. Then the time came when there was really nothing else to be done and they sat back and gazed upon their work with a smile of achievement.

'Not bad,' Robert said, downing a pint of brown ale.

'Super,' Joan declared.

'Spiffendous,' Richard announced, having arrived at an age, when the manufacture of words was considered to be a necessity.

'Make sure you wipe your feet before you come in,' Edna warned.

They decided to give a house-warming party.

The sky rained relatives, for it was rumoured that Robert was well-endowed and had a sympathetic ear for those in need. Aunts came from the suburbs; pretty nieces and distant cousins drifted in from bed-sitter land; old uncles floated over from seedy residential hotels, and one mother-in-law motored down from Chalfont-St-Giles. Edna was in her element, handing out strangely shaped sandwiches, sausages on sticks, bits and pieces on biscuits, and answering the never-ending calls for coffee. Robert contented himself with serving sherry and a concoction of white wine and gin he had invented. After the third glass even he rather liked it.

Voices became blurred; the room appeared through a faint mist, and he was warmed by a delicious feeling of well-being. Even his mother-in-law assumed a kind of golden glow, and her acid-tipped barbs glanced off his armour of reinforced self-esteem.

'Bit remote, I should have thought,' she stated, sipping from a glass of grapefruit juice.

'Distance,' he said airily, 'is a great protector.'

'And personally,' she went on, 'I find the house much too large.'

'But the question is,' he wagged a forefinger at her, 'would the house find you too large?'

She disappeared into the deepening mist and was replaced by one of the pretty nieces, who had a long-haired boyfriend in tow.

'Uncle Robert,' she said, showing him more leg and bosom than is usually considered an uncle's just due, 'this is Jason. He's in the dress-designing business.'

'Good for Jason.' Robert nodded with ponderous solemnity. 'May his designing never grow less.'

'That is to say, he is thinking of going into the dress-designing business,' the niece corrected.

'Tell him never to think,' Robert advised, 'it's bad for the liver.'

'If only he had a little capital,' the niece went on, nudging Jason, who appeared to have indulged in the gin concoction rather too well, 'I am certain he would make a fortune.'

'Tell him to try Dublin.' Robert gave her one of his lop-sided smiles and moved on. He was beginning to feel rather bored when he spotted the young girl in the white dress. She looked sad, lonely and very pretty and his heart warmed to her. He found himself looking down on the rich auburn hair which was tied back with a white ribbon, and adjusted the room by swaying gently back and forth.

'Hullo,' he said.

She looked up and presented a long pale face. Her hazel eyes were the most beautiful and sad he had ever seen. Her face crumpled into a wavering smile.

'Hullo.'

'Are you enjoying yourself?'

She looked round the crowded room. The mother-in-law was talking most earnestly to Edna and kept glancing in Robert's direction.

'It's all rather frightening.'

He nodded very slowly. 'Too true. This lot are enough to frighten the living daylights out of anybody.'

She seemed rather surprised. The smooth forehead was

creased by a tiny frown and the beautiful eyes widened.

'Are you frightened too?'

'Sweet child,' he swung his arm out in a gesture that embraced the entire room, 'this room is full of vampires, and they are all after my blood.'

A fleeting look of alarm crossed her face, then she smiled.

'You are joking? You are – what is the expression – pulling my leg?'

'It's not such a joke,' he said thoughtfully, just as he was captured by a middle-aged aunt who wanted him to meet her new son-in-law. A little later when he remembered to look round, the girl in the white dress had disappeared.

*

It was a month to the day before the unusual happened.

The sun was setting and Robert was looking out of the window; wondering where to put his summerhouse, when the man walked across the lawn. He was tall, with a red, hooked nose, and was attired in an old, faded army overcoat. Robert watched him for a few seconds with almost dispassionate interest. The man slouched – there was no other way to describe his loose-limbed action – across Robert's line of vision, with bent shoulders and lowered head, giving the impression he was treading a familiar path. Robert turned and going quickly to the door, shouted across the hall.

'Edna, have you hired an old rough to do some gardening?'

She came out of the kitchen, wiping her hands on a glass-cloth.

'No, I haven't engaged anyone. I leave the garden to you.'

They went outside, and after looking around rather anxiously, proceeded to search the garden with methodical care, occasionally making a weak joke as to the possibility of invasion. Neither of them wanted to admit the unthinkable suggestion, the secret fear. Their search revealed nothing out of the ordinary; no sign of the man or a trace of his passing. Once back in the house there was a ridiculous urge to keep looking out the window and start at every passing shadow. Presently Edna said; 'I will begin to believe in the ghost if this sort of thing goes on,' and then they both laughed. But when a few days had passed, the incident was pushed into the back of their minds, where memories lay, waiting to be recalled.

A week later the children found the girl in the white dress standing by the front gate and requested she be allowed to come in. Robert was delighted: Edna was not so pleased.

'What does she want?' she asked.

'Probably lives nearby,' Robert said, 'and has come to say thank you for the party.'

'But who is she?' Edna demanded, watching the white figure being led up the garden path.

'God knows.' He grinned. 'But then, I didn't know half the crowd that came to the house-warming. It was a free-for-all for most of London and the suburbs.'

She came into the sitting-room like a stray kitten, uncertain of its welcome. Joan and Richard both wore an expectant expression, as though contemplating praise for a novel discovery. Edna advanced and held out her hand, creasing her face into a polite smile of welcome.

'So pleased to see you, my dear.'

The girl allowed her hand to be shaken, then gravely presented it to Robert. He was much more effusive.

'Delighted. We don't get many visitors, especially young and pretty ones. Do you live hereabouts?'

'Yes.' She nodded and the long auburn hair danced. 'Yes, I used to live here.'

'Did you hear that, Edna?' He appealed to his wife who still wore her fixed smile. 'Eh – what is your name?'

'Julia.'

'Julia used to live here.'

'I heard,' Edna said, adjusting her smile to one of pleased surprise.

'It must be rather sad to see other people living in what used to be your home,' Robert observed.

'Yes,' Julia answered with rather sweet simplicity.

'She didn't want to come in,' Richard stated, 'but we made her.'

'I think she did, really,' Joan added, 'but was too shy.'

'I came the other night,' Julia raised her beautiful eyes and looked at Robert, 'because lots of other people were coming in and it seemed to be all right.'

'Indeed!' Edna exclaimed.

'The lady who lived here before you,' the girl went on, 'never welcomed me.'

'You must feel free to come any time you like,' Robert ignored Edna's look of disapproval. 'We will always be pleased to see you.'

'Absolutely,' Richard hastened to add. 'You can tell us all about the ghost.'

A look of bewilderment clouded the young face and she turned her head slowly from side to side as a gesture of denial.

'Ghost! This house was never haunted when I lived here. It was a happy place.'

'There you are.' Robert grinned at Edna. 'I always said it was a lot of piffle.' He again addressed Julia, whose face wore an expression of rather fearful bewilderment. 'The house agent relayed a message from the last owner, who warned us that the place was haunted. Why should she do that?'

'Mrs Ames,' Julia said slowly, 'was a lady who was easily frightened.'

'Rattling windows, wind in the chimney, and shadows at sunset.' Robert nodded. 'Imagination can do the rest.'

Edna was still watching the girl with some concern, and her eyes narrowed when she asked: 'Why did you say the lady was easily frightened?'

Julia shrugged. 'I don't know but she was. Once she screamed when I came in by the window.'

'Perhaps,' Edna observed drily, 'she wasn't expecting you. If someone were suddenly to appear uninvited, I would possibly scream.'

'But I'm always around,' the girl protested. 'I wasn't a stranger.'

'Well, no one will scream when you come in now,' Robert promised. 'What would you say to a spot of tea?'

Julia nodded. 'I would like that. It's been a long time since anyone invited me to tea.'

'Well, talk to the children while I get it ready,' Edna instructed. 'Robert, come and give me a hand.'

He made a face but dutifully followed his wife into the kitchen, then looked surprised when she closed the door.

'What's the idea? She'll think we are talking about her.'

'We are.' Edna filled the kettle and placed it on the stove.

'Robert, who is that girl?'

'I don't know. I saw her at the party and thought she looked a bit lonely so I spoke to her. She seems a nice enough kid.'

'Kid my foot.' Edna unwrapped a sliced loaf, then proceeded to butter each slice. 'Get the jam out of the cupboard. She's a minx if you ask me. Sliding in when she's not invited. And that meek, I am so easily hurt, expression! That might go down with you men but it cuts no ice with me.'

'Oh, be your age.' He slammed two pots of jam down on the table. 'Surely you don't think I ... ? Look, she's just a child who wants a bit of company. So far as I am concerned she can come here as often as she likes.'

Edna appeared unmoved by his outburst.

'She's not so much a child as you seem to imagine. Don't be taken in by that unlined face and innocent eyes. I bet my best cotton socks she's every day of twenty-five.'

'Rubbish,' Robert ejaculated. 'I'd say sixteen – certainly not more than seventeen. Honestly, you women, once you get it in for one of your own sex, you cover the impossible with a thick layer of imagination and call it logic. Why don't you like her, anyway?'

'She never looks you in the eye,' Edna pronounced.

'Oh, for heaven's sake. It's not everyone that goes round staring into your eyeballs. It's embarrassing, anyway.'

Edna did not answer but loaded the tea trolley while Robert made the tea. When he wheeled the trolley into the sitting-room, the two children were bubbling over with excitement.

'Daddy,' Joan grabbed his arm, 'Julia has been telling us about the pimpkins. They are little people who live behind the skirting boards and under the floor. And they come out to play when we are in bed.'

'Indeed!' Edna, who had been following close in Robert's footsteps, frowned. 'My name for them is mice.'

'No.' Richard sounded a little scornful. 'Julia says pimpkins go for rides on mice. But what I like best is the horrible little thing that lives in an oak tree, and on windy days, jumps down on people's heads and tangles their hair.'

'I think you'd all better get on with your teas,' Edna said. 'Julia appears to have a very vivid imagination.'

'No I haven't. Mother used to say I had no imagination at all. I just see things that other people don't. I have sort of special eyes.'

Edna frowned again. 'Joan, pour out the tea, there's a good girl. And Richard, see that your guest has everything she wants.'

Robert sat back and closed his eyes. The rattle of teacups was soothing. The children's chatter was a comfortable reminder that his life ran along well-ordered lines. Someone nudged his arm, and he opened his eyes and blinked as Joan said: 'Your tea, Daddy.'

He smiled indulgently, then took the offered cup and saucer, while his glance automatically went to the young girl seated on the sofa. She was holding her cup with limp fingers and staring at the window with an expression of horror.

'What is it, my dear?' he asked.

She turned a white face towards him, and there was great fear in the lovely eyes.

'There is ... there is someone in the garden.'

'What?' Edna rose quickly and shot the girl an impatient glance. 'How can you possibly know? You are too far away from the window to see.'

'I know.' She dropped the cup and an ugly brown stain began to spread over the new carpet. 'Someone is walking across the garden. There is an awful loneliness – I am frightened.'

Robert walked quickly to the window, where he pulled back the curtains and looked out into the gathering gloom. At first he saw only the long shadows cast by the trees as they reached out for the last golden rays of the dying sun. Then he stiffened as he saw the reason for her fear. The man in the old army overcoat was once again walking across the garden.

For a while Robert could only stand by the french window, with his nose flattened against the glass and watch the brown figure as it walked very slowly across the grass and into the shadow of the first tree. Then Edna's voice, its tone sharp with anxiety, cut into his consciousness.

'Robert, what on earth is the matter? Who is it?'

He knew he must take some form of action. Cover his rising fear with a light blanket of anger, reinforce his courage – such as it was – with cynical disbelief.

'I've had enough of this. Bloody layabouts using the place as though it were the main road.'

Edna was still calling after him, when he flung the windows open and stepped out into the garden. 'Don't go out ... come back ... come back ... ' As though he dared not go out; could possibly live with the knowledge that he was afraid to find out who – what – walked across his green, well-tended lawn at sunset. The memory of those beautiful, fear-bright eyes went with him as he moved out into the gothic-grey of expiring day. The soft breeze that heralds the coming of night caressed his face with cold kisses. But the garden, save for deepening shadows, was as empty as a dead man's brain, and although he ran back and forth with desperate courage, even into the blackness that lurked beneath the trees, no trace of the intruder did he find. Finally he stopped and listened. A bird twittered in its nest far overhead; some small creature scampered among the plants that grew against the tall, red-bricked wall; the leaves muttered as the breeze disturbed their peace – but otherwise all was still in the garden. He could do no more than go back to the house, and once there, laugh away the atmosphere of gloom.

'No one there. The old devil must be able to move fast when the mood takes him.'

'You must report this,' Edna insisted. 'We can't have some horrible old tramp coming and going as he pleases.'

Robert grinned ruefully, and marvelled that he was able to act so well. 'I suppose I must. But I'd like to know how he gets out. The wall surrounds the entire house and he walks away from the front gate.'

'Perhaps he shins up the wall,' Richard suggested.

'But he's too old ... ' Robert began, then realized he was entering a maze where questions and conjecture led to a central point that he had no wish to find. 'Where's Julia?' he asked.

There was a turning of heads and questioning glances, before Joan spoke for them all. 'I don't know. She was very frightened, and must have slipped out when we were at the window.'

'If you ask me,' Edna said, 'that girl is not all there. I am not at all sure she should be encouraged to come here again.'

Both Richard and Joan protested and Robert gave way to a sudden surge of unreasoning anger.

'Why must you condemn anyone who does not toe your line of mundane normality? Maybe she is a bit eccentric. But I'd rather have that, than the "thank you very much and I'd love to come again" types, you go for. Sometimes you make me want to throw up.'

The ensuing silence told him he had stepped out of character. He had showed a depth of feeling unusual to a man who prided himself on being cool and collected at all times. Edna's face was a picture of hurt surprise.

'I'm sorry I spoke. I had thought I was entitled to express an opinion as to who should be a guest in my house. It seems I was wrong.'

She turned and hurried from the room and presently they heard the kitchen door slam, a sure sign that although a retreat had been effected, peace overtures were expected from the antagonist. The children looked decidedly uncomfortable. Presently Richard asked: 'What are we going to do about the man, Dad?'

'What man?'

'The one that walks in the garden.'

Robert went to the window, then resolutely pulled the curtains. 'I'll think of something.'

When Joan asked the next question, it was like a hot needle on a raw nerve. 'Daddy, do you think the man is a ghost?'

'Don't be so damned silly,' he snapped.

*

The house agent was as urbane and non-committal as ever.

'My client was most insistent that her identity and whereabouts should not be revealed, Mr Erwin.'

'But I am also your client,' Robert pointed out, 'and I consider it essential that I contact the late owner of my house.'

The man seemed a little uneasy. 'To be frank, I have never met the lady. All business was transacted through a firm of solicitors.'

'May I suggest then, that you write to them and say I would be most grateful for an interview.'

'Yes. I can do that.'

Robert rose and looked down at the round, red face.

'You are very kind,' he said.

'Not at all,' replied the house agent.

*

Edna was waiting for him in the hall. She was pale and seemed to have forgotten the atmosphere of polite restraint which had lain between them for the past twenty-four hours. She put a hand on his arm and whispered loudly: 'I've seen him again.'

Robert hung his hat on the hall stand, then carefully placed his umbrella in the rack.

'Who?'

'The man. He came into the kitchen, did something at the sink, then went out again.'

He frowned. 'Then why on earth didn't you speak to him? Ask him what the hell he was playing at?'

Edna gripped his arm and shook it, while she struggled for words to describe her fear.

'I did ... I did. I yelled ... said, "get out ... get out ... " but he ignored me ... then went out through the door.'

He was trying not to understand, doing his utmost to put off the final moment of realization, but then Edna screamed out the four terrifying words.

'THE DOOR WAS SHUT.'

He led her gently into the dining-room and poured her a generous measure of whisky. She emptied the glass with the dutiful obedience of a child. Then she burst into tears.

'Now, now,' he comforted her with the awkwardness of a man who is embarrassed by displays of emotion, and patted her rather heavily on the shoulder. 'Tell me about it. Were you in the kitchen when ... he entered?'

She sniffed, dabbed her nose with a ridiculous scrap of white linen, and gradually returned to a state of coherency.

'No ... When I went into the kitchen, he ... it was walking towards the sink. I was too astonished to speak for a minute ... it was such a shock ... then I shouted: "What do you want? Who are you?" He took no notice, but went to the sink and did something there. It looked as if he was washing his hands.'

She collapsed again and while Robert continued with his

shoulder patting, he was surprised to find that his fear was giving way to a feeling of growing excitement. The house really was haunted. One read about such things; sometimes a friend related an experience that had happened to a friend of his, but here was a rare phenomenon actually taking place in his garden and kitchen. He said: 'Go on. What happened next?'

'I was frightened, of course. But it was only the natural fear that any woman would feel on finding a strange man in her house. Particularly when he refused to speak. But I never really believed ... When we saw him in the garden, the thought did cross my mind ... But I couldn't ... I shouted at him again and he turned and walked back towards the door. His face! I saw it close up. Robert, it was like that of an animal. Dull, great, watery, expressionless eyes. A thing that would just follow its instincts. Then it walked through the closed door and I just lost my head. Thank God, the kids were upstairs. Robert, what are we going to do?'

'Get to the bottom of the matter.' He smiled at her, feeling almost light-hearted, not really appreciating her deep-seated terror. 'I've asked the esate agent chap to contact the last owner. If we can find out why, perhaps we shall know what must be done.'

'But, Robert,' her voice rose to a cry of protest, 'we can't live in this house with that – that thing liable to walk in at any moment.'

'I don't see why not,' he said. 'It can't do us any harm.'

'Can't do us any harm!' She came up from her chair. 'Do you realize what you are saying? Something unnatural that stalks round the garden, comes in through shut doors and has the face of a witless fiend – is harmless? Let me tell you this – stay here if you like, but I'm taking the children out of this damned place tonight.'

'Now, don't be so bloody ridiculous.' He was surprised to hear the note of harshness in his own voice, and actually rejoiced when he felt the wave of anger flood his being. 'You will stay here and try to behave like a rational person. What you saw was a coloured shadow without substance or intelligence, and no reason for you to act like a hysterical schoolgirl.'

He left her and went over to the fireplace where he stood

looking down at the electric fire. The anger receded and he said calmly: 'Go upstairs and lie down. We'll talk again when you are more yourself.'

He heard her get up, and a little later the sound of her footsteps ascending the stairs, followed by the quiet closing of the bedroom door. Discord was coming into their lives, where before there had always been tranquillity. The house and that which pertained to it was responsible, and yet, try as he might, he could not dispel a feeling of deep satisfaction. The placid sea of his life was ruffled by exciting waves, and he was sailing a course that he knew instinctively was fraught with danger, yet he would not – even if it meant his eventual destruction – have missed a moment of it.

Robert went into the sitting-room and the two children turned speculative eyes in his direction, while Julia sat with lowered eyes in a chair by the fireplace. It was then that truth unveiled her face and he knew himself.

He said: 'Hullo, you with us again?' She looked up and his heart beat a little faster when he saw the look of undisguised pleasure in her eyes; the shy, tremulous smile that played around her lips. Then she lowered her head again and her voice came to him as a low, husky whisper.

'Yes. I am afraid I am a nuisance.'

'What utter nonsense. You are always welcome. Always.'

'Daddy,' Joan too, perhaps, found pleasure in discord, 'what upset Mummy?'

'Nothing that need concern you.' He frowned at her, and because this was unusual, she backed away. 'I want to have a private word with Julia. You two push off somewhere. But don't disturb your mother.'

They went with obvious reluctance, and Richard dared to look back with a questioning gleam in his eye. Robert got up and closed the door, then came back and sat opposite the girl.

'Julia, it's strange, but I've never asked you this before. Where do you live?'

'Round the corner,' she said simply.

'How long ago was it, that you lived in this house?'

'Oh, a long time ago. I grew up here.'

He began to marshal words with great care.

'This house has a reputation, hasn't it?'

He had reason to remember Edna's remark that this girl never looked you squarely in the eye. She was now staring at a point just over his right shoulder, while the now familiar smile played around her mouth.

'I don't know what you mean.'

'Julia,' his voice was reproachful, 'you do. It is said to be haunted. A man in a brown coat wanders across the garden at sunset, and this afternoon he came into the kitchen. What do you know about him?'

A blast of terror twisted her face into a mask of pain, and she began to wring her hands and contort her shoulders. Her voice rose and became a wail of protest.

'I don't know. I can't remember.'

'Try to,' he pleaded, 'it is so important. Don't you see, if this goes on, I will have to leave the house? I am not frightened, not any more, but my wife – the children. You do see? I must know who he is – was – and why he walks.'

Her eyes met his now. Only for a second, but he was able to see the wild fear, the longing, the loneliness. Her words evoked a surge of protective tenderness, so that it took all his will-power not to cover the distance that separated them and take her in his arms.

'You can't go away. I'd be all alone. Something horrible happens to me when I am left alone.'

'Then you must tell me who the man is. Why does he walk?'

'Because of something he did ... ' She creased her white brow into a frown of deep concentration. 'Something awful. He did ... did ... did ... something dreadful a long time ago.'

'What? Julia, what did he do?'

She put a hand on either side of her head and stared, wide-eyed at the ceiling. Then, suddenly, she screamed. A terrifying, long drawn-out shriek that filled the room, then went echoing round the house. Even as Robert leaped to his feet and moved towards her, she ran to the door, jerked it open and raced into the hall. When Robert followed a few seconds later, he bumped into Richard, who clutched his father to avoid being overthrown. 'Dad, what's wrong?' he gasped. 'Why did Julia scream like that?'

Robert pushed him roughly to one side and looked anxiously round the hall. 'Where did she go? The state she's in, anything could happen.'

Richard jerked his head towards the dining-room. 'She went in there.'

The girl was crouched on the floor near the fireplace; huddled together, with her arms clasped firmly round her legs and her face hidden beneath a screen of auburn hair. He went over to her and whispered: 'Julia, please my dear, don't be frightened. I won't ask any more questions – not now. Please get up.'

There was no movement, no sign that his words had been heard, and presently he reverted to his characteristic gesture of comfort: he patted her shoulder. She rolled over to one side, still in the grotesque position; an inanimate object that displayed no sign of life, seemingly in the throes of some kind of seizure. Robert ran back to the hall and bellowed up the stairs. 'Edna, come down quickly.'

It seemed an age before the bedroom door opened and Edna came walking slowly down the stairs. She seemed listless, displaying neither fear nor curiosity, and Robert's impatience flared into anger. 'For God's sake get a move on. Didn't you hear that scream?'

'I heard,' she said softly.

'Julia seems to be ill. She's rolled up on the floor and does not move. Look at her, see what you can do.'

Edna came down into the hall and looked at him with a quiet smile. She was like a person who has gone beyond the frontiers of fear, and now exists in a limbo where emotion of any kind could not survive. 'Don't you realize,' she said simply, 'it's this house? It's mad.'

He seized her by the arm and pushed her roughly towards the dining-room door. 'Get in there. What's the matter with you, for heaven's sake? The girl may be dying.'

Once back in the dining-room, Robert looked around with helpless amazement. The room was empty and the french window was open, allowing the night breeze to sigh along the walls, playfully ruffling the curtains and causing a solitary dead leaf to dance across the carpet. He went to the open window and called out: 'Julia ... Julia ... '

Edna laughed sardonically. 'She won't come back. Not tonight. Don't you realize what she is? An unbalanced girl who will play any number of hair-raising tricks to draw attention to herself. Particularly your attention. That scream. The stories she tells the children. Then laying herself out on the floor. But when she heard me coming, she knew here was someone who could see through her. So, wisely, she made a bolt for it.'

Robert came up close to his wife and stared hard into her face. 'She's different from anyone I have ever known. She has the soul of a butterfly. But you haven't the slightest idea what I am talking about, have you?'

Edna smiled grimly. 'I should close the window if I were you. One never knows what might come walking in.'

*

Robert took the early morning train to town next day – just one hour after the post had arrived – and on arriving at Waterloo, hired a cab which set him down at Emmwood Mansions, near Bryanston Square. A lift took him to the third floor and a door numbered 27. A middle-aged woman in maid's uniform answered his knock.

'Yes. What is it?'

'I have an appointment with Mrs Ames.'

She moved to one side with apparent reluctance.

'You'd better come in. I will see if Mrs Ames is disengaged.'

He entered a small hall, to wait while the maid announced his arrival. In five minutes she returned and then led him down a narrow passage into a large room at the rear of the house. Mrs Ames proved to be a little old lady with a mass of piled-up hair, clad in a plain black dress, relieved by a white gorget. She was seated by the window and gestured her guest to a chair by an imperious wave of her hand.

'Good morning, Mr Erwin. Being of a retiring nature, I do not as a rule grant interviews. But as I believe I can be of service to you, I agreed that my identity should be revealed.'

'I cannot thank you enough,' Robert began, but the old lady interrupted him with another wave of her hand.

'I must express some surprise that you are still living in Ennerdale House. In the past, few prospective buyers have stayed more than three weeks, and one, in fact, was out within two days. What I had hoped to find was a nice matter-of-fact family who lacked, what I believe today is called extra-sensory perception. Who, in other words, cannot see ghosts. You are clearly not such a person. Perhaps you can enlighten me as to why you did not take advantage of my probationary offer and leave by the end of the fourth week?'

'Mainly,' Robert said, 'because I liked the house, and also I suppose, I refused to believe in the existence of ghosts.'

Mrs Ames laughed shortly; a harsh little crackle that made Robert flinch.

'But I should imagine you were soon disillusioned. I am aware that the phenomenon is both fearful and possibly dangerous. You have a family?'

'Yes,' Robert admitted, 'a wife and two children.'

'And they have seen the manifestation?'

'My wife has. Now you come to mention it, I am not certain about the children. But they know of it.'

Mrs Ames nodded. 'With both parents so gifted, it is unlikely they are not also. I am, Mr Erwin, a timid person and frankly, I was terrified at what I saw in that house. But I am also obstinate, and I refused, until my age weakened my resolve, to allow it to drive me out. I stuck to my guns for over twenty years and during that period, I never ceased to hope I could find a solution.'

'You are a brave woman,' Robert said with deep sincerity.

'I don't think so. Probably a silly one. Have you made enquiries as to the history of the house, Mr Erwin?'

'No,' he confessed, 'it never occurred to me.'

'Just as well. Such accounts are often coloured by imagination, and grossly inaccurate. Briefly, these are the facts. Tom Jenkins was what is broadly described as a tramp. One of those unfortunates who were unable to settle down after the First World War, and took to living, if that is the right word, on the casual charity dispensed by anyone who felt compassion for him. The owner of Ennerdale House in those days, was a Mrs Fortescue, a widow with a young daughter. She, I suppose you could say, encouraged him. She gave him food and allowed him to sleep in a small outhouse at the bottom of the garden. I had it demolished. You see, Jenkins first raped the daughter, then strangled her.'

'How horrible.' Robert shuddered and Mrs Ames permitted herself another grim smile.

'You may well say so. The house has been – how shall I put it? – troubled ever since. But I must stess, Mr Erwin, you are not just contending with a ghost. You are plagued with an entity. An intelligence, that if balked, will I am sure, prove malignant. Have you allowed it to enter the house?'

'I don't know about *allow*,' Robert said, 'but it certainly came into the kitchen.'

'Then someone must have invited it,' Mrs Ames said sternly. 'I would never allow it beyond the french windows. For heaven's sake, Mr Erwin, drive it out. Treat it as you would an unwanted stray cat. Wave a pillow case in its face, curse it, and do not be put out by its apparent distress. Better still, if you find it is firmly established, get out yourself.'

'But,' Robert frowned, 'he does little harm. I grant you, the sight of a disembodied tramp walking round the garden, not to mention the kitchen, is not an experience I relish, but he has never even spoken. Surely he's in no condition to rape, let alone strangle anyone now?'

The silence lasted for a full minute, then Mrs Ames spoke.

'I think, Mr Erwin, we have been speaking at cross-purposes. I was not referring to the shade of Jenkins, who walks the garden at sunset, and occasionally is seen in the house. I agree, he is completely harmless and will in time, no doubt fade away. No, it is the other one you have to fear. The girl in the white dress. Julia Fortescue. The victim. If she can be so called, for it came out at the trial that she had so tormented the poor half-witted wretch, he went berserk.'

It was some time before speech returned to Robert Erwin, and then he could only blurt out a torrent of words.

'But ... but ... she's a living person. Don't shake your head ... She told me ... told me ... she lives round the corner.'

Mrs Ames' smile was positively sardonic.

'You are not very observant, Mr Erwin. Round the corner from your house is the cemetery.'

*

The exterior of the house was deceptively comforting.

The windows smiled out over the countryside, the red brickwork gleamed warmly in the sunlight, and the door was wide open, waiting for him to enter. The man who crossed the hall fully intended to order his family to pack a few essentials, then move out as soon as it was practicable. But when Robert came into the kitchen, he was already entertaining other thoughts. It was as though someone was whispering to him: You are experiencing a unique situation – what have you to fear? The old woman lived here for twenty years, and she is still alive and well.

There was also an urge to see the girl again, now that he KNEW. A fear-tinted curiosity clamoured more and more for satisfaction. Edna who was going about her work in the kitchen, ignored his entrance. She slammed the dishes down on the Formica-topped table with a little more energy than was strictly necessary, and concentrated even more intensely on the task in hand. He said: 'Hullo, I'm back,' and he might have been an invisible ghost himself for all the heed she paid him. He fought down the rising wave of irritation, that he knew could soon flare up into rage, before remarking casually: 'I've been to see the late owner. A Mrs Ames. A weird old body.'

Edna broke her silence. 'Oh, yes.'

'She ... she says, we should be careful.'

'Look,' he hesitated, the old self was warring with the new, 'perhaps it would be better if you ... '

Edna straightened up and stared at him with an expression he found it hard to analyse. It was half-expectant, half-fearful, as though she was afraid he would say something distasteful. She snapped abruptly: 'What?'

They stood facing one another for several minutes, each trying to hide their intimate thoughts from the other, then Robert sighed and turned away. 'Nothing,' he said, 'nothing at all.'

The children were in the garden, cheerfully pulling up weeds from between the flowers, and greeted his arrival with a certain polite reserve that would have been unthinkable yesterday.

'We're busy,' said Richard.

'Weeding,' added Joan.

'Well done.' He affected hearty approval, feeling like a stranger who must win their confidence. 'Marvellous. Anything I can do to help?'

'No thank you,' said Richard.

'We can manage,' said Joan.

'I see.' Robert put his hands in his pockets, shifted from one foot to another, then enquired with terrifying indifference: 'Have you seen Julia? Has she been around today?'

'No,' Richard answered briefly.

'We've gone off her.' Joan stood up and rubbed her hands on the already stained skirt. 'She's silly – and funny – all those stories. As if things called pimpkins could live behind the skirting board.'

Robert caught his breath. Did they suspect? If so he would have to move out, empty the house and leave her to cry alone. Suddenly the prospect was completely unacceptable.

'I'm sorry to hear that. I thought she was ... ' He could not say *nice*, that would be stupid. 'A rather imaginative girl who would be company for you.'

Richard shrugged. 'She was all right at first, but then ... She's a weirdie ... likes to make trouble ... always crying.'

'She's not our sort of person,' Joan stated gravely.

Robert went back to the house and began looking for her. Questions, that up to now he had not bothered to consider, now presented themselves and demanded answers. Was she always here? Were there periods when she could not appear? Was she in fact a – he stumbled over the word – a person? Or something that was built out of atmosphere – terror – unrequited lust? He shuddered but continued to search.

Minutes passed and became hours; the sun sank down behind the tall trees, and shadows crept across the lawn and approached the house. Edna laid the table for the evening meal, then called the children, who had long since deserted the garden and were now romping in one of the upper rooms. When Robert entered the dining-room they were all seated at the table, and he took his seat without a word being said.

They ate in silence only broken by the rattle of cutlery on china, and the occasional hushed word that died almost before it was uttered. Now and again Edna would rise and go to the kitchen to fetch another course, or something she had forgotten and it was then that Robert's rage would bubble and threaten to erupt. Not until coffee was being served did he take a deep breath and attempt to break through the wall which surrounded him.

'Look here, let's ... '

A sound came from the sitting-room. It could have been a door being softly closed, or the french windows protesting as they were slowly opened. But it might have been a thunder-clap, or even a trumpet-blast to announce the end of the world, for the effect it had on the four people seated round the table. Edna cried out: 'Don't go. Please don't go,' when Robert sprang up from his chair, and the two children whimpered and looked at him with terror-wide eyes.

Julia was seated on the sofa when he came into the room; her long-fingered hands clasped, her head lowered. She looked pitiful and rejected. Robert walked slowly towards her and lowered himself on to the sofa. He then leaned forward and whispered: 'You've come back. I thought you had gone forever.'

Her head came round and he saw her eyes gleam softly, possibly with pleasure – maybe even triumph. The smile was almost imperceptible. 'You know?'

He nodded. 'I know.'

'And it makes no difference? You are not afraid?'

He moved nearer; sidled along the sofa until a bare two feet separated them. 'I am afraid. Just a little. But it makes no difference. Perhaps, in my heart I have always known.'

The smile became more pronounced. 'I have been looking for someone who would overcome his fear. You will have to travel a long way.'

He sank down upon one knee and dared to lay his hands on hers. They were cold. Death cold. 'I will build a bridge that will span from your world to mine. I will melt your coldness with my warmth, and take the burden of your sins – if sins there be – upon my shoulders.'

Her eyes were brilliant and their fire set light to the dead desires that littered his brain. He felt the great *resolve* grow stronger with every heartbeat.

'Do what you must,' she said, 'and we will be together always.'

Robert heard the gasp from the doorway and spinning round saw Edna standing there, her face a mask of disgust and terror.

'Get away from – from that thing,' she said. 'In the name of sanity, get away from IT.'

He got up and moved towards her, the great resolve was a voice; a mighty roar in his head that must be satisfied.

'She is lost, lonely, needing love and understanding.'

He was still trying to convince Edna – and himself. As always endeavouring to evade his responsibilities, put off making the final decision. But Edna too could not change, had to blurt out the truth, no matter how distasteful it was.

'You KNOW what she is. A monster ... something that belongs to dark places, and you are giving it life. You have from the moment we set foot in this house. Lie to me if you must, but don't lie to yourself.'

He was drawing nearer to her, smashing down the barriers, walking over ground he had hitherto only glimpsed in half-forgotten dreams. As he moved, words poured off his tongue. Thoughts that had festered in acid for fifteen years.

'Talk ... talk, will nothing ever still that tongue, shut that mouth and give me peace? Soft words, maybe, wrapped in velvet and soaked in oil, but the sting was always there, while you waited for the unguarded flinch, the grimace of pain, who knows, the unexpected tear. Now it is my turn.'

Edna shrieked. 'Don't. You must understand. You are doing what she wants. Turn round, look at her face.'

'I can see yours,' he said gently.

A great joy exploded when he fastened his hands about her throat, and her slowly diminishing, gurgling screams were sweet music to his soul. Then it was over: a broken body lay at his feet, and he was a frightened man who had just murdered his wife. When he turned round, Julia was coming up from the sofa. Her white dress had slipped from one shoulder and she was giggling. An awful, immature giggling, such as a schoolgirl might make if she had played some silly practical joke on an unsuspecting friend. She began to back towards the window, and the giggles gradually merged and rose into a shrieking, ear-splitting laugh.

Somewhere near the window she vanished. Just sank to the floor and dissolved into a patch of coloured air, as though there was now no need for any pretence. Only the echo of that dreadful laugh lingered for a timeless second, then that too faded away, and Robert for a while, returned to full sanity.

The body at his feet stared up at him with bulging eyes; from somewhere came the sound of children crying, and far, far away a dog barked.

Then, Robert Erwin, like a drunkard being drawn back to the bottle against his will, walked over to the open french window and stood looking out at the night-shrouded garden. He raised his voice and sent out a cry that echoed along the avenues of space and time.

'Come back … come back … '

III

The Night Watch

It was Harry's first experience of sentry-go, two nights on, four off, and he could not regard the prospect with anything like equanimity. Drifting up and down a mist-haunted street, keeping his eyes open for shiver-makers, was to say the least a tiresome chore. Sergeant Denham, the guard commander, who had been a stockbroker during most of his flesh and blood life, was a stickler for detail.

'Now look here, lad,' he addressed an unhappy Harry, 'you've read standing orders and I'll expect you to abide by them. To the letter. Keep to the middle of the road. Never mind the occasional car, it will pass through you. Never mind what's taking place in the houses, that's none of your business – not any more. Stay away from F and Bs. If they've got the right mixture, you could be drawn into their auras, then we'll have the devil's own job in digging you out again ... If you do spot a shiver-maker, send out an alarm signal. Don't try to tackle it yourself. It's a team job. Got all that?'

Harry said, 'Yes, sergeant.'

'Hope you have. Can't spare you a side-kick, our forces are spread too thin over the ground. But keep to the rules and you'll be all right. Report to the guardroom every hour. But make sure the street is clean first.'

The guardroom was situated in a disused cellar that in the past five years had only been invaded by two F and Bs: two tramps who soon decamped, for although they could not see the ghostly squad, the atmosphere was not conducive to comfort.

'Right,' Sergeant Denham ordered. 'Get out there and relieve Private Smith. And tell him to come straight back. No peering in through windows.'

Harry rose up through the ceiling and emerged onto the pavement of Bradley Street. The mist which always came up from the river at sunset had transformed the lamps into blurred orange balls and cut down visibility to a few yards, but of course one did not have to see shiver-makers; one sensed them.

Harry had been killed in a car crash six months earlier and had spent the ensuing time in training for the Astral Guard Corps, having apparently the right qualifications for this organization. What they were he had not the slightest idea, unless the ability to mount unnumbered street guards, take part in borderland patrols in search of escapees, was not granted to the average passer-over.

Then he remembered Bob Smith who was somewhere along the street waiting to be relieved and must be doing his nut by now. He drifted forward and soon spotted the black-clad figure leaning against a front door, looking anxiously to the left.

Harry stopped in front of him and said quietly, 'Hope I'm not late, but I got lost in this mist.'

Bob – who had been a hairdresser and dropped dead behind his chair – grinned. 'Beginners always do. So long as you didn't drift up to that blonde's bedroom at number 28. I know we're supposed to have left all that behind us, but there's still an urge to play Peeping Tom.'

'You haven't though?' Harry asked.

'Only a quick glance. Just to make certain that a shiver-maker hadn't crept in there, you understand.'

'Well, I think that Sergeant Denham has his suspicions, as he wants you to hurry back.'

Bob spat. 'That basket! Keep to the book – don't do anything I wouldn't. Well, the street's clean, all its respectable residents seem to have gone to bed, save for that lot at number 19, who are throwing a party.'

'Right. See you back at the guardroom.'

Bob waved his right hand and drifted off into the mist; instantly the street became the most lonely place in the universe. A crowd of well-lubricated revellers poured out of number 19, making the night hideous with their raucous voices, but so far as Harry was concerned they could have been a million light years away. Unless of course one had that mysterious something that could draw a poor weak-willed ninny like him into his aura. And this – despite the sergeant's warning – was a rare occurrence, requiring an unconscious desire on both sides to get together.

He broke law 7 which stated emphatically that no sentry remain within three feet of an F and B; and allowed the entire crew to flow around and through him. For an instant he experienced the brain numbing effects of alcohol, a host of conflicting emotions that ranged from black depression to a mischievous desire to trip someone up. Then they were gone, running down the road, each one certain they would live to see a million tomorrows.

If.

If he had not gone to that party, drunk too much or not attempted to drive home. Then he would be alive now, blissfully unaware that the dead were sometimes given the task of guarding deserted streets. He moved forward, his senses alert for the unexpected and stopped outside number 28 – the house where the blonde lived. All the windows were black oblongs of glistening glass, which must mean she had gone to bed, probably with her boy friend, who – according to report – turned up most nights.

Opposite at number 25 an old lady stood framed in her lighted window, staring down into the street, probably not seeing anything at all, but deriving a meagre amount of comfort at *not* looking at the over-familiar walls of her room.

From loneliness were ghosts born.

There was trouble at number 12. A man wearing a black overcoat and a hat pulled well down over his face, was engaged in cutting a square of glass from a side window. A burglar without doubt.

Standing Orders. Paragraph 2. Under no circumstances whatsoever, will a sentry endeavour or even consider the possibility of interfering in F and B affairs.

So he must remain in the middle of the road and ignore – or at least only watch – a crime perpetrated, that in F and B life would have demanded prompt action. Harry seemed to remember that number 12 was the home of a dark-haired girl, whose husband worked five nights out of each week in the local collet factory. That must mean she was alone in the house now.

He drifted into the side passage and was in time to see the burglar raise the lower sash, then swing a leg over the window sill. He disappeared into the interior of a dark room.

Harry dare not follow, in fact he had no business being in the passage, as that alone technically amounted to deserting his beat. Should he enter any building occupied by a F and B, it was more than possible he would not be able to leave it. Become that most despised of beings – a housebound ghost. Sergeant Denham's warning had been most explicit.

'Enter a house and the corps washes its hands of you. And rightly so. An unguarded beat could mean an invasion of shiver-makers, with ensuing madness and mayhem. Apart from which there's no known way of getting you out.'

Harry went back to the street and peered in through a front window. Dim spears of lamplight faintly illuminated the room beyond, but did not reveal the presence of an intruder, which must mean he was either rummaging in the back room or mounting the stairs. Two rooms up, two down and a built on kitchen did not leave a housebreaker much space to manoeuvre, and lead him to suppose that money and valuables would be kept in the one bedroom in constant use.

Harry ascended to the top window and sent a silent cry shuddering along the street; demanded an answer to a question that sooner or later is asked by the newly dead.

'If something dreadful happens, what can I do?'

The answer of course was brief and simple. Nothing. He must resume his beat, ignore screams, shots and cries for help. In any case a passer-over had no power to render help to a F and B.

But he could create a disturbance. Send out a blast of energy, break glass, cause small objects to fly across the room, only, he had no idea what effect it would have on him. Certainly he would be breaking a basic law.

But basic laws did not take into consideration the reason why he now floated in a sea of loneliness, or why his fellow sufferers in the guardroom could not provide so much as a shred of companionship. Harry whispered:

'That is the crime for which I am being punished. When the ship of passion sank, I ignored a cry for help.'

Jennifer had committed suicide when he had walked out on their short-lived romance. She had telephoned several times and he had been brutally kind. Even derived certain pleasure from her continued infatuation. He had cast poisoned crumbs to a starving soul.

He was about to drift down to street level when a gasping cry came from behind the curtained window, followed by two dull thuds, and now there was no time for coherent thought, or to remember the warnings; the safety valves blew and a blast of released energy cracked window panes and created minor havoc in the room beyond.

Harry felt himself being drawn in, hurtling across space, blind, deaf, but still capable of experiencing fear. Then he was standing upright against the far wall, knowing he had committed the unforgivable, but as yet unable to accept the fact there was no way he could leave the house ... He drifted to the bed and looked down at the pathetic figure. A large bruise on the forehead, the head lay at an unnatural angle; there could be no doubt that the girl was dead. From below came the sound of a crash, suggesting that someone in a hurry had stumbled into a small item of furniture. Then running footsteps down the side passage.

Harry looked around the dimly lit room and whispered: 'Come alive. Wake up. It's all over.'

She materialized by the window, a slender, naked white form that seemed to be composed of lamplight and mist. Harry whispered further encouragement. 'Make yourself more solid. It's easy once you get the hang of it. And imagine you're dressed in the clothes you wore every day. Don't be afraid.'

A green blouse and a tweed skirt emerged on the white figure, followed by flesh-coloured stockings and black, sensible shoes. Her hair flowed back until it was arranged neatly round her head. Then she looked at him and ejected a shrill scream.

Harry raised his hand. 'No, I'm not the burglar. He's gone.'

She found her voice and spoke in a harsh whisper.

'Then who are you? What has happened?'

He smiled ruefully. 'I'm a sentry who has deserted his post. And ... I'm afraid you're what is commonly known as dead. That chap – well – he killed you. Although I'm certain he didn't intend to. Just wanted to keep you quiet.'

Her face seemed to be composed of two immense eyes and a gaping mouth. 'Dead! I'm dead!'

'Not really. Just changed. Take my advice, don't look at the bed. Let's go downstairs and talk.'

'Why mustn't I look at my bed? I think you're a madman who broke into my house.' She deliberately looked at the bed, then clasped shaking hands to her mouth. 'Who is that? Dear God – who is that?'

Harry spoke gently. 'No one at all. Not now. Just a discarded shell. Come away. Downstairs. You can even make a cup of tea. Everything has an astral double, even tea leaves.'

He put an arm round the slender waist and guided the girl down the stairs and into the small lounge, there to will the overhead light on. She said with a hint of dawning interest: 'How did you do that? Turn on the light without touching the switch?'

'I don't know. One can just do that kind of thing. You'll soon pick it up. Now, go into the kitchen and try to act as you did in – well – life. Put a kettle on the stove and don't worry if you see everything double for a while. That will pass. Just think the gas alight. As a point of interest if an F and B … '

'What's an F and B?'

'A flesh and blood person. If one were to enter the room they would not see either of us or what you're doing. Not unless they were exceptionally gifted.'

The girl looked round the room, then shook her head. 'I can't accept that I'm dead. Everything looks so normal. I feel as I always have. I breathe, my heart is beating. I know the room is cold – how can I be dead?'

'Forget the word,' Harry instructed. 'Understand you're as much alive now, as when you went to bed. I'm Harry Morgan. What's your name?'

'Wendy. Wendy Allen.' She began to cry and wring her hands. 'What will happen when George comes home? He'll find me upstairs – and you say he won't be able to see me as I am. He'll most likely go mad.'

'No. He'll be shocked and grief-stricken, but gradually, against his will, he'll begin to forget. Time begins its healing process almost at once. Unless … '

Wendy shouted her protest. 'But I don't want him to forget. He mustn't.'

'When do you expect him back?'

'Tomorrow morning. About eight.'

'Then that's when the action will begin. After all you were murdered. Within seven or eight hours this place will be swarming with cops. Questioning neighbours, looking for fingerprints, photographing ... And we'll have to watch.'

'That's horrible. Can't we go to sleep or something?'

'Go and make a cup of tea. It will be good practice in self-control.'

When she had gone into the kitchen Harry sank down on to a sofa and willed his body to feel the padded back and seating, then faced the grim prospect of his future. Outside the street would remain unguarded until Sergeant Denham came to find out why he had not reported in. And he was housebound, whereas Wendy would be with him for a short time, probably only a matter of hours, before she departed for an unknown destination. Then he would be lonely as never before.

Wendy came in from the kitchen carrying a tray on which stood a teapot and two cups and saucers, her face transformed by an expression of wonderment.

'What do you know? You're right! I'm carrying this lot, but left behind their duplicates. I'll never get used to it.'

'Maybe you won't have to. Sooner or later – probably sooner – you'll move on. Don't ask me where.'

She placed the tray on a table. 'And will you come too?'

He grimaced. 'I fear not. It's a bit complicated to explain, but I'm stuck here for ever and a day.'

'How awful! I wouldn't mind staying here for a bit, because it is my home, but not forever. George and I were going to move next year anyway.'

She began to cry again and Harry said: 'Pour the tea while I fetch the sugar and milk. You forgot it.'

'I don't use either. It's fattening.'

He smiled. 'I don't think that matters now. Your present body won't change, no matter what.'

Having found an unopened bottle of milk in the refrigerator and a basin of sugar in a small cupboard, Harry realised that neither of them wanted to talk, for the girl was still trying to adjust to her bizarre situation, while he brooded on his which was so much worse. He sipped from his cup and decided Wendy made excellent tea, then started when the thud of footsteps came from the side passage. Wendy made a fearful enquiry.

'Do you think it might be – that man come back?'

Harry shook his head. 'Most unlikely. He'll be far away by now. No, I'd say it's a neighbour who was disturbed by the noise I made coming in through your bedroom window. Maybe the action will start sooner than I expected.'

They heard a man's voice say: 'Someone got in through this window. Look, there's a square cut out – and the bloody sash is pulled up.'

A woman's voice replied. 'Then you'd better go in. I heard a godalmighty crash from her bedroom. There must be something wrong.'

'But do you think I should go in? I mean she might just have had a row with her husband.'

'George wouldn't cut squares out of his own window, would he? Anyways, he's on night work and not due back until tomorrow morning. Now, are you going in there, or shall I?'

'All right – all right, I'm going. But you can't be too careful.'

Harry turned to the girl. 'Who are they?'

'Mr and Mrs Florence from next door – on the left. She always keeps an eye on me when George is away. She was in earlier this evening.'

Harry smiled grimly. 'Her reluctant husband will be in here soon. If he finds the courage to go upstairs, I'd imagine he'll come down much faster.'

A large, grey-haired man with a protruding beer-belly entered the room and blinked in the bright light. He called back over one shoulder.

'The light's on, Vi. There can't be much wrong.'

A thin, tiny woman attired in a flower-pattern dressing-gown, emerged into the doorway and gave her husband a look of withering contempt.

'You might have helped a lady over the window sill and if there's anything wrong, it will be upstairs. See that you're in a state of blue funk, I'd better lead the way.'

'But she may be asleep.'

'Let's hope that's all she is. Come on.'

Mr Florence still muttering futile protests, followed his wife out of the room and up the narrow staircase. Wendy shuddered.

'It's so strange that they can't see us. And rather dreadful. It's like being continually snubbed.'

'The pathetic are rarely seen,' Harry observed with some bitterness. 'Ah! Stand by for commotion.'

A feminine scream announced Mrs Florence's reaction to gazing upon the grotesque, while a sound not unlike that of a rogue elephant on the rampage came thudding down the stairs. Mr Florence erupted into the room and sank into a chair. Mrs Florence made a much more dignified entrance, looking shaken, even distressed, but capable of coherent thought. She now glared at her husband.

'There's no point in sitting there like a month of wet Sundays. The poor girl's been done in and we'll have to get the police. Is it to be you or me?'

The big man shuddered. 'I couldn't sit by myself in this house, knowing she was upstairs … '

'She never did you any harm when alive, poor dear, and she certainly can't now. But you'd better get yourself down to that call box at the end of the road. Dial 999 and ask for police. Best tell 'em there's been a terrible accident at 31 Bradley Street. Let them work out what really happened.'

The man jerked his head round and gave birth to another fear.

'Here! Suppose they think we done it?'

The woman made a sound that was not far removed from a snort.

'Don't be daft. Why the hell should we want to do the poor dear in. Someone broke in, went into her bedroom, for some reason smashed the window, woke her, and as they say on telly – over reacted. Now, for God's sake stir your stumps and get down to that call box. The sooner the flatties get cracking, the better chance there'll be in catching the bastard.'

Harry took Wendy's hand in his and tried to will some of the horror away. 'Do you want him caught?'

She watched Mr Florence heave himself out of the chair before answering. 'Yes. Having killed once, he may do it again, and it will be better for him to be caught. If he suffers for his crime – well – on earth, then it should be easier for him here. Is that right?'

Harry nodded. 'You are a very wise lady. Just maybe fifteen years in nick will save him from doing a hundred years sentry go. Now, sit back and watch the show. Remember it has little to do with us.'

Left alone Mrs Florence seated herself and began to cry, her thin shoulders shaking, demonstrating such grief, Wendy half rose from her chair. Harry quickly intervened.

'Sit down. There's nothing you can do, and sorrow is a flame that soon burns itself out. Soon Mrs Florence will only remember you as a dramatic incident in a drab life.'

Wendy sighed. 'I suppose you're right. But George won't remember me as a dramatic incident, will he? Not even when he marries again. He will – I know. Someone who looks a bit like me.'

'Bound to,' Harry agreed.

'Which doesn't mean I wouldn't be grateful for a bit of an argument.'

Mrs Florence got up and walked to the window, where she looked out at the deserted street; then she muttered: 'Why the hell couldn't I have stayed in bed?'

'See!' Harry exclaimed triumphantly. 'You're already a nuisance.'

'Fear curdles affection,' Wendy replied. 'I think I read that somewhere. But it is true, isn't it?'

'Indeed it is. But Mr Florence has come back. Soon we'll be able to watch a murder investigation at close quarters ... '

'Yes, mine. I'm not certain I want to watch ... '

'Nonsense. It will be an unique experience.'

Mr Florence trudged back into the room, looking more lively, even cheerful, than when he left. He perched on the arm of a chair and poured out a torrent of words.

'I got through to the CID and they'll be round anytime now. They ask me what sort of accident it was and I said we thought she'd been done in, seeing that someone had broken in ... '

'You stupid clot,' Mrs Florence interrupted.

'Well, I had to. And they said we were not to touch anything. Definitely not to touch anything.'

'Why the hell should we touch anything? Mind you, I fancy a cup of tea, but I suppose we hadn't better touch the kettle. And you – mind where you put those great hands of yours, or they'll find your fingerprints everywhere.'

Mr Florence thrust his hands into his trouser pockets.

'Bloody hell! I hadn't thought of that.'

'You never think – period. Is that a car I can hear? Them without a doubt. Listen, keep your trap shut. Let me do the talking.'

Her husband nodded violently. 'Suits me. The less you say to coppers the better.'

'And stop looking so guilty. One look at your face and they'll have the handcuffs out.'

'I keep thinking about my fingerprints ... '

'Shut up. Here they are.'

There came the sound of at least two car doors being slammed, followed by the tramp of feet along the side passage. A masculine voice shouted through the open window: 'Mr Florence, are you there?'

Mrs Florence raised a warning forefinger. 'We both are. I'm Mrs Florence. From next door.'

'Right, we're coming in through the window. Don't want the door touched, until it's been tested for prints.'

'Bloody hell! I touched it,' Mr Florence whispered. 'When I went out and came back in. The bloody thing is on the catch.'

Three men clambered over the window sill and formed a compact group in front of the sofa, looking down at Mrs Florence with impassive faces. When her husband got up, their united attention was switched to him. The one in a grey overcoat and a shapeless hat spoke.

'Right, then. I'm Inspector Watkins. These gentlemen are Detective Sergeant Manfield and Detective Constable MacGregor. Why did you enter this house?'

Mrs Florence raised her voice to a near shout. 'Because I heard what sounded like breaking glass from the bedroom window next to mine – which is a little problem for you lot to work out, seeing the geezer came through that window – which being open, we came through thinking poor Mrs Allen might be in trouble. Which she was.'

'It never occurred to you that the intruder might have been still in the house?'

'Wish he had. I'd have given him what for.'

Inspector Watkins grimaced. 'And you went upstairs?'

'Yes and found the poor dear ... '

'Never mind, we'll find out for ourselves.' He turned to MacGregor. 'Mac, go over the lower rooms for dabs, although I don't expect much joy. But you never know.'

'You might as well know,' Mrs Florence stated, 'that my husband opened and closed the front door. In fact it's on the catch now.'

The inspector said: 'Damn and blast! We'll have to take both of your fingerprints anyway. MacGregor, do that first. And send the cameraman upstairs when he arrives. Dick, come upstairs with me.'

Harry nudged Wendy, who had been watching and listening with wide-eyed amazement. 'Pity they can't hear us. I could give them some kind of description. I suppose you didn't get a good look at the villain.'

She shook her head. 'Not what you could call a good look. I was too frightened. But there was one thing I did see. Just before he hit me, his hat fell off and a streak of light that came in through a parting in the curtains, lit up his face. And he had a lazy eye. The left one. You know the lid sort of drooped half way down over it.'

Harry sat upright and emitted a low whistle. 'That is a real clue! The chap is bound to have a record and there can't be that number of crooks who have a lazy eye. If we could only pass that bit of information on.'

'We can't. They don't even know we're here.'

Harry stared at Mr Florence who was submitting to having his fingerprints taken with ill-grace. 'I suppose there's not a gifted one among this lot? Certainly those neighbours of yours aren't and the coppers look as solid as two planks. Let me think for a moment.'

Wendy shuddered. 'I can only think that at this moment those two upstairs are examining my dead body.'

Harry waved a languid hand. 'Forget it. Look, I can create a bit of disturbance round here. Not much, because it burns up a lot of energy and I used a lot bursting into your bedroom. But probably enough to attract their attention. Then we'll carry on from there.'

Wendy displayed growing interest. 'What sort of disturbance?'

'Well, I can probably make that vase leave the mantelpiece and go floating across the room. One of our chaps once overturned a night watchman's fire to frighten off a shiver-maker, so a vase should be easy.'

'A shiver-maker!'

'Never mind that now. Look, you can help. Concentrate on the vase and imagine it floating across the room. Between us it should be a piece of cake.'

'Don't you think we'd better wait until that inspector-man comes downstairs. He's the one we want to impress.'

Harry nodded slowly and patted her hand. 'Clever girl. I'd have wasted precious energy on that finger-print clod and your one-time neighbours, who no one would believe anyway. Ah! Footsteps. The lads are coming down. Get ready.'

For the first time Wendy smiled. A lovely little impish smile. 'I say, this is rather fun, isn't it?'

'Being dead has some fringe benefits,' Harry admitted.

*

Inspector Watkins entered the room, his face set in grim lines, and when he spoke his voice was tense, even contained an element of menace.

'There's no need to wait for the medical report, this is a murder case. So soon as it's light, I want every person in the street questioned. You never know someone might have been awake and looking out of a window. It's worth trying. In the meanwhile, Mr and Mrs Florence, I want you to rack your brains and try to remember anything you can, sounds for example. After all the chap must have left the house just before you entered.'

'We didn't see or hear anything,' Mrs Florence stated emphatically. 'I'd have said if we had.'

The inspector was about to reiterate his request when a vase, which had just been dusted for fingerprints, left the mantelpiece, floated slowly across the room, did a right about turn and dropped at the police officer's feet. It descended so carefully it was not even cracked.

For a while no one spoke, then Constable MacGregor exclaimed: 'Hell! Did you see that?'

'I'm not blind,' the inspector said curtly. 'Doubtlessly there's an explanation if we take the trouble to look for it.'

'A draught,' Sergeant Mansfield suggested, without much conviction.

'Don't be stupid. Let's wait a bit and see if anything else happens.'

Harry grimaced and turned to Wendy. 'What does he expect? I don't know about you, but lifting that thing all but drained me.'

'I certainly feel weak,' Wendy admitted. 'But couldn't we have a go at that picture of Uncle Leslie? He's got rather large eyes and it might be possible to do something to the left one. Couldn't it?'

Harry considered the problem for a moment. 'I could concentrate on it and see what happens. Never tried anything like this before.'

'Maybe if you will the left eye half-closed – it will.'

'Can but try.'

*

The three police officers stood motionless, their eyes darting from one wall to the next and it was MacGregor who spotted the unusual.

'That photograph, sir. The one over there. I swear to God the left eye's going brown.'

'So I see,' the inspector said, having seen nothing at all. 'All very odd. Now the glass is blurring. Somehow it's becoming hot.'

*

'Hold it,' Wendy protested, 'you'll set fire to the photograph.'

Harry closed his eyes for a moment, then reopened them. 'Damn! This kind of thing is difficult to control. But I'd say your uncle's left eye looks lazy.'

'Blurred,' Wendy corrected. 'Wall-eyed. That lot will have to be smart to make anything out of that. Can't you will one of them to half close his eye?'

'Damned if I know. I could have a shot at the one called MacGregor. He looks as if he might be more susceptible than the rest. Hope I don't burn him.'

*

'I suppose,' the inspector said slowly, 'this comes under the heading of what they call psychic phenomenon. But don't ask me what it's all in aid of.'

'Do you think a disembodied spirit is trying to tell us something?' Sergeant Mansfield asked.

'How the hell do I know. Spooks are way out of my line. That picture didn't tell me anything. A blurred eye! Probably isn't meant to mean anything. A murder may stir things up. I don't know.'

Sergeant Mansfield made a suggestion. 'Perhaps the lady upstairs is trying to tell us who did it.'

'Funny way of going about it. Floating vases and mucking up pictures. That's what gets me about this psychic business. – If the departed have something to say, why can't they do so in a straightforward manner?'

'Inspector,' MacGregor raised his voice, 'there's something wrong with my eye.'

'Blow your nose. Sure way of budging a bit of grit.'

'But it feels as if someone is pulling the lid down. It hurts.'

*

'He's covering it with his hand,' Wendy complained. 'They won't be able to see that it's supposed to be a lazy eye.'

'I can see that,' Harry retorted, his face screwed up into an expression suggesting intense strain. 'You concentrate on his hand and try to make him pull it away.'

*

'I wish,' the inspector said impatiently, 'you'd stop making a fuss. I'm trying to solve a murder case.'

MacGregor appeared to be trying to clutch his right hand to his left eye, while that member fought a frantic battle to break free. His colleagues watched with wide-eyed amazement when the hand proclaimed a hard won victory by flopping down to the detective's side, revealing an eye that was half hidden by a half closed lid.

MacGregor appealed for assistance. 'Help me ... I can't open my eye. Something is hanging on to the lid.'

'Can't see what we can do,' the inspector stated curtly. 'Blink the bloody thing.'

'I can't. Something is hanging on to it. It hurts.'

*

'You must stop hurting him,' Wendy protested. 'The poor man hasn't done us any harm.'

'My heart bleeds for him,' Harry replied, still straining to maintain contact. 'Are those block-headed cretins getting the message?'

'I don't think so. The inspector man seems to be more annoyed than anything else.'

'The blithering, brainless clot ... '

'You're letting go. He's opening his eye.'

*

'That was nasty,' MacGregor said, rubbing his left eye-lid. 'Never known anything like it.'

'For a moment you looked like something that had escaped from the chamber of horrors,' Sergeant Mansfield said. 'That droopy eye reminded me of someone, but damn if I can remember who.'

'The hunchback of Notre Dame,' the inspector suggested. 'Give him a hump and he'd have been a natural.'

'It's all right for you chaps to take the mickey,' MacGregor protested. 'But it was a horrible experience.'

'It was a horrible experience watching you,' Mansfield maintained. 'But for a moment you ... Say, Inspector, what was the name of that villain with a funny eye? You know – with a lid that sort of stayed half closed?'

'You mean Fingers Malone. Now you mention it ... Are you suggesting that someone is trying to fit-up Fingers? But he's strictly small time, a bit of house breaking, but mainly dipping in the rush hour. No rough stuff. Unless he panicked of course. Hit harder than intended. Mansfield, get on the inter-com, have Fingers picked up. Might strike lucky. Tell 'em to hold him until I get there.'

*

'We seem to have pushed the right button at last,' Harry said. 'Let's hope Fingers is the right lazy eye and there's not another one around they've never heard of.'

Wendy, who looked rather tired, leaned back and released a vast sigh. 'We've done all we can, but will probably never know if he's the right man, or some poor little crook who had nothing to do with my ... my death.'

It was then that Harry heard the not-to-be-forgotten voice of Sergeant Denham roaring from the street.

'Private Morgan. Show yourself, lad. Don't hide.'

'Who's that?' Wendy enquired.

'My guard Commander. I've deserted my post and he's going to lay the law down.'

'Did you desert it to help me?'

'Yes. And a fat lot of help I was too. Well, I'd better face him.'

He went to the nearest window and saw the sergeant standing in the centre of the street, which was by now dimly lit by the first light cast by the dawning day. The strong florid face wore an expression of anger blended with pity; the voice rose to a stentorian shout.

'You damned idiot! Got yourself housebound and clobbered with a charge of deserting your post. Now, hear this. You're stuck there for all eternity, unless a miracle occurs. And this is the miracle. If an F and B turns up with drawing power. Power to suck you into his aura. Now, I know this something standing orders forbids, but you're so deep in the manure, no action can make matters worse. Once you're embedded in an F and B, sooner or later he or she will take you out of that house, and just maybe one of our squads will dig you out. Means facing a court martial afterwards, but better than spending eternity in that place. Got that?'

'Yes, sergeant,' Harry replied with due humility. 'Thank you very much.'

'Well, even blithering idiots shouldn't be left out in the cold. Particularly the cold that's coming your way. So keep your chin up, lad, and an eye open for a super-sucker-in.'

He turned smartly on one heel and marched down the street, looking as much like a well-trained soldier that an ex-stockbroker could. Harry blinked back hot tears, for it seemed as if he was watching the departure of his last friend, even though up to that time he had not looked upon Sergeant Denham, as other than an unfeeling martinet. But now there was a spark of hope, the possibility of escape from this house, when Wendy was taken, always supposing someone with a powerful aura turned up.

Wendy nudged his arm. 'Two more men have just come in. One has a camera and the other a small black bag.'

'Cameraman and divisional surgeon,' Harry muttered. 'The proceedings will get progressively more boring from now on. Let's amuse ourselves by trying an experiment. Find out what happens when we try to leave the house.'

Her face brightened for a moment, then she shook her head.

'I heard that sergeant man say you couldn't and I mustn't. Poor George will turn up at any moment, and I want to comfort him.'

'You can't,' Harry insisted. 'Only make yourself more miserable. Believe you me, there's nothing more depressing than trying to make a loved one see and hear you, and getting no response. Much better if you're out of the way when he arrives.'

'But I must see him again. Even if it's for the last time and he can't see or hear me.'

Harry shrugged. 'It's up to you. In the meanwhile it can't do any harm in having a shot at leaving the house. It's pretty certain I can't, but there's no reason why you haven't been granted freedom of action. Pop out for a breather.'

'All right. It will be something to do. Let's go to the window.'

Ignoring the men who now walked around the room, ran up and down stairs, and kept relaying orders over a large, two-way radio, Harry and Wendy made their way to the open window and looked out on to the side passage.

'It looks normal enough,' Harry said. 'I mean, there doesn't appear to be anything in the way of my going out there. But I'm frightened to even try. The housebound can never leave.'

Wendy swung one leg over the sill. 'Rubbish. Look, it's easy.' She jumped down into the passage and raised her arms. 'Marvellous. I've never felt so free before. Don't be a scaredy cat. Have a go.'

But when Harry put out a tentative hand it seemed as if the window was blocked by an invisible wall, that if he maintained contact for more than a few seconds, sent a sharp pain coursing up his arm.

'It's no use,' he told Wendy. 'I can't get out. I'm stuck here. But you wander around for a bit. It will be good for you.'

She shook her head. 'No, I'm not leaving you by yourself. Besides, I want to see George when he arrives. Stand back, I'm coming back in.'

Harry watched her scramble back on to the window ledge, raise both hands to grip the upper sash, then push forward. A look of concern slowly transformed her face.

'Harry,' this was the first time she had used his name. 'There's something in the way. It's solid – and hurts me when I touch it.'

For a ridiculous moment he saw the obscene interpretation of the last statement, then the true meaning of what it implied hit him like a hundred mile per hour gale. Wendy had gone out and now could not come back in; he had come in and could not get out. What would happen to her was a matter for conjecture, but he was determined to stay near her until the end. He moaned: 'Oh, my God! My fault. I should have realised.'

Wendy began to cry and attempted to clutch his hands, but of course that invisible wall would not allow intimate contact, so they merely stared forlornly at each other, both desperate for comfort.

'What will happen to me now?' Wendy asked.

'I'm not sure. I think you'll shortly disappear. Ascend to a higher plane where I'll not see or hear you. Sort of die again.'

'But I don't want to go. The other place may be dreadful. Maybe hell.'

Harry grimaced and looked back at the room where the inspector and his team were preparing to leave. 'No, this is hell. Or at least purgatory. I'm certain you'll be happy up there.'

'Why can't you come too?'

'I've told you. I must remain here – for all sorts of reasons. Hopefully I'll make it one fine day.'

While they had been talking he had watched that portion of the street visible from the passage entrance, and therefore saw the tall, red-headed young man who came out of a side road, paused for a moment, while he took in the scene, then came running towards the house. Harry recognized him. He was George – Wendy's husband.

Harry spoke softly, willing the girl not to turn her head.

'Your husband is crossing the road. Please, don't move – close your eyes. Do not ... do not attempt to approach him. Now you're outside, I don't know what effect attempted contact with a loved one might have. It could hasten your departure.'

She obeyed him – to a point. Leaned against the window ledge, eyes closed, shoulders shaking, murmuring: 'He caught the early train. He left early.' Then a voice called out: 'Officer, what's the trouble? I'm Mr Allen. This is my house.'

Wendy screamed: 'George ... ' and ran from Harry's view; leaving him alone, listening to the constable who now guarded the doorway, say: 'The inspector is inside, sir. He'll explain,' followed by the sound of the door opening, a veritable jumble of footsteps, what seemed to be a bedlam of voices, dominated by one that kept shouting: 'I don't believe you ... I don't believe you ... '

Suddenly the street was flooded with pale golden light that made every house, window, door – even a discarded cigarette carton stand out in terrifying stark relief.

Harry whispered: 'She's gone. I will never see her again.'

He turned and for a while could not see across the room for the veil of tears that clouded his eyes, then became aware that George was seated with someone pouring whisky down his throat, while heavy footsteps came thudding down the stairs.

'Stand in front of him,' Inspector Watkins ordered. 'If he comes to, the last thing he'll want to see is his wife's body being carried out.'

They emerged from the narrow staircase; two men carrying a narrow stretcher, closed at the top by means of a zip fastener, and trudged across the room to the front door. All that remained of Wendy left the house, never to return. So far as the F and B plane was concerned, she was an un-person. For all the trace she had left on the sands of time, she might never have existed.

George stirred, then opened his eyes and looked blankly up at the young man bending over him. He murmured: 'I still don't believe you.'

'Just relax, Mr Allen,' Inspector Watkins said gently. 'If it's any consolation to you, we've got the chap who did it. The result of some extraordinary circumstances, that I can still hardly believe. But the main thing is, we've got him.'

'Wendy, if only you had stayed a little longer,' Harry said softly. 'Between us we nailed him.'

The inspector was speaking again. 'We've about finished here, sir. As – the man involved – has made a full confession, there'll be no need to bother you again. Only for the inquest. Get some rest. I've tufted out the people from next door, they were getting under our feet, but if you'd like them back ... '

'No,' George said firmly, 'I'd rather be on my own. Thanks all the same.'

'Up to you, sir.'

The law and its equipment moved to the door and out on to the street, leaving the small house empty save for one being who still retained the right to be called F and B, and one cursed to walk a confined space, unseen, most certainly unwanted; the epitome of isolation.

Harry stood for a long time looking at the grieving widower and presently found the strength to erase the word 'self' from before pity. George was young and time would doubtlessly heal the deep wound inflicted by bereavement, but now – in the never dying present – he suffered and therefore merited compassion.

He placed shaking hands over his face and sent out a terrible question across time and space.

'Why? We loved each other and wished the entire world well. What sin did we commit?'

Harry sank down on to his knees and created a possible answer, even though he knew the man opposite could not hear a word.

'We are not punished for our sins. Our sins punish us. The

road to fulfilment is a painful one.' He sat back and looked up into the contorted face. 'But I'm not getting through. A fly would make more impression.'

He reached out and touched clenched fists, then mouthed a silent plea. 'Let me share your pain. I knew her too – for a short while.'

Grief unfolded in his mind like a black flower, Wendy became a living memory that was only a few hours removed from flesh and blood reality; a warm wave of compassion poured through an alien body.

Harry looked out through George's eyes; sat in his brain and so was finally permitted to deliver his message.

'Wendy is not dead. There is only change and life eternal.'

George stood up, making Harry realise that he had not really performed a physical action for six months, and ran to the door. He wrenched it open, went out into the street and shouted the good news.

'No one dies. Wendy still lives.'

At the far end of the street Sergeant Denham stood surrounded by his squad. His face was lit by a rare smile.

'The lad has wiped the slate clean in one go. He forgot self. Something I still can't do. There'll be an investigation of course, but I'd say Private Morgan will be moving upwards. Upwards ... '

IV

The Astral Invasion

From the Casebook of the World's only Practising Psychic Detective

'There can be no form of life after death,' the man in the brown suit maintained. 'Life is life – death is death. Stands to reason.'

'Ah!' The little man with the big pipe smiled mysteriously and tried to give the impression he knew much, but was prepared to reveal little. 'What about the soul?'

Brown-suit released a derisive laugh. 'No such animal. A mythical nothing invented by our ancestors who couldn't face the prospect of sliding quietly into oblivion. Death is the great eraser and a good thing too.'

An attractive young woman of some twenty-eight years, with an oval sensual face framed by black hair, who may possibly have imbibed a trifle too unwisely, said in a soft, hesitant voice, 'One could have been supplied with an extra body. One that sort of grows up with the one we have now.'

A rather uncomfortable silence was broken by Brown-suit asking:

'Where, my dear, is this extra body of yours now?'

The young lady blushed and examined her fingernails with apparent interest. 'Perhaps just behind me. Made of high vibratory matter. Attached to me by an invisible cord.'

The little man with the big pipe nodded thoughtfully, a personage with flaming red hair blew out his cheeks, while a tall, lean young man, who had been listening to the conversation with an amused smile, said quietly:

'An interesting theory, but one that demands proof. At least a glimpse of this extra.'

The young lady lowered her eyes and traced an invisible pattern on the table. 'Actually I've seen one. More than once.'

The little man with the big pipe got up and announced, 'Wife's brother is coming to dinner, must be off,' which was a cue for everyone – save the tall lean young man – to empty glasses, push back chairs and button up coats.

'Seems you've frightened them away,' the young man said gently a few minutes later. 'The commonplace becomes embarrassed when faced by the unusual.'

The young lady raised her head and studied the handsome face with shy interest. 'But you're not embarrassed. You believe me.'

He shrugged. 'Let's say interested. The unusual lies in my stretch of country. Perhaps I'd better introduce myself. My name is Francis St Clare.'

'I'm Sophia Danglar.'

Francis St Clare permitted himself a slight frown. 'You *may* not have heard of me, although my principal cases have received wide publicity. I'm a psychic detective. In fact the world's only practising psychic detective.'

Sophia Danglar assumed an expression denoting delighted surprise. 'Of course! I read somewhere – seen your photograph – I never expected to meet you in a pub.'

'Even I get thirsty. About this astral body … '

'Pardon?'

'Secondary body. You say you've seen one. More than once.'

The pretty head was lowered again, a long finger began to trace a pattern on the table. 'My sister. My half sister that died eighteen months ago. She comes quite regularly – shifts the furniture about – hits me.'

The psychic detective leaned back in his chair. 'My fee is a hundred pounds a day, plus expenses.'

*

Frederica Masters was extremely pretty with ash-blonde hair and clear white skin, but she wore an expression of cynical amusement, as though her blue eyes had seen too much and forgotten too little in her short life. She wore a colourful costume that bordered on the bizarre. The bright green blouse had a dangerous split down the centre that revealed the valley between her full breasts, the matching mini-skirt was the stunted offspring of a broad belt, and her splendid nylon-clad legs were guaranteed to widen the normal masculine eyes with appreciation.

She addressed her nominal employer who sat behind a vast desk.

'You're bonkers.'

'Eccentricity is the hallmark of genius.'

'You pick up some bird in a pub. Swallow a tall story about a dead sister who comes back to move the furniture, then take the case without a word to yours truly.'

Francis fitted a cigarette to a long holder. 'But if true – unique. Dearly departed sister must be a catamado.'

'Balls.'

'Please, vulgarity sears my sensitive soul. I know it's asking a lot, but try to think. For dear departed sister to move furniture, she would have to lower the vibratory matter of her secondary body to such a degree, it would be impossible – except to a catamado.'

Fred placed her hands together and assumed a mock, pleading expression. 'Please, sir, tell me – what exactly is a catamado?'

Francis smiled amicably. 'It is always a pleasure to instruct the ignorant. A catamado, dear child, is so rare, I doubt if more than one is born every hundred years. Which is just as well, as they're very nasty. Their bodies are nigh indestructible, due possibly to an enormous willpower that can heal wounds in a matter of seconds, negate the effects of every known poison and sustain life under water for a long period. I'd say Rasputin was a catamado. Remember the trouble they had in disposing of him? With these extraordinary gifts goes a monstrous greed for carnal pleasures; eating, drinking, sexual deviations which include a strong element of cruelty.'

'If they're so god-darned powerful, how come they die?'

'Every catamado reaches a point where they self-destruct,' Francis replied. 'Usually when their will has been thwarted on some important issue. But they gain rather than lose by the death of the earth body. Apart from being welcomed with open arms by the nasties on the limbo plane, they inherit a secondary body that is even more powerful than the first. Von

Holstein maintains that a catamado can with practice, so condition the secondary body, it will exist on this plane for long periods, if not forever. Walk around and be accepted as normal.'

'That I would like to see,' Fred murmured.

'And maybe you will, child. But of course we must bear one fact in mind. If a catamado decided to take up residence in this vale of tears, it would be for a purpose. Possibly to help less gifted nasties across the great divide.'

Fred thought for a few moments, then announced a decision:

'I'm not going.'

'Help me get the gear together, then find a coat to cover that blood-stirring outfit you're wearing. I dislike not being the centre of attention.'

*

Springfield Mansions proclaimed by ornate verandahs, well-tended lawns, an intricate pattern of crazy-paved paths and a collection of gleaming cars, that here resided a section of the community that were well-blessed with healthy bank accounts. Fred remarked on this fact.

'Our Sophia must have a few quid tucked away.'

Francis nodded. 'Married briefly to one Michael Canford, of Canford, Canford and Bayswater, Solicitors. After less than one year of marriage, he died and left the grieving widow twenty-five thousand a year. She instantly reverted to her maiden name. How do I know? Two unethical telephone calls. Enough said.'

'So she's good for your hundred a day, plus expenses. There's no flies on my Francis.'

'But if she was skint, I'd still take the case. In fact I might pay her a hundred a day, if there's the slightest chance of tackling a catamado.'

'She could have been having you on,' Fred remarked caustically. 'Had she been knocking back the old gin and tonic?'

'Malt whisky,' Francis confessed. 'But I think that was because of, not why.'

They went into a large, carpeted foyer and approached a

uniformed porter who presided from behind a small mahogany counter, and seemed to regard their arrival as the bright spot in an otherwise dull day.

'How can I help you, ma'am – sir?'

'Miss Danglar – she's expecting us.'

'Apartment 22a – second floor. The lift is just across the hall.'

'Now there's a funny thing,' Francis observed once they were in the lift. 'Few women, having acquired the right to put Mrs before their name, revert to Miss. Might suggest the lady was not enamoured with the married state.'

'Probably a raving les.'

'Didn't strike me that way. Could have a sister complex. If she turns out to be a weirdo, we can always leave. Ah! Second floor! Soon all will be revealed.'

Before Francis's finger had reached the bell button, the door swung back to reveal Sophia Danglar attired in a long, pink dress and a pale smile. She stood to one side and allowed them to enter, before closing the door and leading the way into a room where modern décor contrasted with heavy old-fashioned furniture. Coffee simmered in a glass percolator and a collection of assorted biscuits, cream cakes and doughnuts were laid out on a nearby table. Francis made a brief introduction.

'Frederica Masters – answers to Fred. Sophia ... '

Fred grabbed the offered hand, said, 'Hi,' then moved quickly to the table. 'Good. Cakies!'

'Which you will not touch,' Francis instructed. 'I want your tummy empty, until we know what to expect. You know the rules.'

'Pig.'

'A much maligned animal.' He turned to Sophia. 'You must ignore our bickering, but this creature is so monstrously greedy. I just have to put my foot down. Now, Fred, behave yourself and test the atmosphere.'

Fred instantly sank into a chair and closed her eyes, while allowing her body to relax. Some two minutes passed before she spoke.

'Reasonably clear. I think a man fell from the scaffolding outside that window, when this place was being built, and just maybe he left something behind. And … yes … the faint sound of a child crying, but that's probably a relic of the building that was on this site years ago.' She giggled. 'What do you know? At least three little puppies are playing at my feet – and one is trying to get on to my lap.'

'Right, shut down,' Francis instructed. 'We can assume that this floor at any rate is fairly normal. Now, Sophia, you may pour me a cup of coffee with milk and three spoonfuls of sugar. I'll also partake of two doughnuts and two eclairs. Fred, one cup of black coffee. Let there be no argument, the young master has spoken.'

'Have you heard of sexual equality?' Fred demanded.

'Surely you mean sex equality?'

'Whatever I mean, have you heard of it?'

Francis thought for a moment. 'Heard yes – taken notice of – no.'

'One of these days I'll turn the women's lib loose on you.'

Francis accepted a cup of white coffee from Sophia, helped himself to doughnuts and cakes, then sank back with a sigh of content.

'Sophia, while I fortify the tissue, perhaps you'll fill in the blank spaces. To begin. Let's hear all about your sister when alive.'

Sophia sat down on the sofa and after sipping from a cup of weak coffee, began to speak,

'Her name was Margaret and she was twenty-five when I was born, being only my half-sister. My father had been married to her mother twenty-seven years when my mother – who was only eighteen – first went to work for him. Although he must have been in his middle fifties, they were soon engaged in a hectic love affair, which … '

'Dirty old … ' Fred began.

'Shut up,' Francis ordered. 'Sorry, Sophia, go on.'

'Which resulted in a rather sordid divorce case. Actually the entire business ended tragically. A year later my mother died giving birth to me, my father had a fatal heart attack some six weeks after, and Margaret's mother committed suicide.'

'And your half-sister never married?'

'No. She agreed to raise me, why I do not know, for she hated me. Mainly I suppose because she saw me as the cause of her mother's tragic death. But it wasn't until I was twelve or thirteen I became the object of cold, calculated cruelty. I've been told since that at that age I began to display a remarkable resemblance to my mother.'

'So you became a substitute punching bag,' Fred observed. 'Figures.'

'When did your sister die?' Francis asked.

'About eighteen months ago, when I married Michael. Frankly it wasn't so much a marriage as an escape, but I really do think this was the cause of my sister's death. She suffered a kind of stroke and never regained her power of speech. Within two days she was dead.'

'Well,' Fred remarked cheerfully, 'it's an ill wind that relieves no one's stomach.'

'If you can ignore the child's coarseness,' Francis said, 'perhaps you will tell me of your sister's return. When did it first happen?'

'Last week. On Tuesday morning, just after I'd finished hoovering the carpet. Footsteps came into being in the hall. Suddenly, moving quickly the way she always did. Always in a hurry. Then the door was flung back and she came in and began to rearrange the furniture, saying – so far as I can remember – that I had as much idea of how a room should look as an imbecile donkey.'

'Was this the kind of remark she might have made during her lifetime?' Francis asked.

'Yes. It was her favourite expression. But the mere sight of her dragging heavy furniture across the room, lifting that table and placing it by the window, was just too much, and I must have fainted, because I was brought back to full consciousness by two stinging slaps across the face.'

'Then?' Francis prompted.

'She began to rave – like always – said I was responsible for her death, but now she'd found a way to come back, I'd be seeing a lot of her.'

'And have you?'

'Almost every day. There's no way of knowing when she will appear or how long she'll stay. Yesterday she came at seven and left a little after eight. But last Thursday she only remained for a few minutes.'

Francis frowned at Fred who was gazing longingly at the plate of doughnuts. 'When you say appear and leave, what does that mean?'

'She seems to arrive at some point in the hall and so far as I can tell, departs from the same place. Her footsteps certainly cease when she's halfway across the hall.'

'Don't you go out to watch?' Fred asked.

Sophia shook her head. 'No, I just couldn't. Anyway Margaret orders me to stay here. Says there's things not meant for me to see.'

Francis got up and crossing the room opened the door. He stood looking into the hall for a few minutes, then spoke without looking back.

'Fred, come out here and do another atmosphere test.'

The girl rose from her chair with the air of one who has been called upon to perform an irksome chore and followed the psychic detective into the hall. There she walked slowly back and forth, then repeated the action from side to side until every inch of the floor space had been covered. She raised her shoulders and made an enchanting grimace.

'No cold spot. Not a dicky bird. Wait a sec – I don't know what it means – but I have a feeling – that I want to fall.'

An expression that was not devoid of alarm crossed Francis's face as he said quietly, 'Back into the sitting-room and be careful where you tread. I must be slipping.'

When they were again seated and Fred was pouring herself another cup of coffee – unrebuked – Francis asked softly: 'You do realise what we have here?'

She turned her head and looked straight at him and parted her full lips into a bleak smile.

'It's as clear as the nose on your face. Someone is opening an astral hole. Sister Margaret must be a very powerful lady.'

Sophia pleaded for information. 'An astral hole? I'm sorry. What is it?'

'A hole that can on rare occasions be driven through the fabric – the only definition I can think of at the moment – that separates this plane from the next. And the personage who can perform such a trick has to be very powerful indeed.'

'Even so,' Fred added, 'I think she must be having some help. Has teamed up with a super-nasty on the other side. We have a tricky situation and I wish I'd stayed at home.'

'With a catamado and a king-pin, I'm inclined to agree,' Francis confessed. 'But having taken the case ... '

'Should I move?' Sophia asked.

'Wouldn't do much good if you did. Let me explain. You must be a feeder. Help in some measure to build up your sister's secondary body; you are also connected to her by blood ties, so no matter where you go, she'll be drilling her way through. No, we must take what's coming and do our very best to bash the lady and whatever she eventually brings with her.'

'What can we expect in the immediate future?' Fred enquired.

'She'll come over, shift the furniture again – setting up exercises – possibly bash Sophia around – make her more compliant – then shove off. After a few days she should be strong enough to enlarge the astral hole, help king-pin and other nasties over, and bob's yer uncle. We're all set for a full scale invasion. Result – big upsurge in violent crimes, quite a few important people will do some very stupid things and chaos will reign supreme.'

Fred shuddered. 'And you and I are all that stands between so-called civilised society and that lot!'

'Our burden is heavy,' Francis admitted, 'but our souls are strong. But fear not. I intend to cut the programme by several days. Attack the lady before she has got into full stride. Then seal up the hole.'

'How?' Fred demanded.

'Never ask leading questions. At the moment I haven't the slightest idea, but my genius is certain to come up with a solution.'

Fred made a rude noise and helped herself to a doughnut, then poked her tongue out when Francis glared.

'Whatever happens I'll be in the manure. Why didn't I apply for a job at Marks and Spencers?'

'You wouldn't hold it down for a week. They could never trust you in the food department. Now, let us relax, talk of things weird and wonderful while our client prepares the lunch I will thoroughly enjoy. Sophia, Fred only requires two Ryvita biscuits and a weeny slice of cheese.'

'No I don't. I want ... '

'The child dreams,' Francis murmured. 'But her pretty tum-tum must remain reasonably empty, so the psychic juices can flow.'

'Stuff the psychic juices.'

'Such a statement, my angel, is not only vulgar, but borders on the impossible. Sophia, don't let us detain you. I expect you're anxious to get cracking in the kitchen.'

Sophia – clearly not knowing whether to be offended or amused – got up and said, 'Yes, well, I'll do my best,' and all but ran from the room. Francis waited until the door had been slammed behind her, before gazing intently at his assistant.

'Fred, I fancied I saw that delicious little organ you call a nose, twitch a moment ago. Can it be there's something I should know?'

The girl did not look up, but sat motionless, examining one slender hand. Presently she spoke.

'Things are beginning to happen in the hall. Nothing much. A kind of stirring – a hint of things to be. I think we should sit tight and wait for nature to take its course. Francis, can't I have a good solid lunch? I'm starving.'

He took one of her hands in his and kissed the soft palm.

'Angel, this may well be our most dangerous case. Strangely one I came across quite by chance. Or maybe not. What we call chance could well be the guiding hand of destiny. You well know that marvellous gift of yours only works one hundred percent when your tummy is empty. So be a good girl and eat some nice rye biscuits and please the young master.'

There was a more than usual brightness in her eyes as she brushed back a lock of hair with her free hand, before sitting upright and saying, 'Soft soap and balderdash. Anything to stop me getting my fair share of nosh. If I drop dead through mal ... mal ... '

'Malnutrition?' he suggested.

'Yes – I think. Then maybe you'll be sorry.'

'True, I would be heartbroken. But it could be convenient to have a gifted lady working for me on the other side.'

'Selfish, egotistic pig.'

'With a heart of gold.'

'Yes, solid – right through.'

Presently the door opened and Sophia stood in the entrance, staring at the fully engrossed couple with startled eyes. A deep flush slowly stained her face as she said:

'I'm sorry. I should have knocked. Please ... '

Fred turned her head and gave the embarrassed woman a dazzling smile. 'It's all right. I was just rummaging through Francis's hair. Can't be too careful.'

'Oh! I see. I just wanted to ask if grilled sole would be all right? With french fried potatoes. And cream crackers and Danish blue cheese for the young lady?'

'Fine,' Francis replied gravely. 'But could Fred have her Danish blue in the kitchen? I've a sensitive stomach and she's a messy eater.'

A push in the chest sent him sprawling on to the floor.

*

Lunch had become a digested memory, the psychic detective and his assistant, relaxed in armchairs, while Sophia watched them with something akin to disgust. Several times she was on the point of awakening them, but perhaps Francis's remark before closing his eyes, restrained her.

'Even while we sleep, we work. Or rather Fred does. I blunder along as best I can.'

This could have been another of his maddening jokes, if the mocking, inexplicable play of words could be so designated. But one thing was certain. Only someone like herself involved in a bizarre situation, would dream of employing this strange pair.

The girl woke first, opened those lovely eyes, that were not devoid of an element of alarm. Then Francis St Clare stirred, before parting his lips in a deceptively lazy smile.

'OK, Fred, collect yourself and make a total recall. Me, I blacked out the moment you reached the door. How went the voyage through the barrier?'

She clasped trembling hands and began to recite an account that was complete gibberish to the watching woman.

'Went up to D four – made blue C and kept out of harm's way. You're right – all kind of nasties are waiting for entrance pass, but the king-pin is a six-time has-been – a real know-all who intends to set the world on fire. Maggie *is* a catamado with bags of aggro and has strong links with our Sophia. Two way feed. One more visit, plus a spot of furniture humping and she'll be here to stay. Likewise King-pin.'

'Is she a has-been?' Francis asked.

'Can't be sure. Maybe. Strong hint of sado power that may go back a long way. Had a glimpse of rank and file nasties, but no sweat – if we can put paid to Maggie and King-pin. Mostly lower types with bowel emptying aspect.'

'When are we likely to expect a visit?'

'Anytime now. Maggie using a lot of power activating AH.'

There was a hint of impatience in Sophia's voice, when she said, 'Please – what is she talking about?'

Francis shrugged. 'Briefly – we all move into the secondary body while asleep and move up and down other planes of existence, but few of us can remember where or what we've seen, when this body wakes. Fred can. She has total recall. The result of years of self-training. Hence she has been able to overlook the limbo plane and get some idea of what is likely to happen.'

'Most extraordinary!' Sophia exclaimed. 'But I do not find such a possibility comforting. Thankfully I do not remember what happens.'

'And I am more concerned how we are going to stop a catamado and a king-pin from organizing a break out. They have occurred before and the dead have been seen walking our streets, but they lacked the power to stay long. Anyway, they rarely mean harm.'

'What about the phantom motorist of Guildford?' Fred enquired.

'Running that man down was an accident, although I'll admit he'd no business pinching that car in the first place. But, Angel, we're up against a proposed invasion with malicious intent. It means we have to clobber the two principals.'

Fred was about to make some retort, when the sound of footsteps came from the hall; a loud thumping that had Francis on his feet, sending out words in a harsh whisper.

'Fred – into the kitchen – now. Sophia, try not to think about us. Act as though we had never been.'

The girl moved with the speed of a startled cat and in less than three seconds they were both behind the kitchen door, which Francis left slightly ajar. Scarcely were they in position, when the sitting-room door was flung back and a shrill feminine voice began a furious tirade.

'So there you are! Glad you decided to stay put. Not that running would do you the least good. Wherever you go, I'll be there. Told anyone about my little visits yet? No? Wise. Because you won't be believed. Think you're mad. Put you away most likely, then I'll have to get cracking in a loony bin.'

There was a pause and Fred took advantage of the break to whisper, 'Aren't you going to have a look?'

'Not yet. Want her to go on as long as possible before putting in an appearance. You must stay out of sight.'

The voice spoke again.

'Not a word from you, which must mean you're scared out of your tiny mind. I wouldn't mind betting that when I'm gone, you'll try to imagine I've never been here. But I'm solid. And a bit stronger than last time. Watch. A bit more furniture shifting. Let's see if I can lift the sideboard.'

Fred nudged Francis in the ribs. 'This I must see. Come on, don't be a scary cat.'

'OK. But not a sound.'

Silently they drew back until both, with Fred in front, Francis's hands resting on her shoulders, could command a view of the room beyond. Sophia sat in her chair, her face devoid of expression, staring at a woman who was lifting an immense mahogany sideboard well clear of the floor. A tall woman with wide shoulders and grotesquely developed forearm muscles. She lowered the sideboard, then turned and revealed a strong, florid face and dark, deep-set eyes that were magnified by a large pair of horn-rimmed spectacles. Iron-grey hair, cut short, looked not unlike a close-fitting steel helmet and completed a portrait of a woman whose strength of mind would equal that of her body. She was dressed in a blue woollen jersey, grey tweed skirt and square-toe sensible shoes.

'Why the specs?' Fred whispered.

'She must have worn them all her life. Feels more comfortable in them now. Exercises about to continue.'

The woman began to move chairs about the room, lifting them high above her head and placing them against the wall, then utilizing two small tables as dumb-bells gripping each one by a leg and jerking them up and down with amazing rapidity.

'All part of preparing the secondary body for a prolonged stay in an alien environment. This is enthralling. I wonder if she can eat and drink?'

Fred's whispered reply all but erupted into a giggle.

'How could she? When her vibrations went up, the nosh would remain as it was and she'd have indigestion such as you've never dreamed. Say – can the secondary body die?'

'I don't know. But I think it's about time I took part in the proceedings. You stay here, but be prepared to send out a restraining loop if I get into trouble.'

'That will mean me opening up.'

'I know, but it can't be helped. The pursuit of knowledge is worth a few risks.'

'Your knowledge – my risks.'

He stepped round her, felt a brief grip on his left hand, before he walked boldly into the sitting-room. Sophia emitted a gasping cry, while the creature that had been Margaret Danglar dropped both tables and became as motionless as a statue. Francis was fascinated to see his own face reflected in her glasses. For a while neither spoke nor moved, then the shrill voice broke the silence.

'So, the stupid fool talked and found one willing to listen. I should have remembered you were always inclined to snivel to strangers. Where did you find him? In a pub? And what do you think he can do?'

Without removing his eyes from the white, strong face, Francis St Clare moved round the room until he stood facing the kitchen door and was relieved to see that Fred had retreated well back into the shadows. When he spoke his voice was soft, soothing, almost humble.

'I am but a seeker after truth, who can scarce believe he is looking upon a miracle. Forgive me, but when your sister told me ... I did not believe. Even now I can hardly accept the fact that the dead can return.'

A scornful smile parted the thin lips. 'I can assure you they do and in large numbers, but few have my power to stay. But I dislike the word dead. Do I look dead?'

'By no means, ma'am. But I used the term loosely. Let us say instead, those who have left time and joined eternity. As a student of the occult, I am enthralled. Could you satisfy my burning curiosity and tell me – what is it like there – beyond the barrier?'

The smile became a sneer. 'You will know soon enough. Limbo is a plain that glowers under a fire-flecked sky. The plane above that is much the same as this one – plus a few extras. Higher still? There is talk of colour language – sounds that take on glorious shapes, a gradual blending with the universal mind ... I have no burning desire to rise that high. Satisfied?'

'I am greatly obliged to you, ma'am. It is reassuring to be given proof that this life is not the beginning and end.'

Margaret Danglar sank into a chair and Francis heard the springs groan under her weight. Suddenly she snapped:

'Now, who are you? And what's your game?'

'My name is Francis St Clare. My game is the pursuit of knowledge. Permit me to retaliate. What are your intentions?'

Her head began to nod ponderously; her eyes invisible behind the spectacles, that due to some trick of light resembled gleaming discs. A dry chuckle escaped from between parted lips.

'My, but you're a sly fellow. Instead of genuine astonishment, terror, disbelief, we have a coolness that might be expected from a master of the eighth circle. Yet you have no power. If there had been the merest hint, you'd have been writhing on the carpet by now. I wonder why you're so confident?'

Francis did not feel confident, neither was he free from the mind-dulling effect of fear. This woman – and he used the term without reservation – was extremely powerful, just how much so, time would tell. And if she detected the near presence of Fred, the unique beautiful vessel, then indeed would all hell break loose. He shrugged and created a mundane reply.

'Knowledge breeds confidence and I have long suspected much that would alarm those who walk an uncomplicated path. But knowledge is a bottomless jug, and no matter how much I drink, my thirst is unquenched. I trust that answers your question, ma'am.'

The sneer broadened to a terrifying grimace. 'In other words a long-winded nosy-parker, with more brains than one might suppose. But can you keep your mouth shut? More important ensure that this sister of mine keeps a clamp on her tongue and out of public houses? Well?'

'And my reward for this vigilance?'

'Your lust for knowledge may be satisfied – in part.'

The psychic detective bowed. 'Crumbs from a rich man's table are a banquet for a starving man.'

Margaret Danglar emitted a deep chuckle. 'Crumbs from a rich ... ' She clasped large, useful hands together. 'Very good! A fellow of wit. I look forward to our further acquaintanceship. Now, I must get back. But you may expect me back in a short while. Don't follow me into the hall, as the lowering of vibrations is not a pretty sight and I'd rather not have an audience.'

Francis waited until she was half way to the door, before he said quietly, 'But it would be an interesting spectacle, ma'am.'

The face that looked back over one shoulder for the first time, suggested that this was not a creature of normal flesh and blood. Her voice had reached a higher pitch when she spoke.

'You will not – will not – move – move – until the sound of my footsteps has died away. Or by Beldaza and all his angels, you will curse the day that gave birth to that body. Do you hear me?'

'I hear and obey. Might always takes precedence over curiosity.'

She continued her journey to the door, opened and then closed it very slowly behind her; loud footsteps came into being, created the impression that they were descending stone steps, before abruptly ceasing. Francis expelled his breath as a vast sigh, and turned a pale face to Fred when she emerged from the kitchen.

'We got away with it – this time. Thank God it never came to a test of power, for, Fred my angel, I have grave doubts if you would have come off best.'

The girl sank into a chair and began to blow on her hands, while she endeavoured to control her trembling body.

'Sophia, you wouldn't have drop of the hard stuff handy? If anyone needs a stiff drink, it's me.'

Sophia seemed at first to have difficulty in talking, but she finally nodded and said, 'Yes, yes, of course. I could do with one myself,' and walked unsteadily to the sideboard. But Francis St Clare crouched down beside Fred's chair and glared at her with eyes that glittered with anger and fear.

'Fred, you didn't open up?'

'Mind your own business.'

'Did you open up?'

She grabbed a glass from Sophia and emptied its contents without pausing for breath. Almost at once a tinge of colour returned to her cheeks. 'Yeah, well – maybe just a bit.'

His voice rose to a shout. 'Do you realise the risk you took? If she had got wise to the fact that a medium of your power was present, it would have been curtains for both of us.'

She handed the empty glass to Sophia and silently mouthed a request for a refill. 'Well, she didn't. Francis, I just had to. You said I was to throw out a restraining loop if you got into trouble, and there's no way I could do that from cold. You know that, so why the panic act?'

He sat on the floor and leaned against her chair arm.

'OK. So you got away with it. How? She's a catamado. A super-sensitive. How come she didn't spot you?'

Fred half-emptied the second glass of neat whisky and smacked her lips in appreciation.

'That's better. I guess you must underestimate yours truly. I kept tight control, sent out the merest whisker of a probe, and it worked.'

Francis shuddered. 'Of all the bird brain ... '

'Don't you want to know what I found out?'

He shrugged. 'Of course. Since you broke into the orchard, we might as well taste the fruit.'

'Grub and bashing.'

'Elucidate.'

'Pardon?'

He sighed gently. 'Explain. In detail.'

'Can I have some more whisky?'

'No.'

Fred grimaced and slid back in her chair. 'OK. King-pin may be using her to make a big break through, but our Maggie drools for fish and chips and whacking the daylights out of Sophia here, or any other likely candidate.'

Francis turned to Sophia and raised an enquiring eyebrow.

'Would you say she enjoyed these weaknesses during life?'

The young woman blushed. 'Fish and chips was most certainly her favourite food and as for the other thing ... I explained that I was subjected to ill-treatment, and I'd say she enjoyed inflicting it.'

Francis nodded thoughtfully and narrowed his eyes until they were grey slits. 'In keeping with what little I know about the make-up of a catamado. I very much doubt if we'll ever share fried plaice and chips with her, but ... '

Fred sat upright and pointed a quivering forefinger at her employer. 'This is one time when I refuse to be a thinny-goat. I refuse ... '

'Will you shut up?'

'No one's whacking me.'

'I'm not suggesting any such drastic action. But if you were at some point to tempt her – taunt her – it might be a way to distract her attention at a vital moment.'

'So long as it's all talk.'

Francis got up and yawned in a rather pathetic attempt to appear unconcerned. 'Right, you stay here and chew the fat with Sophia, while I go and collect some special gear.'

'What do I do if Maggie comes back?'

'Go hide in the loo and shut down. Do you hear me? Shut down and on no account make contact.'

Fred put a forefinger under her chin and performed a little curtsey. 'As always, I obey, kind sir.'

'Mind you do or I'll put on a performance that will make Maggie wet her astral knickers. And no more booze for either of you. That's an order.'

'We'll both remain as dry as a pebble in a desert.'

*

Frederica Masters sat watching Sophia Danglar with an unblinking intensity, that finally made the older woman voice a mild protest.

'Please don't stare like that. It's ... it's most uncomfortable.'

The girl's flawless face assumed something like a smirk. 'You haven't much time for men, have you? I bet your late husband had a lean time.'

'I beg your pardon!'

'Granted. But it's a fact. Even our Francis, who could raise interest in a week old, female corpse, does nothing for you. Neither do I think you're les. What do you do for kicks?'

Sophia got up and glared down at her tormentor. 'You are the most insolent, irresponsible creature that I've ever met. I will not remain here to be insulted.'

'Sit down,' Fred ordered. 'I said – sit down. Do as I say or I'll belt you one.' She waited until the white-faced woman was again seated opposite, then continued. 'So, you obey the harsh word! That's interesting. I wonder – what was your relationship to your dead half-sister? A blood tie – you an A3 feeder – a catamado. Why do I feel that there's something dodgy about all this?'

'I don't know what you mean. I hated and feared my sister in life and even more so now she's – well – dead.'

'But you'll do whatever she tells you. Anything at all. And you're taking the entire business much too calmly. I mean you should be crawling up the wall. But apart from a spot of bottle bashing and a heart-tugging display of fearful helplessness, you seem to be bearing up very nicely. Suppose you hadn't, accidentally like, bumped into Francis in a pub?'

'I would have most likely gone mad. But I'm not going to talk to you anymore. After all you're only Mr St Clare's assistant. An insolent girl whose one asset is a rather bizarre gift.'

Fred screwed her face up into a parody of a contrite expression.

'I forgot me place! Me a miserable wage slave – only I'm a partner and I don't like seeing Francis taken for a ride.'

Sophia got up and began to walk resolutely towards the sideboard. 'I've said all I'm going to say until Mr St Clare comes back. Now I'm going to have a drink.'

'No, you're not,' Fred stated in a deceptively gentle voice. 'Not so much as a sniff of an empty bottle.'

Sophia did not reply, but continued on to the sideboard where she poured a generous ration of whisky into a glass. Fred rose and with sinuous grace crossed the room, until she stood behind the older woman. She placed long-fingered hands on rounded shoulders.

'Understand this. I sometimes cheek Francis, but when the

chips are down, he's the boss. And when he says no booze for either of us, then it's no booze for either of us. So you put that there glass down and go back to your chair like a nice and obedient girl.'

An elbow came back and butted Fred violently in the stomach, causing her to gasp and double up in agony. Then her head came up and she stared at the other woman with wide-eyed astonishment, while struggling to regain her breath. Sophia turned and raising the glass, said mockingly, 'Maybe that will teach you to mind your own business.'

Fred slowly straightened up and displayed signs of making an amazingly quick recovery from the unexpected blow. She creased her face into a wry grimace.

'Well I never, what a surprise. Who would have thought that helpless Sister Sophia was capable of packing such a wallop! But you're knocking back the corn juice. Put it down.'

'Make me, you stupid little fool.'

There was a blur of movement as Fred's hand lashed out, knocking the glass from Sophia's hand, to go hurtling across the room. The older woman instantly retaliated. Her right hand cracked against Fred's left cheek, leaving the imprint of four fingers on the smooth skin; forcing the girl's head back and forcing another gasp from her gaping mouth. Then she spun round, drove a foot into Sophia's stomach, before bringing her forearm up under the woman's chin. She looked down at the motionless body and swore.

'Bloody hell! Why can't people be peaceful?'

Looking round she spotted a cut glass vase that contained several splendid red roses. Having removed the flowers, she poured water over Sophia's face. Her restorative action was rewarded by a stream of obscene words that both shocked and amused.

'Poor Francis is never going to believe this,' Fred remarked as she pulled the spluttering woman to her feet. 'Just goes to show what a spot of aggro will uncover. Where did you learn all those rude words?'

Sophia backed slowly to a chair and sat down, her face ugly with rage. 'You'll pay for this. When I tell Margaret what you've done – she'll make you hop.'

Fred helped herself to a small whisky and explained this

departure from the path of total abstinence. 'Medicinal. That little set-to took it out of me.' She too sat down and surveyed the glowering woman with a mocking smile. 'Well, well and well again! So frightened little woman who couldn't say boo, was just an act. Goodbye, pussy cat – hello tiger. And even the great Francis St Clare was taken in, not I might add, that it takes much to take him in. If I make myself clear. My word he's going to be surprised.'

'You hit me first,' Sophia protested, rubbing a bruise on her chin. 'If you hadn't hit me, I wouldn't have hit you.'

'I hit the glass, which resulted in a waste of good whisky. From then on it was a case of self defence. Now, you sit there and don't move so much as an eyelid. And should you have some so far undetected gifts, don't you dare send out a call to sister Maggie, or so help me, I'll turn your brain into a speck of seething porridge.'

'I have no psychic gift,' Sophia said quietly. 'You know that.'

'Me, I don't know anything. I'm merely a bag of nasty suspicions. Perhaps it might be better if we didn't talk. Even looking at you makes me nervous.'

'Really ... ' Sophia began, then shrieked and clutched her head, thereby causing Fred to sigh deeply. 'There, look what you've made me do. Send out an offensive probe. Francis doesn't like me to do that. Of course I've only planted a suggestion that your head is being split in half, but you'll never know it's not the real thing. Ah! The front door has just been opened. Francis the Great must have used his skeleton key. Now, let fun and games begin.'

Francis St Clare entered the room carrying a large leather case in one hand and a bulky bag in the other. He placed both carefully on the floor, then stared at the young women with growing concern.

'What,' he asked quietly, 'is up?'

Fred pointed a quivering forefinger at Sophia. 'She's a fraud. Packs a star maker punch – knows a lot of rude words – told me Sister Maggie will make me hop. Nice frightened lady? Not on your nelly.'

Francis sank into a vacant chair and stared sadly at the empty fireplace. Presently he asked a question.

'Why isn't she saying something?'

'I gave her an offensive probe and told her not to even think.'

He nodded, then shook his head. 'I always said the child had a brain the size of a split pea. As usual I was right.'

'What the hell ... ?'

'Didn't it occur to you that if our Sophie is a fraud, then the little act we saw from the kitchen was also a put up job? That Sister Maggie knew we were there, rejoiced when you made contact, for that gave her the opportunity to estimate your power potential. That my acquiring a client in a pub was not accident, that, not to put a too fine a point on it, the young master was led up the garden path. We, dear child, are being used.'

'Oh!'

Francis gave Sophia his most brilliant smile. 'Would I be correct in assuming that you read the accounts of my previous cases, took note that I was always accompanied by an addle-brained creature, who quite by chance, is possibly the most powerful materialistic medium alive today, then nailed me in my favourite pub?'

After a fearful glance at Fred, Sophia spoke.

'Margaret made me do it.'

'Fred.'

'Present.'

'Help me set up the pentacle.'

'That won't do much good. It's only big enough for us and we daren't leave Sophia on the outside.'

'Allow the young master his wonders to perform. It is not my intention to put us in the pentacle, but put it round the astral hole so Sister Maggie can't get out.'

'You're mad.'

'I prefer brilliant and resourceful. Maybe it won't work, but damned if I can think of anything better. Now, you keep a fix on Sophia, while we get the doings set up.'

Fred watched with raised eyebrows, Sophia with apprehension, as Francis opened the flat case and spread out a number of silver rods that had slots at one end and flat projections on the other. These he proceeded to slot together until a five-pointed star, measuring about fifteen metres in circumference, lay on the floor.

'My own invention,' he stated with some pride. 'Charged water in every tube, made of pure silver, no nasty can get in, or hopefully, get out.'

'Shouldn't you,' Fred enquired in a gentle voice, 'have erected it in the hall. I mean – how are you going to get the bloody thing through the doorway?'

Francis sighed deeply and gazed upon his assistant with sad reproach. 'Would it not have been kinder to give the young master a word of warning, before he had expended so much precious energy? Genius cannot be bothered with minor details.'

He disconnected the pentacle, carried component parts into the hall, then reappeared in the doorway.

'Fred.'

'Sir.'

'I would like you to locate the exact location of the astral hole.'

'Dicey. If the damn thing is open, I might get blasted.'

'If it was open Sister Maggie would be honouring us with her presence.'

'Shall I bring Sophia with me?'

'It might be wise. Left alone she may get lonely.'

Sophia displayed marked reluctance to move from her chair, but after Fred enquired sweetly, 'Got any aspirins, love?' rose and walked quickly into the hall. There Fred closed her eyes, advanced a few paces, then got down upon her knees and crawled across the carpet. Suddenly she sat up and pointed to a spot which was situated a few feet away.

'There. I'd say it's about three feet wide and is bubbling.'

'What!'

'Bubbling like a saucepan of porridge. No sign of anyone or thing trying to get through.' She got up and placed both hands on the small of her back. 'You've no business making me crawl around like a demented frog. I've got a crick.'

The psychic detective rubbed his hands. 'Right. Let's do the job properly. First the blessed sheet.'

'Who blessed it?' Fred enquired.

'I did. Merely a matter of knowing the right words. Keep well back while I do the necessary.'

Francis went back into the sitting-room and returned

carrying the bulky bag, which unfastened and tipped its contents out on to the floor. White wax candles carefully wrapped in clean silk, silver swastikas with their bent arms pointing upwards, bundles of pungent herbs and a roll of dazzling white canvas, which when unrolled revealed that it had been cut and shaped to fit underneath the pentacle. A small pocket had been sewn into each point, into which Francis slipped a swastika. He then stapled an ornate candle-holder just below every tip.

'Grab hold of one side,' he instructed, 'and we'll lay this masterpiece over the astral hole, then having reassembled the pentacle, bung it on top.'

They laid the star-shaped canvas into position, before reconstructing the silver pentacle and laying it gently until the two outlines merged. There was an element of beauty in the large silver star, that gleamed with light reflected from the overhead lamp, enhanced by tall candles and white 'blessed sheet' that looked not unlike an even coating of snow. But in the centre, in that part which covered the astral hole, a faint rippling movement could be seen; suggesting that a slight draught was seeping through an imperfectly closed aperture.

'Do you suppose Sister Maggie is trying to get through?' Fred asked.

'Extremely unlikely. The disturbance would be more pronounced. In any case I cannot believe that a catamado will find difficulty in rising up through a blessed cloth, but I hope she'll be clobbered by the pentacle. I think it might be wise to tie Sophia up. I don't want her disturbing the proceedings at a vital moment.'

Sophia shrank back against the wall and shook her head.

'Leave me alone. There's nothing I can do. Apart from giving Margaret the power to appear, I have no psychic power. I've told you that.'

Fred smiled sweetly. 'But you've got feet, dear. It only needs a good kick to put the pentacle out of action. So you sit yourself down in that chair.'

'Curtain cords from the next room,' Francis suggested. 'And you'd better get a couple of towels from the bathroom. Useful as a gag in case she starts yelling. Can't abide yelling women.'

'What about you lighting those candles? That thing is not

very effective unless there's a circle of light.'

'Well done. I was hoping you would spot the deliberate mistake. Nine out of ten for observation.'

When Fred had left the room, Francis produced a gold cigarette lighter and lit each candle, then straightened up and looked upon his handiwork with unstinted admiration.

'Made the lot myself,' he informed an unresponsive Sophia. 'Even the candles. Pure wax. Nasties can't stand pure wax and silver. Did you know that?'

From her position near the wall, Sophia shook her head. 'I know nothing about anything. I only do what Margaret tells me.'

Fred returned with four silken cords and three towels, and there followed a slight struggle as Sophia was tied to the wooden armchair, followed by a verbal protest when the girl prepared to stuff the end of one towel into the quivering mouth.

'Please don't gag me. I'll not make a sound. I promise.'

The psychic detective, after some consideration, nodded.

'Very well. But remember not so much as a squeak. Sit there like a good girl and watch the show. So far as I know if my pentacle works, there's no way your sister can influence you. But I can't take any chances.'

'If it doesn't work, we're all in the manure,' Fred said fervently. 'May the hired help enquire what we do now?'

'You may. Wait for it all to begin. So fetch two comfortable chairs from the sitting-room, then when we are at ease, the young master will edify you with brilliant conversation.'

'Why can't you fetch the chairs?'

'I must reserve my strength for the battle to come. Apart from which he of rank does not fetch and carry.'

Five minutes later found the psychic detective reclining in a small padded chair, his feet on a footstool, while his unfaltering gaze was directed at the undulating centre of the blessed sheet. His demeanour was that of a man with an untroubled mind.

'It is not generally known that I am a poet of rare distinction. Words trip across my mind like fairies dancing on a floor covered with upturned tin-tacks. At odd moments – while shaving or sitting on the loo – the muse woos me – and lo

– beautiful odes come into being. I will now proceed to deliver one such masterpiece that I composed this morning.'

'Is it obscene?' Fred enquired.

'Most certainly not.'

'Pity. Carry on.'

Francis watched one candle flame tremble slightly, before clearing his throat and reciting the following lines.

'The Sad Saga of Charlie Tunnicliff.'
'There lived outside London Gate,
'A man t'was said was never late.
'Charlie Tunnicliff was his name.
'But he always gave me a nasty pain.
'Now Charlie he lay down to die,
'And his soul soared above the sky.
'Before the pearly gates he stood.
'Without his cap, cloak or hood.

'St Peter gazed upon him with awe,
'And said Gor Blimey show this bloke the door.
'And Charlie on his knees did ... '

Fred dared to interrupt. 'Is there much more?'

'Three hundred and twenty-two verses,' Francis replied gravely.

'Well, don't let me stop you, but I'm experiencing a distinct feeling of unease which is coming from that contraption.'

'Ah! Then perhaps I'd better curtail your intellectual treat. What sort of unease are you getting?'

'Sort of – all is not well unease. Same as a burglar would feel if he found some swine had fitted a chain on the front door, since he last did the place over. He'd wait a bit, wouldn't he, before getting the old hack-saw out?'

'And it is possible that our burglar is having a little think before breaking in?'

'Most certainly, but she'll be bursting through anytime now.'

'It will be nice to see her again,' Francis declared, shifting to an upright position in his chair. 'Dare I hope that another meeting will lead to a tender relationship? All things are possible.'

'The BS is bulging,' Fred pointed out.

They watched a circle of cloth gradually rise up, seemingly stretching the fabric and permitting a dim red light to filter through the extended strands. It grew in height and circumference, took on the shape of an illuminated figure, then after a loud popping sound, emerged into the undoubted likeness of Margaret Danglar. She gave one glance at the bound form of her sister, then glared at the psychic detective.

'So!' the high-pitched voice held an undertone of sardonic amusement, 'with the help of my blundering sister, you caught on. Eh? And,' she looked down at the silver star and lighted candles, 'it would seem you are a knowing fellow. Even better than I supposed. Not that this contraption will be of much use – in the long run.'

'Why not try to get out,' Francis suggested. 'But before you waste precious energy, allow me to explain a few points. I've used pure silver tubes filled with charged water. The candles were also charged while still in liquid form. Once you leave the astral hole, your feet will be in contact with blessed – or if you prefer – charged cloth. But maybe you are a very gifted lady and will – given time – overcome these obstacles. If so, I will order Fred – who is indeed very gifted – to send out a blue protective loop. Has a nasty effect even in a secondary body, and creates an impression of being strangled with white hot wire.'

The eyes magnified by the horn-rimmed spectacles, were turned in Fred's direction and the strong teeth bared in a mirthless grin.

'That's the one I want. A shapely font of power. Sooner or later you and I will have an interesting session together, my dear.'

'Would I not be right in assuming you are not drawing power from your sister,' Francis asked with a harsh voice, 'and you must be operating on what I can only describe as your battery? It might be wise to go back to Limbo without delay.'

For a while it seemed as if Margaret Danglar was considering breaking out of the pentacle. She swayed like a tree buffeted by a strong wind, glared at the lighted candles that blazed up into a spluttering flame, while thin tendrils of steam seeped out from where the silver rods joined.

'Go on – have a go,' Fred jeered. She held out one well-shaped hand and said in a little girl voice, 'I'm very naughty and need correction.'

'And I believe there might be some frozen fish and chips in the fridge,' Francis added thoughtfully. 'Would you like to organize a fry-up? We can make it a real kinky party. Rod and cod. Sorry.'

The strong face crumpled into a mask of uncontrolled rage and the voice rose to a near scream.

'You dare to taunt me! Think you're safe, eh? Well let me tell you this. There's one greater than me. And you can be certain he'll take action. Make use of the fragments that drift through the rooms in every house. We'll see how your pentacle stands up to an attack from the *outside*.'

'We'll be ready,' Francis replied with a confidence he did not feel. 'Send 'em all in.'

'You may gamble your body and soul on it.'

Her face and form began to disintegrate, gradually merged into the original illuminated figure, that in turn sank downwards and became a fast shrinking mound of cloth; after the lapse of a few seconds the pentacle was unoccupied, although the slight quivering in the centre still continued.

Fred wiped her forehead and blew out her cheeks.

'Francis, the situation is very dodgy. Did you hear what she said? King-pin will make use of fragments. Personality debris, build them up into something very nasty. Why can't I go home?'

'You don't mean that. Think of all the fun you'd miss. And the satisfaction of knowing you'd help repulse an astral invasion.'

'Always supposing we do.'

'I often stumble, sometimes fall, occasionally stray in the wrong direction, but eventually I stagger across the finishing line. Therefore let us advance with girded loins and upstanding knickers, secure in the knowledge that all will be well.'

'Shouldn't we be doing something about the nasties that will soon be belting round this place?'

'We are fortified for such an eventuality. Perhaps you'll give me a hand in transporting Sophia – chair and all – back to the sitting-room, where we'll be more comfortable.'

Fred frowned. 'And leave the pentacle unprotected?'

'Dear child, the kind of nasty that will shortly put in an appearance will draw a certain amount of essence from us, then have a go at breaking up the pentacle. Hence, the further we are away from it the better. See?'

'I suppose so. Why isn't Sophia saying something?'

'The wise remain silent when the strong speak.'

*

Francis had switched on a tall standard lamp and closed the curtains, before the first disturbance made Fred raise her eyebrows. A bright, red luminous ball of approximately six inches in diameter, rolled across the floor from the direction of the door and exploded without making any sound. A foul stench spread throughout the entire room and caused Sophia to retch.

Fred wrinkled her nose. 'I suppose you want me to get rid of that? I ask you – an ele-ball! Not very original.'

'But unpleasant,' Francis retorted, 'and I'd be pleased if you'd neutralize the bloody thing without delay. But I must point out that this is only a trial run. A little tester, so to speak. Further visitations will get progressively worse.'

'Thank you, mate,' Fred replied, making some complicated passes with her hands. 'When they reach the stage where I can't handle 'em, I'll let you know.'

Francis gave her a beaming smile. 'My faith in your ability to cope with the unusual is complete. Whatever puts in an appearance will go down in flames. I will relax and watch your performance with the utmost confidence.'

Fred sat up and directed a glare at her employer.

'Just a moment! Am I to understand that you are relying on me one hundred percent? You've got no plans of your own?'

'Why should the most brilliant general plan when he has such a gifted chief-of-staff? But fear not, when battle is joined, I will be right behind you.'

Fred looked anxiously from left to right. 'Francis, don't joke. This is going to be a terrible dust-up. Waterloo will seem a nun's picnic in comparison. A king-pin chucking his all at us. To say nothing of a sado-catamado who has cruel designs on my person.'

'Should the worse happen you will have suffered in a noble cause.'

Sophia spoke for the first time in a long while. 'Why not be sensible and leave? I only carried out Margaret's instructions and now you know what to expect, she can't blame me if you disappear. There's no way you can win against Margaret and her – her friends.'

'But we'll go down in a blaze of glory,' Francis insisted. 'At least Fred will and I'll make a point of covering her grave in forget-me-nots once a year. But do not imagine for one moment that I am not fully aware of what we are up against, hence the inane chatter. But I cannot walk away from the prospect of an astral invasion, without putting up some kind of fight.'

The sitting-room door suddenly opened, then just as quickly closed again. This appeared to be a signal for every door in the flat to open and slam, creating such a racket, both Francis and Fred covered their ears. Sophia, being unable to take this elementary precaution, began to cry. After a few minutes of this unnerving phenomenon, all sound ceased, to be succeeded by an equally disturbing silence. Francis was the first to speak.

'Still warming up. Poltergeist action. Stand by for flying objects. Sophia, get your head down. Fred, get ready to hit the floor.'

'I'm on my way. Would you like that I clear the flat? Bit of an effort, but I'll do my best.'

The psychic detective shook his head. 'Save your essentional, angel. We'll need every dram later on. What happens now is for frightening purposes only. That which follows will have a go at knocking us into next week.'

A picture left the right hand wall and crashed against its opposite neighbour; a foot stool rolled across the floor and came to rest at Francis's feet. 'Very kind,' he murmured, 'but not at present.' A particularly ugly vase rose up from the mantelpiece and with a peculiar whistling sound went hurtling past his head to make violent contact with the door. The clatter of falling broken china seemed to be unnaturally prolonged.

'That's interesting,' Francis remarked.

Fred spoke from the floor. 'It would have been had it hit your head.'

'Don't be facetious, child. Don't you realise these objects are not being thrown, but tele-ported? Lowered vibratory matter travelling through time-space. Enthralling.'

Fred raised her nose from the carpet. 'You be enthralled in silence. Just let me wet my knickers in peace.'

Sophia made another of her rare utterances. 'I think it's too bad Margaret breaking up my home like this.'

Francis hastened to reassure her. 'Please don't blame your charming sister for this orgy of destruction. It's the master mind who's responsible. King-pin. Not being able as yet to put in an appearance himself, he's activating elemental forces that ... '

Fred sat up and turning her head looked fearfully at the window. 'Francis, that ... '

'Don't interrupt the young master when he's talking.'

'That time image I sensed a while back. The man who fell off the scaffolding – well he's building up on the balcony.'

'So we'll be entertained by one of yer actual hauntings.'

'But he's malignant.'

'A time image malignant! How come?'

Fred shook her head, making the blonde curls dance.

'I don't know. Maybe he's been given an extra ingredient. But I'm not what you might call happy.'

'Shut down. Don't let him get to you.'

'I don't think he can get at my mind. That's him having a go at the french windows.'

The double french windows were tall, comprised of rows of glass panes that permitted a view of the waist-high balcony wall, that stood some four feet beyond. But now the view was impeded by a tall shadowy figure that pressed against the glass, making the casements rattle.

'Only semi-solid,' Francis observed. 'Never reach full maturity. I mean – how can it? Unless ... ' He glared at the trembling Sophia. 'Are you feeding that thing?'

'No, I don't ... don't think so.'

'Do you feel a sudden coldness? A draining of strength?'

'No. But I never do. Not even when Margaret comes. I don't think I've got much – whatever it is – and Margaret doesn't need much.'

'If he's only been fed from the other side, there's not a lot to worry about,' Francis said, without however his usual conviction. 'He may be able to shift things around, give you a nasty knock if you get in the way, but I doubt if there's any intelligence. Possibly a residue of instinct, plus whatever instructions King-pin can get through.'

'Those bloody windows are about to call it a day,' Fred pointed out, 'and when they do I'm all for hiding in the loo.'

'The loo was never intended for hiding in, so pull yourself together and talk sense. Get back into your chair and let nature take its course. Remember this is not the worst we have to face.'

The french windows crashed open and what Francis would later describe as a reinforced time-image, glided into the room. It resembled a tall, well-set man with red hair and a white dirt-stained face, attired in a faded blue boiler suit. From the waist up he appeared solid, but his lower half suggested a hint of transparency. He made no sound, but moved across the room, his deep-set eyes glaring at the psychic detective, his teeth bared in a death-grimace. In contrast to Fred's former alarm, she now watched the apparition with icy calm and rapped out a stream of information.

'Just over fifty-percent solid ... no kind of personality ... has been built up to put us out of action. Then break up the pentacle.'

Francis St Clare spoke quietly. 'I would like you to place a psychic barrier across the door and hold it until this thing loses power and disintegrates. Can you do that?'

Fred nodded slowly. 'Do my best. Can't promise more.'

She sank back and closed her eyes, then appeared to collapse, every indication of life leaving her face. But a faint whisper escaped from between her parted mouth.

'I have erected the barrier, erected the barrier ... '

The apparition, still staring directly at the psychic detective, glided slowly towards the door, one arm raised as though threatening anyone who might impede its progress. When it reached the door, the outstretched hand appeared to be groping for the handle, before the figure froze. A full minute may have passed until it slowly turned and presented a face that lacked both eyes and nose, although a pulsating hole could have been accepted as a primitive mouth. For a moment

Francis thought the battle was over and disintegration had set in, but in a short while the former features slowly reformed, then assumed an expression of intense rage.

The eyes flashed from Francis to his assistant, then the right arm came up and the forefinger pointed – and Fred screamed. The psychic detective ran to the writhing girl and grabbed her hands.

'Fred – fight it. It is only auto-suggestion.'

She managed to eject half-strangled words. 'A – red – hot poker – in – my stomach.'

'King-pin is trying to make you drop the barrier. Dismiss the pain – it doesn't exist. And keep the barrier up. You can do it. Draw strength from me. Fight, darling – fight as you've never fought before.'

Her grip tightened on his hands until he flinched, her gasping cries sank to moaning sighs, then ceased altogether.

'It's almost gone,' she whispered. 'But I'm terribly tired – and it's still there.'

'Are you maintaining the barrier?' Francis asked, looking back at the terrifying figure.

'Yes, but I don't know for how much longer.'

'Just hang on for a few minutes more. The damned thing is looking a bit ragged round the edges. Just take a deep breath, push out your what-its and in next to no time, it will fade away.'

In fact the apparition suddenly vanished, its passing marked by a soft swishing sound.

'Air displacement,' Francis explained. 'Semi-solid object suddenly removed – air rushed in to fill the void.'

Fred wriggled her shoulders. 'I know that. What I want to know is – can we rely on a little break now? Is King-pin as buggered as I feel? I only require a little information.'

'I'm not certain, having never dealt with a king-pin before, but I'd say he needs a short rest. Say – five minutes.'

'Five minutes!'

'Angel, you must see the situation from his point of view. We're mucking up a well-planned astral invasion and quite naturally he's somewhat put out. We've got to be clobbered. On the other hand, we're ... '

'Buggered.'

'That remains to be seen. You, my loved one, must take an another astral stroll. Put yourself into a self-induced trance, slip out of that pulse-stirring body and seep that atom of awareness you call a soul, in blue essence. You've done it innumerable times before. Do it now.'

Fred murmured, 'He-who-must-be-obeyed has spoken' and instantly snuggled down in her chair and appeared to fall into a deep sleep. Francis nodded his approval, before moving over to the confined Sophia and kneeling down before her.

'I'm truly sorry we have to keep you trussed up like a Christmas turkey, but I must protect Fred and myself from your involuntary actions. Do you understand?'

Sophia nodded. 'But I cannot believe you will beat my sister. She seems to have retained those terrifying aspects that were hers during life and merged them with ... '

'Her post-crematian gifts that are hers now. I understand. Of course you know nothing about a king-pin?'

'Margaret said she had a powerful friend on the other side, but that's all.'

'A king-pin is a being that has completed at least six long life-times on this plane and a timeless period on one or the other of those beyond the barrier. Although it is doubtful if such a creature could exist on or above the third. Now, when the action starts keep your mind shut down. Imagine an iron door fitted with seven locks. Can you do that?'

'I'll try. Is – Fred – now again spying on – my sister and King-pin?'

'Not exactly. She's still in this room keeping guard. The moment something nasty starts, she'll wake up and warn us. Can see, hear and sense the super-normal on the astral. Remarkable girl, but for heaven's sake don't let her know I said that.'

From the balcony, just beyond the open windows a dog howled, causing Francis to spring to his feet. 'Fred,' his voice rang out, 'wake up. What's going on?'

The girl opened her eyes, stared blankly at the opposite wall for a few moments, then jerked her head round and spoke quickly.

'Those sweet little puppies – they're being used to build up something very close to hell-hounds. Taking on form now.

Soon be as solid as a double-decker bus.'

'But only for a short while,' Francis replied calmly. 'Can you rebuild the barrier across the door?'

'Yes. But if I do the brutes will go for me. I don't fancy a dangling windpipe.'

'Rely on the young master to protect you.'

'Heaven help me!'

He bent down and took from a gladstone bag that crouched by his chair a large garden syringe and pulled back the handle.

'Filled with charged water, which if used sparingly will keep ele-beasties at bay until King-pin is exhausted. Right, put the barrier up.'

They came into the room, black as midnight, eyes glittering like fire-tinted rubies; three dog-shaped creatures that spread out across the room and became black statues.

'Building up power,' Francis explained. 'Soon they'll make a dash for the door and if the barrier drops, at least one will smash its way through. But if it holds ... '

'Wrong,' Fred said quietly. 'Two will go for the door – one will go for me.'

The young man nodded slowly, but not for one moment removing his gaze from the three ele-dogs. 'Fool that I am. I should have realised. At least I'll only have to deal with one – at first. Then when the other two fail to get through the door ... '

Three black heads were raised, but one growl came from three throats. All sprang into action, one streaked for Fred's chair, the other two for the door. Francis waited until the creature was a scarce two feet away, before depressing the syringe handle. A thin stream of water hit the ele-dog between the eyes and sent it hurtling backwards, while emitting a high-pitched howl. Francis aimed another stream at the throat and waited until the thick fur began to dissolve into a sizzling, smoking, foul-smelling black liquid, before turning to watch the remaining two.

Both leapt repeatedly towards the door, only to bounce back as though they had struck a resilient wall. On each impact Fred shuddered and moaned softly, her white face drawn and gleaming with perspiration. Suddenly one dog spun round and came bounding towards the psychic detective, leaving its companion crouching by the door, as though exhausted or waiting for a suitable opportunity to renew the attack.

Francis depressed the plunger again, but this time his target swerved, went bounding round the room, then approached Fred from the far side; crashed into the chair, overturned it and sent the screaming girl rolling across the floor.

Francis released an involuntary cry of anger and distress as he sprayed the snarling beast with charged water, not stopping until it was a steaming, seething mass that gradually disappeared. For a fatal moment all was forgotten but the girl who lay motionless and silent on the floor; he knelt beside her and took one slim wrist between thumb and forefinger. Her pulse was strong if somewhat erratic and presently she opened her eyes and murmured:

'You berk! The barrier's down.'

He jerked his head round in time to see the third dog crash through the door, leaving a jagged hole that permitted a limited view of the flickering candles that marked the outer edge of the pentacle. Then a giant dog that reared up on hindlegs, disarranged with front paws; whimpering, self-destructing when it made contact with silver, wax candles and charged water that seeped out from fractured joints, but when it at last sank down into dissolution, the object for which it had been created had been achieved. The pentacle had been wrecked.

'Not one of my most successful cases,' Francis murmured. 'Are you hurt?'

Fred got up, righted the chair and sat down. 'Only in spirit. Sorry I couldn't hold the barrier, but when that thing hit me, I could only think of the body beautiful. Our Sophia has passed out.'

Francis spared one glance for the slumped figure and shrugged.

'Only to be expected. I should imagine she's been drained by now to give her sister staying power. And you, dear child, will soon be giving substance to King-pin himself.'

'What!'

'Well, that was the purpose of the exercise, wasn't it? The young master set-up, so he'd bring his gifted side-kick along. His well-shaped reservoir of body-building power.'

Fred looked upon him with righteous indignation. 'Well don't stand there looking so helpless. Do something.'

'Such as?'

'I don't know. You're the genius. I don't want to be drained.'

'Not drained. You've enough essence to build up a dozen super-nasties.'

'Precisely. King-pin is only the first. There's a bloody army over there, all hungry for a nice, very much physical body. I provide the basic materials, so they can belt out of here and feed on less succulent fruit.'

Francis nodded. 'True. I had overlooked that little fact. You may well become the mother of nations.'

'What are you going to do about it?'

He gazed thoughtfully at the shattered door. 'Play by ear. However, there's a bright spot to every dark cloud. At least we'll meet a king-pin, which is an experience granted to the select few. So relax. Let the storm rage and keep your feet dry.'

'But, Francis, we're whacked. Beaten.'

'Every general loses at least one battle.'

'Fine. What about the troops? Me?'

'Smile in adversity. Now, I wonder what's holding up the proceedings?'

'I should think King-pin is whacked too. Must have taken it out of him building up those dogs. To say nothing of the fight you made two of 'em put up.'

'That's a point. Well, as the eunuch said to the actress – we must hope that something will turn up.'

Before Fred could think of a suitable reply, the by now familiar sound of footsteps came from the hall, to be shortly followed by the door gliding back, revealing the figure of Margaret Danglar. She entered the room and looked first at the bound and unconscious figure of her sister, then at the girl in the chair. A triumphant smile parted her lips.

'So, my dear, the battle is over and you are rendering my master the trifling service he requires. You are a pretty thing, who in due course it will be my pleasure to – educate.'

'Francis!' Fred spoke in a low voice. 'He's in contact. I can feel ... '

'Don't resist,' Francis ordered. 'Just relax and let the juices flow.'

Margaret turned and smiled her approval. 'The only wise decision you have made yet. But be warned – no interference. Frankly I think you're a self-opinionated fool who would be lost without this gifted girl. It will be interesting to see you react when King-pin appears.'

'With becoming humility, ma'am,' Francis replied, lowering his head. 'You are aware of my desire for knowledge.'

'Then sit down – do not move – and enjoy the unique performance.'

Francis did what he was told and sat with one leg slung nonchalantly over the other, his face wearing an expression that suggested deep interest. He cleared his throat before speaking.

'I trust you will go easy on poor Fred. After all she's not a bottomless well. Building up a king-pin will surely be rather exhausting?'

Margaret turned a face that seemed to be one great sneer in his direction. 'How thoughtful you are. But we have no intention of incapacitating the little dear before it is absolutely necessary. Besides I have plans that necessitate full awareness if she is to enjoy them.'

'And what plans have you for me?'

The sneer became decidedly more pronounced. 'Your strong healthy body should provide accommodation for at least six tenants. Or maybe not. It depends how you behave yourself.' She shot an almost joyful glance at the damaged door. 'At last! The master comes.'

The footsteps that came into being were soft, a gentle, slow tread such as might mark the progress of a man who walks with confidence and has no wish to disturb those who await his arrival. All of Francis' professional interest was aroused when the door slid back and a black figure entered the room.

A tall black man with white hair; a three dimensional photograph negative. A long face of terrifying beauty; high-cheek bones, straight nose, full lips and vivid green eyes that glittered with intelligence. He wore a long black robe that covered his slender, but powerful figure from neck to ankles, relieved by a golden medallion, suspended on a thin matching chain.

He nodded affably to Margaret who bowed her head, then

turned to Francis, who, after meeting the full gaze of those wonderful green eyes, experienced a nigh overwhelming urge to sink to his knees and pay homage. A beautiful deep voice spoke:

'Ah, the renowned Francis St Clare! Your fame is possibly even greater beyond the barrier than here, where alas, great men are often unappreciated. Your handling of the *Wailing Waif of Battersea* was masterly. Really one in the eye for we poor super-nasties. It is a great pleasure to meet you, Mr St Clare.'

He bowed and the glittering green eyes held no hint of mockery.

Francis returned the courtesy. 'And I, sir, consider it a great privilege to make the acquaintance of a king-pin. But may I point out that much of my success is due to the exceptional gifts of the young lady who is now at your mercy.'

King-pin turned and walked slowly over to the unconscious Fred, who slumped in her chair. His large, delicate hand lightly touched her hair. 'The beautiful and as you rightly say, gifted Frederica Masters. How strange that the Light Lords have granted so much power to such a young soul. For as you must know this exquisite body houses the soul of a celestial child. But she has provided the essence from which this perfectly adequate vessel has been formed and I am not ungrateful.'

'Then perhaps, sir,' Francis suggested, 'you will use her gently and restrain the sadistic intentions of your – your underling.'

King-pin directed an amused glance at Margaret Danglar. 'I will temper necessity with consideration, bearing in mind that devoted labour must be rewarded. However, you may be assured that I will allow nothing to disturb our charming supplier until she has brought over at least three of my – my associates. Afterwards, who knows. We must wait and see.'

Francis shrugged. 'I fully understand that the fate of the individual cannot be considered, when such an achievement is in the pipeline.' He paused and forced an enquiring smile. 'I wonder, could I possibly see the manifestation for myself? To be present when a number of elementals come up from an astral hole, housed in some kind of body, would indeed crown my not unsuccessful career. If you grant me this favour, I will not be over-concerned as to the fate of that girl.'

Margaret glared at the psychic detective. 'Don't believe him. I don't trust his interest. He hates us and all we intend to do.'

King-pin chuckled. 'Perhaps, but I can understand a lust for knowledge. Like all deep-rooted vice, its gratification demands complete surrender. I am prepared to grant your request, Mr St Clare, on the understanding that Margaret goes with you. She will never be more than three feet away. Try anything naughty and I'll blast your brain to jelly.'

'Why not come with us?' Francis suggested. 'With both of you watching me, I'll be as helpless as a week old kitten.'

King-pin bowed. 'Your invitation reassures me, but I must remain close to the source of power. Go along and enjoy yourself.'

Francis followed Margaret Danglar through the doorway and into the hall, where the wrecked pentacle had been transformed into a jumble of scattered rods, overturned candles and a rumpled charged-sheet. He gave them a quick glance, then directed a charming smile at the woman.

'We might as well make ourselves comfy. Draw up chairs and wait for the lads to come over. Will we have long to suffer joyful suspense?'

Margaret waited for him to be seated, then moved to a position a little to the left of his chair. 'Not long. The two way connection was made when the master came over; now the girl is providing power for the lower orders.'

Francis frowned and gave the impression he was rather confused.

'Am I to understand that for me to enjoy the pleasure of your company, there must be an uninterrupted flow of power between Fred and the next plane? You have to be plugged in at both ends?'

The catamado smiled scornfully. 'Of course. You're not such a know-all, are you?'

'I'm but a seeker after truth,' Francis admitted ruefully. 'But of course it makes sense. Two way connection.'

'Look!' she pointed to the centre of the Blessed Sheet which was pulsating with a bright red light. 'The first one is about to come up. Once we are re-inforced the master and I are safe. Then ... then that girl will be mine.'

'Something to look forward to,' Francis murmured. 'Ah! Charlie one is making a tentative appearance.'

A head came up from the gleaming material; bald, oval, a skull covered by loose skin. A thin-lipped mouth opened several times as though gasping for air; large, lidless eyes stared blankly across the room with as much expression as those of a dead man.

'You know,' Francis said in a conversational tone of voice, 'I'm not all that keen on him.'

He moved with the speed of a panther; left the chair and down on his knees, hands outstretched to grab scattered rods, which, before Margaret could take any form of action, he flung direct on to the quivering head. There was a loud bang, a bright flash of red light, then a dense cloud of grey smoke, which quickly dispersed. A rough circle of scorched cloth was all that remained to record the existence of an astral hole and that which had attempted to emerge from it. Francis rose and assumed a wry grin.

'I seem to have blown a fuse.' He raised his voice and shouted:'Fred, you back with us yet? Fit and kicking?'

Her voice came from the next room; not very strong, but still clear. 'With knocking knees and wet knickers, but ... King-pin is doing his nut. He doesn't look well.'

Margaret Danglar tried to grab his arm, but he neatly side-stepped and maintained a respectable distance between them. 'What have you done? In the name of the dark lord – what have you done?'

'Chucked silver rods that still contained charged water over the astral hole,' Francis replied cheerfully. 'When you confirmed my suspicion that a two way flow of power was necessary for your existence, I knew what must be done. Now you and Charlie next door are sort of – well, shipwrecked. Can't get back, losing power every second, which means true-death in a very short while. You should last longer than your master, due to those setting-up exercises, but he – anytime now.'

King-pin appeared in the doorway, his beautiful face tinged with a strange pink flush; a fine network of lines framing his eyes and mouth. He smiled gently. 'You caught me unawares. I permitted myself a moment of distraction – with fatal results.

As you say I have not got a great deal of time left, running as I am on a battery that cannot be recharged.' He turned to Margaret Danglar. 'Your unguarded tongue has brought us to this pass, but there is little point in my wasting strength rebuking you now. If you still wish to be rewarded for services rendered, the girl is weak and will be at your mercy for some little while. I will remain here to deal with Mr St Clare.'

The catamado bowed her head. 'Forgive me, master. At least we will go down into oblivion well revenged. The girl at least will have reason to remember me for a long time to come.'

King-pin waited until she had gone back into the sitting-room, before again addressing the psychic detective. 'Revenge is wasted energy, but when one is on the point of true-death, it can afford a certain amount of satisfaction. You too, Mr St Clare will have occasion to remember me.'

'Perhaps I should remind you,' Francis pointed out, 'that if you attempt to blast me, the effort will completely drain you and bring about total oblivion that much sooner.'

The smile never wavered. 'Of that I am fully aware. But this body will retain full physical strength to the moment of dissolution. I intend to cripple you, Mr St Clare. Turn that handsome body into a useless hulk. A worse fate than mine, wouldn't you say?'

From the other room came a loud cracking sound, followed by a gasping cry. Francis steeled himself to ignore it.

'That will be the crowning act of my career. Crippled by a king-pin. Incapacitated by a solid ghost. No one will believe me. How do you intend to go about it?'

King-pin advanced a few paces, his hands outstretched. 'You are trying to waste time, hoping I will grow weak before the battle even begins. Banish any such hope from your mind. Unless you manage to kill this body, I have power left to finish you and some to spare. Allow me to answer your question with a demonstration.'

He lowered his head and glided forward with hands rigid, sawing the air like twin blades; actually making a hissing sound as they rapidly drew near to the psychic detective's legs. Francis spun round on one heel and aimed a clenched fist at the lowered head; felt a wave of pain run up his arm, then moved quickly away.

The rules of this bizarre game were terribly simple. Not get hit – keep moving until the monster that was approaching again had exhausted his strength. Half an hour? Surely if he could keep King-pin on the constant move, the outpouring of energy would cut that time down to an endurable period. Before his own strength began to drain away and he fell victim to those sawing hands.

A mad dance. Dodging, weaving, pushing chairs across the room hoping to trip the attacker, or at least delay his advance. Francis St Clare was as fit as a man could be, who smoked twenty cigarettes a day, a habit he swore to forego if he should live to see another dawn, but constant movement was beginning to take its toll, while King-pin, his face wearing a sardonic smile, showed no sign of flagging.

St Clare knew he would have to go over to the attack, try to get round the back of King-pin and strike for the head – neck – wherever he could. He would be taking a terrible risk, but no more so than if he continued to play this cat and mouse game. Suddenly, more by reflex than design, he dropped to his knees; King-pin crashed into him and fell flat on to the floor.

Francis jumped up and flung himself on to the prone figure and clamped his hands round the thick throat, digging his fingers into the windpipe, trusting that a secondary body had to breathe and he could maintain the pressure. A terrible gasping, which, when coupled with the grotesque struggling beneath him, created a sick fear such as he had never experienced before.

He never understood where he found the moral and physical strength to hang on, unless it was due to the certain knowledge that if he let go, complete destruction of both body and soul would quickly follow. Even when the struggling grew weaker and there came the awareness of a strange softness of the flesh under his fingers, he did not relax his grip or really believe he could win this terrible battle.

Suddenly it seemed as if his adversary was growing smaller; that a kind of shrinking was taking place; flesh and muscle evaporating, leaving only skin-covered bone. With a loud cry Francis rolled down on to the floor, then over and over, until a space of some six feet separated him from the *thing* that was fast disintegrating. The skin disappeared leaving a white-boned skeleton, which in turn seemed to crumble into a cloud of white mist. This took on a nebulous shape that slowly merged into a transparent likeness of King-pin.

Francis lay gasping, trembling violently, his face glistening with perspiration, he still managed to mutter, 'Reverted to apparition form. Housebound.'

The spectre drifted up from the floor, then when it had risen to a height of some four foot, floated feet first to and through the side wall, without displaying the slightest sign that it was other than a transparent corpse.

Francis wiped his brow before whispering: 'Mort-apparition. Quite common. Will scare the living daylights out of someone one fine night.'

A gurgling screech from the next room caused him to clamp hand to forehead. He called out, 'Sorry, Fred, what with one thing and another, I'd forgotten all about you. Had to shut awareness of you and your little problem out of my consciousness. Be with you in a trice.'

He clambered to his feet, waited for the floor to settle down, then walked unsteadily into the next room. The scene which greeted him, brought a low whistle from his pursed lips. Fred was standing a little to his left, her dress hanging in tatters about her hips, her white back marred by vivid red weals. A few feet away Margaret Danglar stood holding a plaited whip, her face screwed up into an expression of intense agony. Francis voiced his approval.

'Well done, Fred. The astral loop. Keep it up for a few minutes more and she'll join her master in never-never land.'

Margaret's hands opened and the whip fell to the floor as she released a long drawn out howl, then displaying the same shrinking process that had marked the passing of the king-pin. Remaining upright, her form slowly lost muscle and flesh, then the skin-covered skeleton turned into gleaming mist, that also took on the transparent likeness of former secondary body. Francis examined the dead face with lively interest.

'Marvellous! Never thought I'd live to see the like. Must send a full account to that chap who over-dramatizes our cases. Fred, you're worth your weight in gold.'

The apparition drifted to the fireplace, disappeared for a while, then could be seen in the over-mantel mirror, floating towards the reflected opposite wall. She appeared to go through it.

'One haunted mirror,' Francis said cheerfully. 'Should make someone swallow their false teeth.' He turned to Fred who was crouched on the floor. 'How goes it with you?'

She spoke from behind clenched teeth. 'You callous bastard. Look at my back. She almost flogged me to ribbons.'

'So I see. Where did she get the whip?'

'From that cupboard. It's the one she used to wallop Sophia with.'

He sank to his knees and gently kissed one wealed shoulder. 'Sorry, darling. I would have stopped her if it had been possible. Are you in much pain?'

'Not now. I'm getting it under control. Will there be scars?'

'No. The skin's not broken. In a few days the welts will have disappeared and your lovely back as good as new.'

Fred got up and staggered to a chair. 'Actually the pain was a life-saver. It roused me to full power so I was able to project the astral loop. Where the hell were you?'

'Fighting King-pin who entertained designs in making me a cripple. But all is well that ends well. Now, all we have to do is rouse Sophia, tell her the good news and call it a day.'

He walked over to the unconscious woman and after untying the cords, gently slapped her face. Sophia groaned and opened eyes that gazed for a while on the face that looked down at her. Presently she murmured, 'Margaret will be so angry.'

'No, she won't. She and King-pin are no more. Well – almost.'

'You mean – she's gone? I'll never see her again?'

Francis nodded. 'That's right. And the astral hole is no more. A spot of clapping would not be out of place.'

Sophia burst into tears and completely ignored the psychic detective's open-mouthed amazement and Fred's ironic laughter.

Francis straightened up. 'Only goes to show that blood is thicker than pink gin. Fred, you'd better find a coat or something, or passers-by will think I've been inflicting well-merited correction.'

'Unfeeling, sadistic brute,' Fred ejaculated.

'Genius has never been appreciated,' Francis murmured.

*

Francis St Clare sat behind his littered desk and after some reflection tossed a packet of cigarettes into a waste paper basket. Frederica Masters watched the operation with sardonic amusement.

'I bet you fish 'em out again before sunset.'

'Never. The young master has a will of iron. Well, what does it feel like to know you've helped quell an astral invasion?'

'Uncomfortable. Or at least it was. May one ask what happened to our Sophia?'

'Gone to live in Broadstairs. Something nasty in the mirror may have been a deciding factor. But she paid up. A thousand quid.' He kicked the wastepaper basket under the desk. 'Strange how she hated, feared and yet loved that awful sister. Wouldn't be surprised if she doesn't sort of fade away herself. Pity, she was a likely wench.'

'Fancy her, did you?' Fred queried.

'Fancy maybe – desire never. She set me up.'

Fred traced a pattern on her knee with a long forefinger.

'I don't suppose we'll ever have to deal with a catamado again. I mean, they're as rare as apple trees in a desert.'

'True,' Francis agreed. 'Which is just as well. Nasty of nasties.'

Fred raised her eyes and stared at the ceiling. 'I sometimes wonder if I haven't got a touch of the catamados myself.'

He shook his head. 'Nonsense. You're much too kind and gentle.'

An enigmatic smile parted her lips. 'Am I?'

V

Someone in Mind

They met in the Claremont Hotel, one of those rather grim establishments that cater for mainly middle-aged or elderly people, who have the means to spend long periods travelling from one resort to another. It was a cold January morning that had discouraged all but a few hardy souls from leaving the centrally-heated lounge, which meant reclining in ancient armchairs that hid well-worn arms and lumpy seats under loose covers.

Celia Beaumont stifled a yawn, consulted her wristwatch for the third time during the past hour, then looked idly around the room. The old clergyman and his middle-aged daughter were playing chess on a folding board that he carried in his jacket pocket; a fat man and his equally plump wife sat side by side on a sofa, their heads performing a kind of circular movement as boredom and its attendant sleep, gradually took control of their brains. A slightly more lively man with thinning grey hair and a gleam of tired lust in his eyes, caught her gaze and winked. Celia frowned and turned her head away – and instantly experienced a wave of interest.

A stranger had entered the room and after some hesitation, walked to and sank down into a chair that was only a few feet from Celia's own. He opened a newspaper, flicked through the pages, then folded it carefully, took a pen from his top pocket and proceeded to fill in the crossword puzzle with remarkable speed. Possibly forty-five to fifty, Celia decided and extremely good-looking. His blond hair was flecked with grey round the temples and the long face had a faint network of lines round mouth and eyes; but there was something captivatingly boyish about him.

Celia wondered if he was alone and if so what he was doing

in this place, which had to be a rest home for zombies. In fact what was she doing here?

An unanswerable question. At forty-four she was still attractive, having that kind of appeal that did not rely on looks alone, but two broken marriages and any number of unsatisfactory affairs, had left her with a kind of over-lived feeling. The word 'men' had become an explosive expletive. At least for the time being. Maybe that was why she had chosen the Claremont Hotel as a suitable place for a winter's holiday. Whatever men turned up here would either be old, boring or plain repulsive. No danger of being drawn into a romantic attachment that – if experience was anything to go by – would begin on a high note and end at the very bottom of the scale.

She shot another glance at the stranger. He had completed the crossword and was now reading some long-winded article that Celia could plainly see was headed 'Saturn and Beyond' which must mean he was brainy and therefore probably dull. A crashing bore. Like her second who had a string of letters after his name, but whose idea of a brilliant conversation was a lecture on the death of the dinosaurs.

Celia got up and decided to brave the cold wind and go for a long walk. Maybe she could work up an appetite for the stodgy lunch. Better still lunch at one of the better restaurants, then retire to her room with a good book. If she was going to vegetate into a respectable ex-virgin, she might as well do it properly.

*

Of course he had to be seated at the next table at dinner time.

Looking more handsome – beautiful was a better word – than that morning, he had the effect of putting Celia off the curried lamb, a dish that normally she was very partial to. Then her gaze alighted on his long-fingered hands and she knew that without doubt she was hooked.

They made the mundane task of handling a knife and fork an act of grace. Delicate muscles quivered under skin that was covered with golden hair; gorgeous filbert (was that the right word?) nails literally flashed as they reflected the overhead light. But it was the fingers that really sent her. Long, strong; she began to imagine what effect they would have if ...

'Is not the curried lamb to your liking, Mrs Beaumont?' Mr Whitehead, the proprietor, enquired.

'What!' She looked up at him and forced a smile. 'Yes, but I'm not all that hungry.'

'What a pity. Mrs Whitehead is rather proud of her curry.'

There was one consolation the stranger – glamour-pants – seemed to be having difficulty in getting through his. He pushed his half empty plate to one side, ordered coffee from an indifferent waitress (was the wretched girl blind?) and leaned back in his chair with a kind of sad resignation. Celia also ordered coffee, then taking a cigarette from a slim gold case, leaned sideways and asked:

'Could I possibly bother you for a light?'

His head swung round and she became the focal point for a pair of brilliant grey eyes. A beautifully moderated voice made utterance. 'So sorry, but I don't smoke. But if you can hang on for a moment I'll get you one from that desk thing over there.'

Celia gave him what she hoped was her most dazzling smile.

'You are most kind.'

Two minutes later he returned with a box of Swan Vestas and lit her cigarette with the same flowing grace that had marked his use of a knife and fork. Celia blew out a smoke ring and spoke in a low, husky voice.

'You are so wise not to smoke. A filthy habit.'

He edged his chair a little nearer to her table, then sat down.

'In fact I used to smoke, but the doctor made me give it up.'

'Indeed! Anything serious?'

'Not really. I have a heart flutter and smoking makes it worse.'

The last thing Celia wanted was a discussion about his health, but she had to display some interest and trust a more fruitful line of conversation would follow.

'I'm so sorry. Is that why you're down here? For your health?'

He bared splendid teeth in an engaging smile.

'No, it's not so bad as all that. I'm in advertising and its pretty hectic, you know. I come here for a bit of peace and quiet. The very dullness of the place is relaxing.'

'I come here for the same reason,' she said. 'By the way, my name is Celia Beaumont.'

He extended one beautiful hand. 'And mine is Richard Duncan.'

His grip was firm and warm and a delicious shiver ran down Celia's spine; she just stopped herself from leaning forward.

He consulted a wrist-watch and raised an eyebrow. 'Good heavens, is that the time! I promised my stand-in I'd ring at seven o'clock. Will you excuse me?'

She murmured, 'Of course,' while experiencing a ridiculous feeling of disappointment.

He got up, inclined his head and said: 'It has been so nice to meet you,' then walked away, giving a passable imitation of a man who has shared a few minutes conversation with an attractive middle-aged woman, whom he will never see again.

Celia whispered, 'Oh, my God, I've made no impression at all!'

*

For two entire days Celia Beaumont kept out of Richard Duncan's way. She took to eating out, using small and expensive restaurants, spending more than she could afford. Well-authenticated arguments raced across her mind. Love was a four letter word. Lust a sweet fruit that quickly turned sour. Apart from which the man had not shown the slightest interest in her.

The breakthrough came on the morning of the third day when Celia discovered her quarry seated in one of those glass-sided shelters that can be found in most English seaside resorts. He was gazing out across the deserted beach, overcoat collar turned up to cover his ears, looking, Celia thought, more dishy, appealing and bedworthy than ever. She patted her hair, smoothed her coat, then like a sleek and hungry cat that has spotted a saucer of succulent cream, she moved in. She made as though to pass him, stopped and turned her head, before assuming an expression of glad surprise.

'Why, Mr Duncan, imagine bumping into you! I thought I had the entire front to myself.'

He rose and gave her a heart-stopping smile. 'Why it's ... (a terrible pause – he had forgotten her name) ... it's Mrs Beaumont! You could not have come along at a more opportune moment. I am feeling very much down in the dumps and if the truth be told, rather lonely. Please join me in this contraption and we'll have a shot of being lonely together.'

Pride demanded she display some slight reluctance. 'Well, perhaps for a little while. Then I must really get back and write some letters.'

'You are indeed very kind.'

Seated side by side with the wind taking liberties with Celia's skirt, bright conversation was at first hard to come by; in fact after five minutes spent in making inane remarks about the weather, she began to wonder if it would ever come at all. Then suddenly he said, 'I've wanted to talk to you lots of times since we met at dinner, but haven't liked to.'

'Why for heaven's sake not!' she exclaimed, genuinely surprised.

'Well, you know what it's like. Chaps making advances in hotels ... You could have got the wrong idea and snubbed me. I can't bear being snubbed. Sort of upsets me for days.'

She snatched back a hand that was straying very close to his and made the only possible reply.

'That's silly. I wouldn't have snubbed you. Doubt if I know how. It's dreadful to feel lonely. I know.'

From then there was no need for her to make conversation. The cork came out of the bottle. With an occasional prompting word, his life poured out for her delight and edification. He was forty-eight years old, separated from a wife that Celia assumed to have been a bitch; had an unhappy childhood, lost both parents at an early age, had plenty of money, but lived the life of a hermit; suffered from fits of depression – but was happy now.

The seemingly unassailable fortress surrendered without a fight. When they finally set out on the return journey to the hotel, Celia's hand lay on his arm and she had reason to congratulate herself on a good morning's work. They lunched and dined together, this providing their bored fellow guests with some much needed diversion.

Getting him to bed took a further two days.

*

He did not make a very satisfactory lover, but in those early days Celia more than made up for his discrepancy. For a while both moved back into that land which many maintain is the exclusive domain of the young. There the sun always shines and the sweet sound of bells come drifting across a placid lake; memories of long ago spent lives mingled with those newly born and possibly happiness for the first time becomes an understandable word.

It was not until the holiday was over and Celia and Richard had moved back into their respective town flats, that he even mentioned his exceptional and disturbing gift.

Generally they met at her place, for it delighted him to watch her working in the kitchen; also – more important – he did not own a double bed. One night when they were recuperating in her king-size model, he said:

'There's more than one way of making love.'

She giggled. 'I know. We've tried most of them.'

He shook his head. 'Not the one I have in mind. In fact that's what it is – intercourse of the mind.'

'What!'

'Please don't laugh. I have a sort of talent – gift. I can – with your co-operation – enter your mind – send down impulses along your nerve grid. At least that's the only way I can describe it.'

She came up on one elbow and brushed a lock of hair from his damp forehead. 'Are you serious?'

'Never more so. My wife didn't like me to do it – and other ladies were a little frightened. I think it only really works between two people who know each other well and are – well – friendly lovers.'

She ruffled his hair. 'You funny old thing. How can lovers be other than friends?'

'Not always. Sometimes they dislike each other as people. That's why so many marriages break up. But with us it's different.'

Celia was not at all certain about that, for already some of his foibles were beginning to irritate. But she smiled brightly and said: 'You're so profound, darling. Let's hear about this – intercourse of the mind.'

'You look into my eyes and empty your mind. I know it's not easy, but it can be done if you try. Then let me come in – or at least don't resist.'

She shrugged. 'OK. I'll try anything once.'

At first she was determined to treat the entire business as a lot of nonsense and so widened her eyes and stared into his with mock alarm. But after a few seconds it seemed as if the pupils were unnaturally enlarged; that some force was gradually expelling every thought from her mind, leaving it swept clean, like a familiar room with scraped walls and bare floor.

She began to gasp and cry out when he forced an entry; drove some essential part of his being into the quivering uterus of her mind; penetrated the deep recess where unexpected desires burst into shuddering life. Then he was there – packed into her brain – his voice whispering, suggesting, titillating, pouring fire down to every part of her body, until it seemed as if she were dying a million glorious deaths.

Celia had six orgasms in as many seconds.

*

'Well?' he asked.

Celia waited until the trembling of her limbs had subsided, before replying. 'It was great of course. A real trip. But – well – weird. I mean – anything goes between two adult people – but there must be limits. That was a kind of mental rape.'

'How could it be rape if you enjoyed it?'

'I know. But maybe I shouldn't have enjoyed it. God! What an extraordinary man you are!'

He shook his head and she felt a pang of pity.

'No, a very ordinary man, with an unusual gift.'

This first trip into mind-intercourse marked the beginning of the end. Although she allowed Richard to repeat the experience twice more, even that began to pall. On reflection indeed, it was more than a little disgusting. Disgustingly enjoyable at the time of fulfilment, but positively revolting when reviewed in the cold light of day.

Then one morning as she lay in bed, trying to face the prospect of getting up, she became aware of him lurking in her mind. Not the usual way, but unobtrusive, like a burglar who has entered a house and is rummaging through personal effects; reading very private letters, unearthing secrets that lay hidden in bottom drawers; listening to the whispered words that never die.

She gasped and cried out: 'Go away. Push off, you sneaky bastard.'

He left at once. Fled from her brain. Decamped like the startled intruder he was. Alarm gave place to anger and she leapt out of bed and ran to the telephone. She dialled his number and he must have been expecting her call, for his voice spoke almost at once.

'Richard speaking.'

'You dirty sneaking bastard. If you do *that* again, by God, I'll come round to your place and kill you.'

His voice took on a whining tone. 'Sorry, it won't happen again. I promise. But I longed ... Wanted to be with you so much ... I couldn't resist the temptation.'

The end came hurtling out of the past and killed whatever had switched her on – stone dead. 'Now, get this. It's over. Write me out of your life. I never want to see, hear or *feel* from you again. Get lost. Go jump over the moon, but in the name of sanity, don't come near me again.'

For a while the only sound that came from the telephone, was a faint dialling tone that must have been the result of a crossed line, and Celia wondered how this mad conversation would sound to an invisible listener. Then Richard's voice began to plead.

'Please don't say that. Let me come over now. We'll never play that game again, if you'd rather not. But I can't live without you.'

'Don't talk such bloody rot. Even if you hadn't played that filthy trick, it would still have been over. So far as you're concerned I'm switched off. So stay out of my flat and my mind.'

She slammed the receiver down and walked over to the sideboard where she poured herself a stiff drink. Surely she had frightened him sufficiently to ensure that mind-invasion act was never repeated. But if he did ... What would she do? Really try to kill him? Go mad? For the greater part of that night she did not sleep, terrified by the prospect that he might slip into her mind when the defences were down. But just before dawn her brain blacked out of its own accord and there was no recollection of bad dreams next day.

*

Richard Duncan did not bother Celia Beaumont for almost a week, thereby allowing a thin veneer of optimism to form over the running sore of her anxiety. He had given up. Most likely found himself another woman who would more than fill the void she had vacated. Then one evening she returned home and found him sitting on the landing outside of her front door. His eyes were red and swollen and he was in a most pitiful state.

Celia, like most sensualists had a kind heart, although she could never completely subdue a contempt for ex-lovers. Only their failings were remembered, not their virtues. But the sight of him sitting there, knees drawn up, his face the epitome of grief, caused conscience and pity to blend and permitted her a brief glimpse of truth. If she left him alone, neither of them would be in this state now. He looked up at her and said:

'I intended to kill myself – maybe I still will. But I had to see you first.'

She fumbled in her handbag and produced a key, which she inserted in the lock. 'Come inside and I'll give you a cup of coffee.'

He forced a wry grin. 'You mean I am to be permitted entry? Allowed to enter the sanctum?'

She snapped, 'Don't talk such rubbish. For heaven's sake come in.'

Once in the flat he drifted into the lounge and sank on to the sofa and did not move or speak while she made coffee in the kitchen. After he had sipped from the cup, his deep voice broke the terrible silence.

'I have promised that I will never ... never invade your mind again. As long as I live I'll keep that promise. All I ask in return is a tiny crumb of kindness. A smile. The sneer hidden under a look of concern. It is not much to ask from one who before was so generous.'

There was no way Celia could refrain from sending out the barbed arrows of truth. 'Your appeal was being unattainable. Women like me are predatory creatures. The joy is in the hunt. Now the mere sight of you in the place where we used to make love is – well revolting.'

'Then you never wish to see me again?'

'Frankly I think it would be best – for both of us.'

'You want me to go and never come back?'

'Haven't I said so? There would always be the fear of ... that dreadful gift.'

His eyes were suddenly lit by a gleam of anger. 'Distance has nothing to do with that. If I were on Mars I could still enter your mind. But I have promised not to.'

Celia tried to cement that promise, ensure that he would not leave with a grievance.

'Then let us part as friends.'

'How can we be friends if I never see you again?'

That was a question she could not answer – or wanted to.

'You are a very handsome man; the world is full of women.'

'But I only want you.'

She pounded clenched fists down on her chair arm.

'But I don't want you to want me. For God's sake leave me alone. Go ... go ... never come back.'

She closed her eyes and sat very still and when the sound of a quietly closed door told her he had left, she opened them and stared at the chair on which he had recently sat.

She burst into tears and cried as though her non-existent heart was breaking.

*

Weeks passed. The present became the past and gave birth to the future. Celia Beaumont took up the threads of her life and wove them into a mundane pattern. Bought a dog and took it for long walks, entertained girl friends to tea, joined a basket-making class and really enjoyed using her hands. But Richard Duncan was never forgotten.

While exercising her dog Celia sometimes saw him watching her from a long way off, but on investigation it always proved to be someone else. When working in the kitchen, his face appeared just beyond the window, even though it was twenty feet above ground level. She rocketed out of a deep sleep, certain he had been standing but a few feet from her bed, but a few seconds before.

'We can't stop thinking about each other,' she whispered and knew this to be the truth.

She began to visualize years of uncertainty, forever haunted by the fear that one day – night – he would succumb to temptation and creep back like a cringing cur and take possession of her mind; maybe force her to take part in that obscene game. So long as he lived she could never know the true meaning of peace again.

To kill! To stab, shoot, push under a train, all were impossibilities to a woman of her temperament and background. She might threaten, but never perform. Nevertheless he must die. How? Sleep became a beautiful memory, she lost weight, unsightly pouches formed under her eyes; friends remarked how ill she was looking.

Then the fires of anguish forged the appalling idea. He could enter her mind – could she sneak into his? He had formed the link, but she had the stronger personality. The experiment would be the act of a mad woman, but it could be classified as compulsory defensive action.

She made the first approach at a quarter to three in the morning, assuming he would by then be asleep. She closed her eyes, sent out long – limitless – mental feelers – and at once swam into a black sea of misery. She sensed he was indeed asleep, in so far as the five senses were shut down, but the boundless cavern that was his brain, was a seething mass of longing – for her.

In that all-feeling darkness she encountered an atom of his personality that never slept and sent out a whisper – a shout – a scream – that expressed with wordless thoughts.

'She … is … a … harsh … cruel … woman … but … I … want … want … '

Celia spoke in the same language. 'There … is … no … hope … die … die … '

'I … have … no … wish … to … live … '

'Then … die … die … death … is … the … great … eraser.'

'I … will … die … die … die … '

Celia sat up in bed, her entire body drenched with perspiration.

*

The experiment proved to be a one hundred percent success.

The Daily Express relayed the news by a short paragraph on page two.

> Richard James Duncan, joint managing director of Dunwilliam Advertising Agency, was found dead in his Bayswater flat last night. The police have taken possession of two empty bottles, found by his bedside. Foul play is not suspected.

Reprieve written in terse language. What it portrayed stirred the sluggish waters of conscience; informed Celia Beaumont that she was morally a murderess; it also presented her with a certificate of freedom.

A burden of fear slipped from her shoulders; that night she slept for ten hours and awoke next morning feeling at least twenty years younger. She had her hair retinted, enjoyed a facial massage, bought a new dress and ate a fattening lunch. Now she could again enjoy life; rusticate or seek new adventures. God was in his heaven – and Richard Duncan nowhere at all.

Three weeks later 'men' again ceased to be an explosive expletive. She met Martin Forester and embarked on a gay – in the orthodox sense – affair that was certain to end with no complications, for he – Martin – stated emphatically he was for fun and games and a no-hard-feelings-parting afterwards. For three more weeks Celia was a very happy person.

Then one bright silver morning she woke up and knew that Richard Duncan had taken up permanent residence in her mind. A very contrite, tearful, even apologetic Richard who kept repeating over and over again: 'I had nowhere else to go ... please don't be angry ... I had nowhere else to go.'

Celia exclaimed: 'Oh, my God! Oh, my God! Oh, my God!'

Richard shuddered – so did Celia's mind. He tried so hard to explain.

'You forced me out of my brain, so I had to come into yours. Please ... please ... understand ... I had nowhere else to go.'

Celia screamed ... and screamed ... and screamed ...

VI

The Man Who Stayed Behind

Benjamin Howard had never been a particularly good specimen of a man. Now he resembled a dried-up monkey that had lived not wisely, but horribly. The Reverend John Pearce who had arrived armed with a prayer book and a well-used collection of platitudes, found himself shuddering when he saw the bundle of bones wrapped loosely in brown skin, to which he was required to minister spiritual comfort. He seated himself on the bedside chair, unpleasantly aware that a pair of small, but still bright eyes were watching him. So disturbed was he, his opening gambit fell short of being the epitome of tact.

'I fear, Mr Howard, your time is short.'

The little monkey face bared its teeth and a harsh voice said: 'You bloody fool, I don't have to be told that.'

It was not a good beginning, and the clergyman made a weak effort to regain lost ground.

'What I meant was – life is short and all of us must be prepared.'

A hideous mottled hand clawed at the bed-clothes and the rasping voice again assaulted Mr Pearce's ears.

'You meant nothing of the bloody sort. I'm dying. Kicking the bucket. Handing in me chips. Any bloody fool can see that. I didn't ask you here for a medical opinion. The bloody doctors do that. I want your professional advice. I take it you are an expert in your field?'

'I am an ordained priest,' the scandalized clergyman admitted, 'otherwise … '

'Don't jabber.' The sick man shook his head impatiently. 'I have always believed in employing experts. It's cheaper in the long run. Now, what can I expect from this after-life business?'

'Expect!'

'Yes. My soul has a lot of experience in controlling labour, building factories, making money. I should be quite an asset to that lot over there. But what do I get out of it?'

'Heaven is not a business,' the Reverend Pearce said sternly. 'There is no buying or selling in paradise.'

'Rubbish. The place must be packed with financial wizards like me, and I bet they're all cutting each other's throats for the best mansion. And you're not telling me, one of 'em hasn't cornered the market in ambrosia – or whatever they eat.'

Mr Pearce had not been so shocked since the day when the archdeacon had inadvertently made up a four-letter word while playing Scrabble.

'Mr Howard, I fear you have some very strange ideas about heaven. It is a place of joy and light. The material things of this life have been left behind. The attributes you describe, far from being an asset, will I fear, be a great liability.'

The ensuing silence was broken only by the dying man's laboured breathing and the Reverend Pearce was on the point of delivering an improving lecture. The rasping voice forestalled him.

'Do you know what you're bloody well talking about?'

'I beg your pardon!'

Benjamin Howard tried to wave what passed for a hand.

'All right – keep your shirt on. But it sounds funny to me. Take old Peter Sharp who pushed off last year. He bought a factory for a cool million, sacked all the staff, then sold the site for three million. Are you telling me, heaven couldn't find a use for a man like that?'

The clergyman positively glowered.

'I greatly regret to inform you that I have grave doubts if your friend got into heaven at all.'

Benjamin Howard closed his eyes and digested this piece of information for a few minutes. Then his eyes snapped open.

'What about the other place?'

'You mean … ?'

'Yes I do. There must be quite a brain drain going over to the rival concern. I bet Old Nick would give his right horn to have me. Bloody Moses – in a few years I'd probably be able to make a take-over bid … '

'Mr Howard!' The Reverend Pearce was sitting upright, his

eyes blazing with righteous anger. 'Your conception of hell is – forgive me, but I must say it – as warped as your idea of heaven. Hell is a place of retribution. A place of suffering and atonement, where the memory of your past mistakes are a source of untold misery.'

'Doesn't sound unlike the Stock Exchange.'

The clergyman so far forgot himself as to shout.

'It is not the Stock Exchange, neither is it a boardroom, or a factory floor, or a shop, or even a stall in Berwick Market. Get this into your head – once the soul leaves earth, it is finished with material things. Forever.'

Benjamin Howard nodded slowly, like a man who has come to an irrevocable decision.

'Then, I'm not going.'

The Reverend Pearce wiped his brow and attempted to marshal his dispersed thoughts into some kind of order.

'Mr Howard, I fear you have no option. It has been ordained, that very shortly, your soul must leave its earthly home and go forth … ' Mr Pearce hesitated, being unwilling to state categorically what he thought would be Mr Howard's ultimate destination, ' … into eternity. Try to … '

'How big is the human soul?' Benjamin enquired.

Mr Pearce adjusted himself to this new line of questioning.

'The immortal soul cannot be measured. It is as large as the universe, or as small as a pinhead.'

Benjamin Howard actually chuckled. A nasty little cackling sound.

'Then I guess it would fit into almost anything.'

'That is certainly a point of view,' the clergyman admitted.

'Into a shoe-box, for example?'

'Well, I'm not sure … '

'Or a wrist-watch?'

The Reverend Pearce frowned. 'I cannot believe that the Creator … '

'All right then. A mouse. If my soul is as small as you say, I could easily get inside a mouse.'

'Really, this is absurd … '

'No, it's not.' The frail little body began to struggle, and then to the clergyman's horrified amazement, sat up. It seemed as if the iron will that lay behind the little, dilated eyes had concentrated the ebbing strength into a final blaze of energy. Even the voice was firm.

'Hear me. Hear me good. When I was an ugly little runt, running about with me arse hanging out of me trousers, they laughed when I said I'd get to the top. But I knew I could do it – and did. The most beautiful woman in London laughed in my face when I had the bloody nerve to propose to her. I said – I told her – "you'll be in my bed before the year's out." She was. When I was fifty, the effing doctors said I'd a year to live. I said, "Balls". I've lasted another twenty. Now you're giving me this crap – telling me I've got to go to heaven – hell – it makes no difference – because I'm staying right here. I'll use anything – I'm not particular. Boxes, clocks, dogs, cats – even the bloody lavatory pan if it's vacant ... '

He collapsed back on to his pillow and wheezed out the last, defiant words.

'Who knows ... I might find me ... a new body ... one ... day ... day ... '

The voice was suddenly cut off by a rattling sound and the grotesque head jerked up and down as though, even now, the old man wished to endorse his terrible statement. Mr Pearce ran to the door and called for assistance. Then he went back to the bed and saw that Benjamin Howard no longer required anyone's help. The mouth gaped, the eyes glared, the hands were clenched into tiny fists.

The Reverend Pearce shuddered.

*

They were congregated in the library. Twenty people in all: cousins, nephews, nieces, one ancient brother, two sisters-in-law and the one and only son. For the most part they had been drawn together by two powerful magnets – greed and hope. Of greed there was an abundance; hope flickered like a candle in a strong draught, and in some cases was merely a glimmering spark. One distant cousin summed up his situation in three words: 'You never know.'

Mr Brandt, the one solicitor that Benjamin Howard had almost trusted, cleared his throat, then tapped his pen on the desk for silence.

'Ladies and gentlemen, as executor for the estate of the late

Benjamin Howard, I would like to thank you all for coming on this sad occasion ... '

The ancient brother, who appeared to share the dead man's direct approach, if not his ability for making money, interrupted.

'Let's cut out the cackle, Brandt. You know why we are all here. How much, if anything, do we get?'

The solicitor coughed, put on a pair of rimless glasses, then unfolded a sheet of parchment with irritating slowness. He was clearly suffering from embarrassment.

'Before I read the will, there is one point I wish to clarify. Although this document was drawn up in my presence, I dissociate myself from the phraseology and generally offensive style favoured by my late client. Mr Howard was, I fear, a man who believed in calling a spade a spade. He has not hesitated to do so in this, his last testament. I therefore apologize in advance to anyone who may feel they have been slighted – indeed,' Mr Brandt cast an anxious glance down the document, 'possibly even insulted.'

He cleared his throat once again, adjusted his glasses and began to read.

' "I, Benjamin Howard, being sane in all aspects, save that I allowed a crowd of conniving, witless and thieving layabouts, hereby designated as my family, to sponge on me for the greater part of my adult life, hereby evoke all wills heretofore made by me at any time and declare this to be my last will and testament.

' "To my brother, Daniel Howard, whom I can only describe as a crook without drive, a fornicator without potency, but who otherwise has the ability to cling on to a good thing with all the tenacity of a leech, I bequeath the sum of one thousand pounds, with the profound hope that it will choke him.

' "To the rest of my so-called relatives, who are now doubtlessly gathered like a flock of vultures, I bequeath nothing, and strongly suggest that they be searched before leaving the premises.

' "To George Conrad Howard, who I have every reason to believe is my son, but has failed to prove it to my satisfaction, I, with great reluctance, bequeath absolutely the residue of my estate, while expressing the forlorn hope that he will not dissipate it, even worse, give it away; in other words, act according to his spineless, wishy-washy, mushy nature." '

When the will had been read, everyone reverted to their true opinions.

'I never got a bean out of him when he was alive,' a fat lady – second cousin once removed – stated emphatically, 'so I'm not surprised. But I did think he might have remembered little Albert. The child doted on him. Didn't you, ducks?'

Albert, a miniature horror in spectacles, nodded before kicking the table leg.

'I have never,' declared a tall, thin creature, with a nose like a shark's fin, 'been so insulted. I should never have come.'

The storm of rising indignation was quelled by George Howard suddenly rising to his feet. He raised his hand for silence, regarding the family with a compassionate smile.

'Friends,' his smile widened, 'family ... '

Everyone sensed the flame of hope might not, after all, have been entirely extinguished and began, in advance, to murmur their appreciation. 'I deeply regret that Father, whom, although we did not always see eye to eye, I deeply revered, has laid upon my shoulders this awesome burden of wealth.'

'Strewth!' the fat lady was heard to murmur, 'I wouldn't mind staggering under it.'

'So,' George went on, 'I intend to do what Father, I'm sure, really wished. Share it among you all.'

Mark Antony at Caesar's funeral could not have wished for a better reception than the one now given to George Howard after his speech. Scowls were transformed into smiles, curses into blessings and the prevailing air of gloom changed to a spontaneous outburst of joy. The ancient brother gripped George's hand and shook it vigorously.

'I'm proud of you, me boy.'

They flocked round the dispenser of largesse like hungry cats round a liberal-minded butcher. His hand was shaken, his back slapped, his hair ruffled, and little Albert – a youth with violent tendencies – kicked him.

A little spinster – third cousin to the youngest niece – was still a little worried. 'Are you sure you know us all? I feel we should leave our particulars.'

This was considered an excellent idea and there was an instant demand for pen and paper. In no time at all, everyone was printing their names and addresses on Benjamin's headed notepaper, together with any other information they considered needful. Cousin Alfred, whose predilection for the bottle made some kind of support an absolute necessity, was slouched over the desk, trying to write with a pen that would not keep still. He was therefore in a position to observe a phenomenon that caused him some disquiet. A silver cigarette box, a gift to the deceased from a frightened client, opened its lid and hopped across the desk. It skirted the blotting pad and made a direct approach for George's hand that was slapping the desk in an effort to emphasize its owner's remarks.

'Father (slap) was a man who tried so hard to be thought bad (slap), but could never hide his fundamental goodness (slap). He knew (slap) that I (slap) would ... '

Alfred's eyes did not blink, his mouth refused to close, but he did manage to groan. The cigarette box appeared to have reached its objective. It stopped, then when George brought his hand down for the final: 'I am certain that my father is at this moment rejoicing,' slammed down its lid on his fingers with an audible snap.

George screamed and performed a little dance while trying vainly to dislodge the box from his fingers. Little Albert had his face slapped, there being a consensus that he was responsible for the outrage, and Cousin Alfred toyed with the absurd idea of signing the pledge. But it was the fat lady that struck terror in every heart.

''Ere, that's his signing hand.'

Mr Brandt, being the only disinterested party present, eventually restored order. He also steered George back to the desk and examined the cigarette box, which displayed no inclination to release the trapped fingers. Mr Brandt tried to prise the lid open with his bare hands and only succeeded in breaking his finger-nails. He looked helplessly round the room.

'Anyone got a chisel?' he enquired.

No one had but little Albert stated he had a pocket knife, equipped with an implement for removing stones from horses' hooves. He was prepared to hire it out for the small sum of ten pence.

''And it over, you little perisher,' the fat lady ordered, taking a swipe at the embryo-capitalist, which due to evasive action, missed and hit the second youngest niece.

The knife was commandeered and the metal implement, which had a tapered point, seemed ideally suited for prising lids off fingers. But even so, Mr Brandt had to exert all his strength before the hinges parted company from the box, and the lid flew across the room to hit the ancient brother a glancing blow on the head, just as he was pocketing a table lighter for which he had long entertained a partiality.

George Howard's hand was in a bad way. A doctor, who was hastily summoned, diagnosed three broken fingers and in answer to many frantic questions, stated that it would be at least six weeks before George could put pen to paper.

The disgruntled family finally departed and no one took the slightest notice of Cousin Alfred who, with tears pouring down his face, clutched the arm of anyone who came within range, exclaiming, 'It jumped – it jumped.'

*

George Howard, attired in a black dressing-gown, was lying on his bed, trying to ignore the voice of temptation which came to him from the bedside chair.

'No,' he said for the third time, 'it wouldn't be respectful.'

'Why not?' demanded Eve Simpson.

Eve had a mass of dark hair, the face of a lustful child and the body of a well-developed woman. She also thought that a bedroom had a dual purpose. And sleep came second.

George sighed. 'My father is not yet cold in his grave.'

'He was cremated.'

'His ashes are not yet cool in the garden of remembrance,' George corrected, 'and I do think that a certain – well – restraint is called for.'

'Nonsense.' Eve eased her dress down off one shoulder and George groaned.

'Look, I must insist you keep your clothes on for at least the period of mourning.'

'How long will that be?' Eve demanded.

'Well, six months is considered ... '

'Not on your nelly,' Eve retorted, baring the other shoulder.

'If you think I'm going without for six months, you're mad.'

George tried to look away, but his eyes seemed to have developed a will of their own. 'Shall we say – six weeks?'

'What about six minutes?' Eve enquired, slipping out of her dress with accomplished ease.

'A week?' pleaded George.

Eve did not answer. The nylon slip was over her head.

'A day?'

'Give us hand with me bra.'

'I can't. My hand. It's in plaster.'

She looked back over one white shoulder.

'You only need one hand, silly.'

George groaned again. 'Why am I so weak?'

'You will be,' she promised.

A pile of feminine attire lay on the floor. A black dressing-gown hung over a chair-back; a matching pyjama suit was draped over the seat. George Howard had surrendered but like a freshly-landed fish, he still floundered.

'We really shouldn't.'

'You're dead right,' Eve agreed, 'but we will.'

On the mantelpiece was a clock. It had been made back in the days when people thought a clock should entertain as well as tell the time. The case was constructed from rich mahogany, on which were embossed bunches of grapes and some unlikely looking flowers. Under the clock face were two little doors; on the hour they opened so that a small brass man could jerk his way out and wave his right hand. George, still troubled by conscience, found himself looking at this example of Victorian craftmanship, and suddenly realized that the time was moving forward faster than it should.

'Look at the clock,' he exclaimed. Eve stopped what she was doing and regarded him reproachfully.

'Why? We've plenty of time.'

'But the minute hand is moving.'

'I know, darling, it should.'

'But it's moving too fast.'

The minute hand was not moving all that fast, but it certainly displayed more activity than usual. It crept perceptibly from minute to minute, jerked when the chime struck the half hour and then moved remorselessly up towards three o'clock. George clambered off the bed and approached the mantelpiece.

'Must have gone wrong,' he said. 'But why? It never has before.'

Eve yawned. 'You'll go wrong in time. Come back to bed.'

'Wait a minute. It's coming up to three o'clock. This is really most extraordinary.'

The clock made a deep rumbling sound. On the first stroke of three the doors opened and the little man came out to stand on his doorstep. He was not made of brass. Instead – and George opened and closed his eyes to make sure he was not dreaming – a tiny replica of the late Benjamin Howard bared his microscopic teeth in a ferocious grin. He was only visible for three seconds – during which time he poked his tongue out – then he turned round and walked back past the doors, which closed behind him. The minute hand resumed its ordained, imperceptible crawl, and the clock presented its usual, rather yellow, but bland face.

George stood very still and thought about things in general and nothing in particular. It was Eve who brought him back to reality by asking: 'What's the matter with you, then?' He turned slowly and tried unsuccessfully to explain.

'He … he … he … '

He pointed a shaking finger at the clock. Eve frowned and seemed a little hurt. 'Honestly, I can't think why you're making such a fuss about a wonky clock. With all your money you can buy a thousand clocks. Now, please, come back to bed.'

'Father in clock,' George said plaintively. 'Clock strikes … dadda comes out.'

Eve rose, and being a girl who always got her man, came to fetch him.

'I can't understand a word you're saying. You saw your father sprinkled over a rose-bush. Now, come back to bed like a good boy and Eve will play you a tune.'

He allowed himself to be consoled. He wanted so much to be told he was tired, nervous, over-imaginative, and how impossible it was for a defunct father to walk out from a clock. Eve was a wonderful consoler. Moreover, she soon demonstrated an ability to make him forget everything. Four minutes passed very pleasantly. Then the clock struck four and

George sat up so abruptly, Eve went sprawling on to the floor.

'What the blazing hell ... ' she began, but George did not hear. He was watching the clock.

The little doors were open. The tiny figure was on the step; it was shaking a minute fist at him.

George fainted.

*

Mr Hunglebert-Chiffinch, such was the psychiatrist's name, tried to explain.

'My dear boy, this is so simple. Father-time-guilt. Your father was a strong, even possessive personality. Being an only son, he naturally used to *watch* over you. Get the idea?'

'No,' said George.

The psychiatrist frowned, then remembering his fee, smiled.

'Father – watch – time – clock. Association of ideas. Father died – you mourn – eh – were distracted – felt guilt – you had *belittled* him – get it? Be-*little*. Watch – clock. In short – ha ha – in short – guilt projected little father in clock. Very simple.'

George scratched his head. 'Will I see my little father in the clock again?'

Mr Hunglebert-Chiffinch made a pyramid with his hands and raised enquiring eyes towards the ceiling.

'Let me think. Guilt complex – period of mourning – distraction element – belittled father-memory. I would say – yes.'

'Can you cure me?' George enquired.

The psychiatrist lowered his eyes and appeared to be praying silently.

'Possibly – indubitably – in short – yes.'

'How?'

Mr Hunglebert-Chiffinch beamed; his glasses gleamed with an unholy light; his hands came together in an act of worship.

'By smashing the clock.'

George cast an anxious glance at the Victorian masterpiece. It had behaved itself for the entire day and sent out a little brass man every hour with dutiful promptness.

'Are you sure that will be necessary?'

'Absolutely. Object of guilt – little father association – destroy – break pattern – no projecting image – result – cure.'

'Well, if you say so.'

'Perhaps,' Mr Hunglebert-Chiffinch's voice betrayed an inner excitement, 'you will send for a hammer.'

George pressed a bell-button and in due course a soft-footed butler presented himself.

'Oh, Masters, Mr Hunglebert-Chiffinch requires a hammer.'

Five minutes later Masters reappeared bearing a formidable looking hammer on a silver tray.

'One hammer, sir. Cook says, can she have it back when convenient. She uses it to tenderize the steak.'

'Of course,' George reassured him. 'Mr Hunglebert-Chiffinch only requires it to smash a clock.'

'Very well, sir. Will that be all?'

'Thank you, Masters.'

When the man had gone, the psychiatrist rose and removed his coat. He then rolled up his shirt-sleeves before reverently taking the clock down from the mantelpiece and standing it gently on the bedroom floor. He took up the hammer.

'End of guilt complex,' he said and swung the hammer.

He did a thorough job. The tough mahogany fought back, but eventually was reduced to a heap of splinters. The conglomeration of cogs, wheels and springs split asunder and went spinning over the carpet like the intestines from a mechanical monster. The little brass man, Mr Hunglebert-Chiffinch crushed with a single blow. He was completely hollow.

'You're certainly good at smashing clocks,' remarked George wistfully. Little father notwithstanding, he had been rather fond of that clock.

The psychiatrist laid aside his hammer.

'I feel much better now. I've always wanted to do that.'

*

Time is indeed a great healer and as the days passed George began, if not to forget, to view the disturbing episode of the clock, with a certain bravado. The affair of the snapping cigarette box he had already dismissed as an inexplicable accident.

'Do you know,' he remarked to his second cousin Marion, who together with the rest of the family, now made frequent visits, 'I thought I saw a little figure like my father come out of a clock?'

'Nerves,' Cousin Marion assured him. 'When my daddy died, I thought I saw him in a bucket of water.'

'Good heavens!' George gasped. 'Was he?'

'No. It turned out to be a flannel.'

'I guess I am rather worked up,' George confessed after a while. 'I don't seem able to get down to anything.'

'You ought to get married,' she said coyly. 'Some mature woman.' She threw a spiteful glance at a photograph of Eve which stood on the desk. 'These flighty young things have no idea. I doubt if any of them can cook.'

'I have a cook,' George stated. 'The place is simply swarming with servants.'

'But they can't give you the intimate service a wife could,' Marion insisted, then blushed unbecomingly when she recognized the implications of her words. 'I mean, they haven't the same interest.'

'No, I suppose they haven't,' George agreed. 'After all, it's only a job of work to them.'

'Look at this carpet,' Marion pointed out. 'No one is going to tell me it was cleaned this morning.'

'The maid ran a Hoover over it.'

'Yes, and a very quick run it was too.' Marion suddenly jerked her plump figure upright and assumed an expression of extravagant surprise. 'Do you know something? I've got an idea.'

'Good Lord!' George backed away in alarm.

'Yes. I'm going to vacuum the carpets.'

'What – all of them?'

'No.' Marion shook her head so violently that her double chin quivered. 'Just the rooms you use.'

'Really, there's no need,' George protested. But Marion would not be denied.

'I insist. You can't live like this. Where can I find a vacuum-cleaner?'

'Better ask Masters. But honestly, you shouldn't bother ... '

But Marion was already pushing the bell-button and when Masters appeared said curtly: 'Masters, I want a vacuum-cleaner.'

'Certainly, madam.'

He reappeared some five minutes later, with the cleaner in his outstretched arms, holding it as though it were a lost child being brought home to its mother. He placed it upright on the floor, then stepped back.

'Will there be anything further, madam?'

'Yes, plug it in.' Marion wished to demonstrate her ability to command, and watched Masters with a critical eye while he pushed a three-pin plug into a wall-socket, then straightened up.

'That will be all. You may go.'

'Very good, madam. Thank you, madam.'

Masters departed and George prepared to follow him.

'Well, I'll leave you to it, then.'

Marion had rather hoped he would stay and watch her mastery of the vacuum-cleaner, but the speed with which he made for the door dismissed any such possibility. She smiled bravely.

'I'll have it all nice and tidy by the time you get back.'

'Right.' He stood in the doorway and grinned sheepishly. 'Awfully good of you. Very decent.'

'There's so much more that I could do,' Marion began to say, but the door slammed before she could go into further details. Left alone, she rolled up her sleeves and set to work. The room had been the late Benjamin Howard's study and certainly required a lot of attention. Papers were stacked in one corner; books and magazines cluttered the desk and mantelpiece; a pair of old shoes crouched on a chair like two sleeping cats, and there was even a fishing rod standing against one wall.

Marion worked quickly and with quiet efficiency. She stacked all the papers and books on the desk, then looked around for a more permanent home. A large, built-in wall cupboard seemed to be a likely place. She tried to open the doors, but frowningly discovered they were locked. But an extensive search found a solitary key in the bottom desk drawer; tied to it was a label on which was printed in red ink: PRIVATE CUPBOARD.

Curiosity accompanied Marion as she went over to the cupboard and turned the key. The interior was fitted with shelves, all of which were bare save for one at eye-level. This contained a row of books, that can be best described as illustrated literature. Marion took one out and flicked the pages over, then shocked to the depths of her puritanical soul, gasped aloud from pure horror.

She saw pictures of young ladies about to be undressed, half-undressed and not dressed at all. There were also – and Marion, determined to see the worst, pulled out book after book – young men and young ladies engaged in exploits that seemed neither practical nor useful.

Marion said: 'Dirty old man,' before subduing her outraged feelings to a point where she was able to think rationally. She was certain George had not seen, did not know of the existence of this – she spat the word out – 'Filth'. He must never see it. She looked round the room and saw the empty fireplace beckoning.

Stacked in the iron grate, the late Mr Benjamin's collection waited for a match. Marion opened her handbag, took out a cigarette lighter and prepared to consign pornography to ash and smoke. She stopped as a sudden sound attracted her attention. A growl? Such a supposition was ridiculous, for what animal could have got into the room when all the doors and windows were shut? Then it came again.

Marion tried to define it. A whirling growl – a coughing gasp? Then it sprang into continuous, roaring life and she realized what it was. The vacuum-cleaner. She was able to sigh with relief, relaxing her taut muscles, even give a little laugh. The vacuum-cleaner with that irresponsibility, peculiar to machines, had somehow turned itself on.

She rose and turned, then felt the first stirring of alarm. Not fear, certainly not panic, but a little uneasiness, for the machine was moving towards her. It could have been funny – the vacuum-cleaner with its handle sticking up like a stiff tail, gliding across the carpet, dodging a table – really most extraordinary – and making for a plump lady of uncertain years, who held a cigarette lighter in one hand.

Marion – trying so hard to laugh – ran round the desk and took refuge in the window bay. The vacuum-cleaner changed direction and skilfully steered its way between two chairs. It glided round the desk and with what seemed to be a roar of triumph, made for the window.

Marion was certainly frightened now, but she could still rely on her well developed sense of self-preservation. With a little scream she ran forward and clambered up on to the desk. The vacuum-cleaner roared, then turned around and made its way back to the fireplace, where it took up a position on the hearth-rug and waited. Marion whimpered, then told herself she was a weak, silly woman, for who in their right senses, could possibly be frightened of a vacuum-cleaner? All she had to do, was jump down, run over to the wall and pull the plug out. She looked at the wall in question, then almost did something very silly indeed. The plug was out of the wall socket. But the vacuum-cleaner's motor was still running. In fact when Marion almost fell off the desk the motor rose up to an anticipatory roar.

She could not possibly remain where she was. Suppose one of the servants were to come in? Or worse, if George returned? She would never be able to show her face in the house again. No, there was no evading the issue – she must jump down and go full out for the door.

She crawled to the desk edge. The vacuum-cleaner raced its motor. She took a deep breath, leaped to the floor and ran as fast as her plump legs would allow towards the door. The vacuum-cleaner sprang into instant roaring action. It streaked across the floor, turned abruptly and caught up with its victim just as she had laid frantic hand to slippery handle. She screamed when the motor made a rasping, chuckling sound – then the door was mercifully open and she was running across the hall with the mechanized tormentor in hot pursuit. She crashed into a suit of armour, which George had purchased in the Portobello Road thinking it to be both ornamental and intellectual, and measured her length on the carpet.

There she lay, waiting for the end, but the vacuum-cleaner, having floored its victim, now seemed to have lost interest in her. It edged its way towards the suit of armour, tapped its handle on one shining knee-plate, then drew back, slowing its motor as though debating some important issue. Then it took up position beside the pile of gleaming metal and lapsed into abrupt silence.

After a while Marion got up and examined – from a safe distance – the object that had caused her so much distress. It was to all outward appearance, an ordinary, if rather expensive vacuum-cleaner, that would go where it was pushed and no further. Having satisfied herself on this point, Marion opened up her mouth and screamed.

A door opened and Masters, suave in his black jacket and pin-striped trousers, walked slowly across the hall. He stood motionless before the hysterical woman.

'You called, madam?' he enquired.

*

George was seated behind his late father's desk, examining his now sound right hand. It was fully restored to all its former usefulness. He could open doors, peel an orange, turn on bath taps – or sign cheques.

George felt rich in goodliness. A glow of pure self-righteousness warmed him from head to toe. He looked at the twenty cheques, all neatly typed out and waiting for his signature. He chuckled: 'If Father could see me now.'

He reached out his newly restored hand towards his gold-plated pen, but he never completed the action. From the hall came a steady, thumping tread, intermingled with an unrecognizable clanking sound. George thought about it for a little while. What could it be? Most of the servants were out. Masters would have retired to his, doubtlessly, respectable bed, and Eve was visiting her mother. In any case, none of these people would make a thumping, clanking sound.

He decided to investigate. He got up, walked over to the door and opened it. The thumping and clanking came nearer; the floor vibrated; a picture of George's late saintly mother fell from the wall, and a cat which had been sleeping peacefully in the hall, streaked up the stairs.

George backed slowly into the room as a complete suit of armour advanced ponderously towards him. He retreated until the desk cut into the backs of his legs and made further retirement impossible. It never occurred to his paralysed brain that he might step to one side and run for the door. Somehow, there did not seem much point.

The suit of armour, which George had lovingly assembled, was without any doubt, alive. The eyeholes were empty, but nevertheless, he could sense a cold, malignant stare. He had often experienced it before. The metal right arm, which terminated in a steel gauntlet, made a too familiar contemptuous gesture.

George made a sound that resembled the bleating of a newly-born calf. The suit of armour retaliated by chuckling. A booming, echoing rumble, that must have originated from somewhere inside the great helmet.

George bleated again as the suit of armour took a lumbering step forward. For the space of three minutes they stood – face to helmet. Then the suit of armour moved again, but George made no sound at all.

*

The family were once again congregated in the study. It was distribution day.

'Sure he's all right?' the second niece enquired of the ancient brother.

'Hand's as steady as a rock. Can sign cheques all night.'

The second-cousin-once-removed asked the question which had murdered sleep for almost everyone present.

'How much will we get?'

One nephew, who worked in a betting-shop, produced a sheet of paper and began to read the results of some very interesting arithmetic.

'Let's put it this way. After death duties, there ought to be just over two million quid in stocks and bonds and things. Now, there's twenty of us – so twenty into two million – equals one hundred thousand smackers each.'

'Is that all?' the first second-cousin demanded. 'Don't seem much.'

'Wait a minute.' The second second-cousin-once-removed raised both hands. 'Let's be fair about this. If we're going to share out the loot between all relatives, then what about my two nippers? Aye? Ain't they entitled to a share each? I say they are. I mean they've got old Ben's blood in 'em.'

The youngest nephew, who so far had produced no legitimate issue of his own, roared his disapproval. 'You greedy bastard. You want to grab three hundred thousand for yourself.'

Just at this moment George Howard entered the room and

the ancient brother acquainted everyone of this fact by hissing loudly and jerking his head in a most alarming fashion. When order had been established, he, as senior member of the family present, made a little speech.

'I am sure we all wish to thank good old George for all he's going to do for us, and assure him, that we will stand by him through thick and thin ... '

'What about the house?' the fat lady interrupted. 'Shouldn't it be sold and the money split?'

'Through thick and thin,' the ancient brother repeated loudly, 'and we know that George ... will ... will ... '

He stopped, aware that an uneasy atmosphere was drifting across the room and everyone was looking at the man behind the desk with growing concern. George was grinning. It was not a nice grin, or even a mocking grin. It was more like the grimace of a wolf, confronted by a flock of stupid, but succulent sheep. A shiver ran down the spine of even the most unimaginative person present. Such an expression did not fit George's meek, rather inane face at all. It was shocking – even obscene. The ancient brother said softly: 'Anything wrong, George old chap?'

The eyes gleamed with an unholy joy and the grin broadened.

'Not a bloody thing.'

A shocked silence lasted for the space of a minute, then someone ventured to ask: 'How about it, then? How much do we get?'

'Not a bloody thing.'

'Look here ... ' the fat lady started to protest, but a sudden glare made the words die in her throat.

'You conniving bastards.' Even the voice was different – low, harsh, not in the least like George's usually mild tone. 'You rattle-brained, bovine half-wits. What I've got – what the bloody thieving government have left me – I keep ... '

The family were frightened to a man, they were also angry, but so far, they were not terrified. That was still to come.

Suddenly George's head jerked up and down, then sideways, and a voice they all remembered cried out: 'Go away ... you're dead ... you've no business in my head ... '

Then the head jerked again and the harsh voice replied:

'Shut up you soft-bellied imbecile ... Here I bloody am and here I bloody well stay. Get out your bloody self ... '

'I won't ... '

'You bloody well will ... '

The ancient brother was the last to reach the door. He could not run so fast as the others.

VII

Don't Know

Yes ... yes, dear brother-in-law, you want to know what sent Lydia round the bend, not being able to swallow the official crap about a nervous breakdown. I understand that and am quite prepared to tell all, knowing it to be extremely doubtful that you will believe a single word. But it will ease the pressure on my mind to talk about what happened, clothe bizarre facts with words and relive the entire business again. Some kind of therapy, I guess. Nature's way of getting rid of the poison.

Now, before I start. If you want a spot of refreshment, there's tea and coffee in the kitchen, but you'll have to make it yourself – I'm just not up to it. On the other hand there's whisky and brandy in the cocktail cabinet, and should you decide on some hard stuff, maybe I'll join you. What? One third water. Fine. Down the hatch.

*

Your sister made a nigh perfect wife, having a sweet temper, surprisingly good in bed, blessed with all domestic virtues, including being a superb cook. What a pity it is that no man hungers for perfection in marriage. After six months spent in this wedded paradise, I found myself looking for molehills, that would after a little work, make excellent mountains of contention. But rightfully has it been said that it takes two to make a quarrel and Lydia refused to co-operate.

Her usual answer to any accusation was: 'I daresay you're right, dear. Sorry.'

How can you explain the joy of a flaming great row that terminates in a prolonged make-up session, to someone who regards a cross word as a double-edged sword. I began to hurt her by word and deed, in consequence suffered varying degrees of remorse, that gradually grew shorter, of lesser intensity, until they ceased altogether.

I am well aware that my wife – your sister – Lydia, eventually aroused a latent streak of cruelty, that may well have slept undetected until the day of my death, had she been less submissive; but the strands that form our individual characters were woven long before we were born, which means that most of us are destined to glide down a disaster course.

You think I'm trying to avoid responsibility?

Well, listen, you sanctimonious bastard, I'm not trying to avoid responsibility, I disclaim it altogether. How was I to know that the thing in the attic ... ? Yes ... yes, I said the thing in the attic and I mean just that ...

You will listen to the ravings of a madman, if that's what you think I am. You'll take a small nip of my whisky and sit back in that chair and listen ... listen real good, or so help me, devil, I'll knock the living daylights out of you.

That's better ... sorry I had to get rough, but I'm fed up with people going all peculiar when I try to tell what really happened.

I've decided to give you the works. Full dialogue, descriptive narrative – the lot.

So settle down and maybe lay off the whisky for the time being. I don't want you soused before I've finished. Then most likely, you'll wish you were. Anyway ...

*

'If you must skulk in the kitchen, at least employ your time to useful purpose. A pot of tea and a plate of scones would not be out of place.'

I was in a facetious mood and derived sardonic amusement from my ironic humour. The essence of the joke being that she would actually make a pot of tea and toast a plate of scones, hoping to repossess my heart via my stomach.

I returned to the lounge, there to lie back in a deep armchair to await developments, aware – as indeed had been my experience in recent times – of a strange phenomenon that was taking place just beyond my range of consciousness. It is so difficult to explain, as it takes on various forms, without actually escaping from the confines of auto-suggestion.

I suppose the most common was the distinct impression that a dark figure stood behind me, but disappeared the moment I turned my head. Then there was the murmur of voices that never really became audible, but would have done so if I dropped my mental guard for the fraction of a second.

I believe that this strange, but enthralling phenomenon began to take place just after I first began to exile Lydia to the kitchen, but I can't be certain about that. Maybe it has been with me all my life and it took the irritating presence of a loving wife to bring about dawning awareness. Be that as it may, I soon came alive to the fact that the house was infested with all manner of sub-life. Really that is true.

I mean – at this very moment there's something very nasty – large, green head and long arms – trying to get a fix on your throat ... now ... now ... don't be silly. Sit still. *Sit Still, Damn You.* I said trying. It will never succeed. Can't. Hasn't got the substance.

But I digress – and put that whisky decanter down.

Lydia came in from the kitchen carrying a tray on which stood a cup and saucer and a plate of oven-hot scones; displaying those signs of insanity that always manifest when I start to jerk my head to the left, hoping to catch a glimpse of that dark figure before it disappeared. She placed the tray on a nearby table and began to butter scones, a service of which I took full advantage, scoffing them as fast as she wielded knife.

'How do you feel, dear?' she asked.

'With a finger and thumb,' I replied, then half choked on buttered scone and devastating humour. She emitted a gasping cry and ran from the room, but instead of returning to her proper place, the kitchen, ascended two flights of stairs to the attic.

What? I could hear her running up both flights and the sound of the attic door opening before she reached it. That's what I said. Someone – something – opened the attic door before she reached it. Not all that surprising. She was of course going mad, even then, and most of the life forms that infest the house, are not from our point of view, all that sane, so she and at least one of them were bound to find a common meeting place sooner or later. Or so I thought then.

I wasn't actually jealous, but no man can really come to

terms with the knowledge that his wife is allegorically having it off with something shady in the attic. So I climbed the first flight of stairs, shouted up the second: 'Come on down, you fornicating cow. I know what's going on.'

She had the cunning of the insane. Opened the attic door and emerged carrying a pile of clean towels and wearing a watery smile. She said: 'Go back to the lounge, dear. I'll be with you in just a moment.'

The loving wife act might have impressed, had I not sensed something standing behind her. I chuckled and backed down the stairs, never once removing my accusing stare from her face, marvelling that such a fair exterior could hide such deceit ...

What? No, I had no use for her cloying, passive love, but that didn't mean I wanted her to deceive me. Not even with something I could not as yet describe. Everyone knows that deceivers are gay dogs, whereas the deceived are for some reason, figures of obscene fun. At any rate from that time on I was aware of the thing in the attic and made my plans accordingly.

No longer did I banish Lydia to the kitchen and even smiled benignly on her friend, the grey-haired gentleman, who thought I did not know he was recording our conversation on a pocket cassette. I permitted her to sit opposite and took pleasure in the delicacy of her white skin, the gentle curves of her face, the softness of her large, well-shaped hands. There was something immensely exciting in the thought that I only owned half-share in this desirable collection and toying with the conjecture – who – what – my unknown partner was.

Lydia said: 'Don't stare at me like that, dear. It's most disconcerting.'

I grinned. 'I daresay. I daresay. Tell me – does He stare? Eh? Has He eyes to stare with?'

The blood drained from her face and I thought that if any man gazed upon unveiled guilt, it was I. Stark fear peered from behind grey eyes, sent out distress signals by means of shaking hands, and tried to find expression in little muted cries. Thus have guilty wives behaved down through the ages, when the painted veil of pretended innocence has been torn aside. When she ran from the room and snatched up the hall telephone, I had the leisure to consider what kind of being this demon lover was.

He must be part of the world from whence came the voices I did not quite hear and be related to, if not be, that dark figure that stood behind me. But how could He be behind me and in the attic, both at the same time, you may well ask? I did not know. I still don't. If pressed I'll maintain that he was most likely multi-dimensional, and could exist in more than one place, but that's pure conjecture. I was more than satisfied to know he existed, and to all intents and purposes, resided in the attic.

Naturally I decided to give him my full attention and watch Lydia with unwavering intensity, a course of action that should be knowledge revealing, which must always be a matter for great satisfaction to a man with an enquiring mind. Even more so to a deceived husband, only of course, I was no longer deceived.

I sent out mental feelers (good words), up both flights of stairs and into the attic. My God! It took a great deal of courage. The atmosphere up here was like cold, black soup in which swam unthinkable things with spiked tails. A bit fanciful, you say? Maybe, but that's the impression I got, before I exerted my extraordinary will-power and began to sort out light from shadow.

Nothing concrete, you understand. No-nonsense people will say – 'Sick imagination' and leave it at that. But I know better. Up there in the attic there's a connection with another house that used to exist in another dimension. I think that's right. Or maybe it still does exist on yet another dimension. It's very complicated and I get a bad headache if I think too deeply about it.

But I get the impression that people have disappeared in that attic – long ago of course – and they finished up in a kind of 'Don't Exist' place and it's their voices I almost hear.

But something – are you following all this? – a being – a skeleton thing – came over – from somewhere – and sort of took root because of a woman who cried her heart out – poured out a stream of frustration – and there's no way of sending him back.

I strengthened my mental feelers and tried to imagine what

he looked like. What was he made of? Not a wise thing to do. I should have remembered that women are drawn to the bizarre. Something with three heads and six legs will turn them on higher than a kite in a gale force nine wind.

No – so far as I know He did not have three heads and six legs; in fact I think he was once a normal human being, who most likely lived backwards, and had in the course of transient has taken on some strange – how shall I put it? – some strange extras. Even about that I can't be certain, as I never actually saw Him in the sense you and I understand 'saw'. Lydia did. That's why she is now mad and I'm sane.

But I *sensed* what he was and a rough idea of what He might look like, which was only achieved after days of intense concentration and doing something to myself, which I can never explain or even understand. Blew a hole in the left hand wall of my brain is the best I can come up with, which is no reason for you to put on that knowing look and start a love affair with the door. Lydia left the door open and wore a similar look when we had our first 'serious talk'.

'Henry,' that apparently being my name, 'I want you to sit quite still and listen to what I have to say. Mr Henderson, the gentleman who comes to see you once a week, wants me to agree to you being – well – sent to a home, where you'll be looked after.'

I nodded. 'And that would suit you fine. Wouldn't it?'

Of course she shook her head violently. 'No. No. I remember the way you used to be and know – oh, God! – know you'll be like that again. If only I have patience. But you must help.'

'In what way,' I enquired.

'Stop imagining – things. Accept that at this moment there are only you and I in this house.'

'If you believe that, then Mr Henderson should consider putting you away in a home,' I said sternly. 'But you don't believe it. You are well aware that there is at least one other intelligent being in this house, apart from ourselves.'

'Henry, please. Don't let your imagination run wild. Because I'm certain that's your trouble. Your wonderful imagination that has served you so well all these years, has rebelled. Get it back under control and you'll be yourself again.'

I nodded slowly, while favouring her with a look of admiration.

'What a superb actress you are! Absolutely astounding! If I did not know you have formed – how to be tactful? – a close relationship with something nasty in the attic, I'd be completely taken in. But, you silly cow, I can feel him moving around up there and he's waiting for you to go up. Like you did just now.'

She gripped my hands so hard I flinched. 'I have turned the attic into a workshop, as you well know. I do a little dress-making as a means of adding to our income. This is more important than ever, as you have not earned anything for the past three months.'

'But my half-yearly royalty statement is due next week,' I pointed out. 'That when added to my 2½% of the gross profit of the film *False Dawn* is more than adequate for our needs. So don't lie about this dressmaking business. If you work up there, it's merely to establish a pretext.'

This was the first time we had really discussed the subject and the prospect of a thrust and parry argument excited me. Now she came up with a beauty that had me chuckling for pure joy.

'Who am I supposed to have up in there in the attic? A ghost?'

It was some time before I could answer. 'You know perfectly well who – what He is. He could not have come into being without your help.'

'You must be mad,' she said sadly. 'I don't want to believe, but there can be no other explanation.'

'Not imagination run wild?' I jeered. 'Not so long ago you were certain I was the victim of my own imagination.'

'There is only one way to settle this matter,' she said after a pause. 'That is to go upstairs and search the attic from ceiling to floor, and finally prove to yourself there's no one there.'

'If He decided to hide, there is no way we could find him,' I countered. 'You should know that to Him a crevice could become a ravine, or an entire room take on the dimensions of an ant hill.'

'You are playing with ideas. Come with me and we will search together. If we find no one – not even a wriggling shadow, then must you shackle imagination and return to normality.'

'The gateway to boredom,' I protested. 'The dark land that everyone visits sooner or later. Very well, let us go through the farce of looking for your phantom lover. Perhaps it would be better if you led the way.'

The moment I set foot on the first stair, fear ran an icy course down my entire body. The higher I ascended, the more intense that fear became, until it erupted in mind-freezing dread. The trouble was that, like an obnoxious weed, the idea began to grown in my mind, that one glimpse of my wife's lover would drive me completely mad. Now, this was passing strange, as I could not now even imagine what he looked like; only that his appearance was so alien from our point of view, the average sanity must crack if the eyes relayed a faithful picture to the brain.

But Lydia ... !

I kept my head lowered when we passed over the first landing; half closed my eyes as we mounted the second flight of stairs, heard a strange croaking sound that I gradually understood came from my own throat: then we were in the attic.

I had to raise my head, look round that small room with its sloping ceiling, dormer window and faded fitted carpet, and instantly sensed that He was there; hidden, watching, listening, waiting for the ideal moment in which to reveal himself.

I would have turned and run back down the stairs, if it had not been so important to unmask Lydia, expose her infidelity. I said: 'Tell Him to come out. Show Himself,' and marvelled at my own foolhardy temerity.

Lydia laid a shapely hand on my arm and perhaps I did not tremble with quite so much violence. Her voice was that of a mother calming a frightened child.

'There is no one here. You can see that. Nowhere to hide. Unbroken walls, large window, table with my sewing machine and a bale of cloth, a folding chair. Not so much as a cupboard. Only you and I are here.'

'He's under the table,' I insisted. 'Demand that He come out. Or rather ask Him nicely.'

Prod the sleeping cobra, then shut the eyes and pretend it's not there, but surrender to the death wish, feel it slithering nearer.

Lydia said: 'Now you're being silly. Really silly.'

'Invite Him to come out,' I persisted. 'Insist that He comes out from under the table.'

She emitted a low, gurgling laugh. 'Very well, if you really insist. Anything to make you happy. So long as we end this silly game.' She raised her voice and called out coyly: 'Whoever you are that's under the table, come out. I really must insist you come out.'

Thank God or whatever power it is that looks after frightened men, that I spun round and faced the door. I heard the table being overturned, followed by the strange noise that Lydia made. It wasn't really a scream; more like a gargle – you know what people do when they have a sore throat – that went on for a long time, until it abruptly shut off. When she began to bleat like a newly born calf, I knew she was quite, quite mad and He was cuddling her.

I walked out of the room, shoulders erect, looking steadfastly to my front, descended the stairs and went back into the lounge. I believe Lydia remained in the attic for a while, probably because she couldn't leave Him, apart from which I doubt if she knew what time of day it was.

I knew then that I had done her a great injustice. She had never even suspected His existence, even though He fancied her from the start. Yes ... yes ... I will admit that I could have been at least partly responsible for Him being in the attic; maybe He is some kind of off-shoot from my own personality, that I created to act as a substitute, for God knows I often wanted to scare her out of that damnable soft, clinging I-love-you act. If so, why should part of myself be so strange as to drive me mad if I saw it? Answer: because there had to be an alien foundation for me to build on.

But now I have lost interest in Him and I suppose He must be dying, if that's the right word for Him fading out. What? You want to know what happened next? After ... ? Well, Mr Henderson called and I let him in. He'd come to see me – the mad one. Funny, eh? Anyroad, I let him in and said: 'I think you'd better look at Lydia, she's behaving most oddly,' and he belted upstairs.

There can be no doubt that he screamed. Oh, yes indeed. Him didn't fancy Mr Henderson one little bit and didn't cuddle the poor man afterwards, so at least he retained a spoonful of sanity. Otherwise he could not have shouted: 'It's got horns,' just before dropping dead. I say dropping – they found him draped over the banisters.

And that my dear brother-in-law is how your sister came to finish up in the local looney bin, where she yells the roof off if anyone puts an arm round her. Me, I'm as sane as a coven of archdeacons. Everyone agrees on that point. My evidence at poor Mr Henderson's inquest, was commended by the coroner as being the epitome of well-reasoned observation. Of course, it was mostly fiction, there being no way I could tell the entire, unvarnished truth, but such skilful invention must reinforce my claim for unimpaired reasoning powers.

May I present another example. That sound you can hear from the very top of the house. That's Him. As previously stated I am pretty certain He is dying, but that doesn't mean He is without strength. Presently He'll make His way down the stairs and just manage to reach the doorway behind me, where He'll send out a kind of wordless appeal for renewed interest. I am of course careful to remain facing this direction, whereas you – seated where you are – will have a most excellent view.

I do most earnestly request you to turn about. Should yet another person drop dead from pure terror, or go bananas in this house, authority will begin to entertain grave suspicions.

Oh, dear! Disbelief has you in its iron grip! You think I deliberately drove your sister mad and it's my accomplice coming down the stairs. Worse than I thought.

Then I must ask you to excuse me. Watching you blow your top will not be a pretty sight. I should imagine the effort required will finish Him off, which means your sanity (or life) will be well spent. I'll be in the kitchen making myself a cup of cocoa. Start screaming when all is over.

VIII
Travelling Companion

Lesley Dale-Henderson placed half a shoulder of lamb in the range oven, raked the fire until a mass of red-hot coals glimmered through the bars, then went over to the earthenware sink to wash her hands. The bedroom still had to be done and the windows could do with a clean, but both chores would have to wait. First a nice rest in the big armchair, where she could skim through a library book, or maybe have a shot at the *Daily Mail* easy crossword. But of course she'd probably be asleep before five minutes had passed, feeling as she did so worn out after a small output of effort. Strange, as the doctor maintained there was nothing wrong with her, but ever since Geoffrey died ...

She went into the small sitting-room, sank into a chair and picked up the newspaper. Fortunately the crossword was on the back page, so she was spared the tiresome business of searching for it, and could at once concentrate her attention on the list of clues. One across – unimaginative – seven letters.

Geoffrey had often accused her of being unimaginative. But surely that could not be true, for she had only to close her eyes to imagine him being sent hurtling through the windscreen when the car hit a low wall, he having swerved to avoid a child on a bicycle, who had made a sudden appearance from a side road.

Prosaic – that was the word. She wrote each letter carefully with a ballpoint pen, then went on to consider one down. Idiom. What on earth was an idiom? It started with P and had eight letters and might have something to do with ... A tap on the front door interrupted her deliberation and sent a shiver of apprehension running down her back.

The travelling grocer was not due until tomorrow, the

postman had left her meagre mail hours ago, no one else was expected.

Had her isolated cottage attracted the attention of a tramp – or whatever they called them these days? A hawker? A madman? A sex maniac? How often had she been warned of the dangers of living alone in this out-of-the-way place.

The tapping came again, only now it was a little louder, more insistent. Lesley got up and clutching the newspaper crept slowly towards the door, quelling the urge to remain silent and wait for the intruder to go away, for then she would be haunted by the fearful curiosity as to who it had been. She cleared her throat and called out:

'Who ... who are you?'

A young masculine voice came from behind the closed door.

'Merely a traveller, ma'am. Would you mind filling my water bottle?'

Could this simple request be a device to make her open the door? On the other hand had she the right to refuse anyone water? The basic element. And had not Geoffrey often stressed the need to help others whenever possible. She reached out and opened the door.

A tall lean young man stood on the step, whose thick blond hair was bleached almost white by the mid-summer sun. He might have been twenty-five or thirty, even a few years older – or younger – for he was blessed by the Saxon good looks that resist the ravages of time until the approach of old age. He wore a green open-necked shirt, a beige canvas jacket, blue faded trousers and a pair of stout, square-toed shoes. A large, well-filled haversack that had an aluminium kettle dangling from one strap, covered his back from neck to waist, but in no way detracted from his upright stance. He smiled and revealed splendid white teeth.

'So sorry to bother you. But yours is the first house I've seen for miles. If I could just fill my water bottle – and maybe the kettle – I'll be on my way.'

He was young, good-looking, clean and spoke with the right accent; just the kind of young man Geoffrey might well have brought home to dinner. A wave of relief made Lesley expel her breath as a vast sigh and extend her hand.

'Of course. Come in. You must forgive my – well alarm – but

one never knows who is wandering around.'

Despite the heat his hand was surprisingly cool and he radiated a kind of good-natured charm that made her suddenly realise how lonely she had been these past weeks. The young voice contained a hint of laughter.

'Too true. In your shoes I'd have told me to go take a running jump. But I do assure you – I'm quite harmless.'

Lesley stood to one side. 'The tap – that is to say – the sink is in the kitchen. Through the doorway.'

He walked across the sitting-room, entered the kitchen, then made his way to the sink. He looked smilingly back over one shoulder.

'Mind if I take this haversack off? The bottle is in it. The damned thing kept banging against my hip, so I packed it away.'

Lesley raised a hand and smoothed back a lock of hair.

'Please – please do. Have you come far?'

He slipped the straps from his shoulders and allowed the pack to drop to the floor. 'Ten miles since sun-up. No distance at all really, only one gets so devilishly thirsty. And would you believe it – not a pub anywhere.'

He unbuckled the haversack and Lesley saw what could only be a dirty shirt and a pair of grubby underpants, two items he quickly pushed out of sight. The 'bottle' turned out to be an ex-army model, complete with khaki padding and webbing. He removed the cork and placed the mouth under the cold tap. Lesley took a deep breath before saying: 'I've a bottle of cider in the fridge. I suppose you wouldn't care for a glass?'

The smile that lit up his face was wonderful to behold.

'Would I! But I really mustn't. But it's most awfully kind of you to offer.'

'Nonsense.' She moved towards the refrigerator, shocked that she Lesley Dale-Henderson, who still mourned her dead, was dangerously near flirting with this young stranger. She must allow him to drink a glass of cider, fill his water bottle and kettle, then escort him out of the door. But there was no denying the fact, her drab day had been suddenly lit by what could only be described as a flash of light.

Seated on a tall stool he drank chilled cider and created a line of entertaining conversation.

'My name is Harry and yours is Mrs L. Dale-Henderson.' He chuckled. 'I know it's not the done thing, but I did notice an envelope on the mantelpiece as I came through the sitting-room. I've twenty-twenty eyesight and just can't help seeing what I shouldn't. What does L stand for?'

'Er – Lesley.'

'What a lovely name. It suits you. People grow to their names. I mean Lesley suggests someone with a pale oval face, large dark eyes, auburn hair and a slender, but well-shaped figure. I do hope I'm not being personal, but that's you to a T.'

Lesley blushed and said thank you.

'I expect,' Harry went on (how well his name suited him), 'you are wondering who I am. Me – I'm a tramp.'

Lesley repeated the word tramp and looked surprised.

'Yes, ma'am. An honest-to-goodness tramp. I walk as far as my legs carry me, sleep where I can. Hayrick, barn, under the naked sky. But I try to work for my bread. Well, bread and whatever else is going.'

'It sounds rather precarious,' Lesley protested. 'It might be all very well during the summer, but what will you do in the winter?'

A cloud dimmed the light in his eyes and for a while he did not answer; then he said, 'Sufficient unto the day the evil thereof. Each day must be drained, each night endured. Who knows what miracle will transform the future. Perhaps one can walk from near despair into happiness.'

He sat with lowered head and stared at the floor and Lesley experienced a ridiculous urge to comfort him; put an arm round his shoulders, probe into the depths of his mind, forge a link that could never be broken. Then he abruptly raised his head and his eyes were those of a mischievous child.

'And what, beautiful lady, has driven you to live in this lonely place? Can it be that you are hiding from someone?'

'My husband was killed in a motor accident a few months back. I just had to get away.'

At once he radiated sympathy that had to be genuine.

'I know what you mean. Sadness should be nursed in lonely places. And people can be such a bore, can't they? Say how sorry they are, and going on about time being a great healer.

Comfort comes from the soft voices that whisper through the woods on a sunny day.'

Lesley frowned, then parted her lips in a semi-humorous smile.

'What a strange person you are. I've never heard anyone talk like that before.'

He shrugged. 'Mad, beautiful lady. It's best not to listen too deeply to what I say. Is that lamb I can smell roasting?'

It might have been a not very subtle hint or merely an idle enquiry, but Lesley – her former intention forgotten – felt compelled to issue an invitation.

'Yes. Look, would you care to share my lunch? Nothing very exciting, merely half a shoulder of lamb with boiled sprouts and potatoes. And tinned peaches to follow.'

She thought he would put on a display of reluctance, instead he said, 'OK. But you must allow me to do something in return. A job around the house or in the garden.'

'The windows need cleaning.'

He got up. 'Fine. Just bring out the materials and I'll do the job. Then, if it's all right with you, I'll have a shot at that lawn. Have you a mower?'

Lesley sighed and unsuccessfully tried to quell a surge of pleasure. 'There's a rusty old model in that old barn left behind by the last tenant, but I'm not sure if it will work.'

'I'll soon make it,' he assured her cheerfully. 'Leave everything to me.'

It was almost like having Geoffrey back again, except it was doubtful if he would have demeaned himself by cleaning windows. And Harry worked with almost terrifying speed, transforming window panes into gleaming rectangles, later all but running a well-oiled machine across the patch of grass that Lesley had kept in some sort of order with an old rip hook. Then he came in and ate more than his fair share of her lunch, all the while chatting about his adventures on the road, but adroitly sidestepping any question regarding the reason he had adopted this life style, his age and background. He assisted in the washing-up, put the plates and dishes away in their appointed places, then took Lesley by the hand and led her to the window.

'That old barn,' he pointed to the dilapidated structure that stood to the left of the garden. 'Now, I know this is an awful cheek, but if I do a few more chores, do you suppose I could spend the night there?'

'There is a spare room ... '

'Absolutely not. I'll have to leave very early in the morning and it wouldn't be very nice of me to disturb you.' He frowned. 'No, I must not spend the night in the house.'

Lesley gently withdrew her hand. 'If that's what you want, yes, you're free to use the barn.'

'You are indeed, very kind. Straw and leaves will make a cosy mattress and if you will lend me a blanket, I'll be fine.'

The remainder of the day passed quickly. Harry cleared the narrow bordering garden of weeds, gathered, then sawed a number of fallen branches into small logs, mended the front gate, then to Lesley's concern, began to dig a deep hole by the old barn.

'What's that for?' she asked.

'To bury rubbish,' he replied without looking up. 'You learn to leave no trace of your passing on the road. I suppose it's a basic instinct.' He paused and looked up. 'But don't let me keep you. Having someone watching me while I work is rather off-putting.'

Lesley – not knowing if she should be offended or amused – said: 'Sorry, I'm sure,' and went indoors. Later, watching him from the sitting-room window, she realised there was a bizarre element in this apparent insatiable desire for manual labour. He had completed the hole to his satisfaction and was now throwing hedge clippings, scraps of wood, sweeping sawdust into it, before shovelling the earth back into place. A frantic tramping down, followed by a careful replanting of grass roots, until finally all traces of his work had either been removed or hidden.

Then he cast an anxious glance up at the darkening sky and went out into the lane, where he stood for a long time, looking intently to the right, as though waiting for someone to appear. Presently he came back into the cottage and sank down into a chair and closed his eyes.

'I'll make a pot of tea,' Lesley said. 'And some sandwiches. There's some ham in the fridge.'

His eyes opened and the charming smile lit up his face.

'You're very kind.'

After tea they sat watching the small portable television, but Harry soon fell asleep, looking so young and vulnerable, Lesley again felt an almost overwhelming urge to put her arms round him, comfort, beg for terrible secrets that would be forever locked in her brain. Then a gust of wind rattled the window frames and he came up from the pit of sleep, stared at her with unseeing eyes and whispered: 'There was no good reason why. No reason for her to pursue ... '

He sat up and looked wildly round the room. 'I must leave at once. I've remained too long. Far too long.'

'That's nonsense,' she said gently. 'It's dark now and raining. Listen, you can hear it pounding on the windows. Remain 'til morning. Seven or eight hours can make little difference.'

'It can. Indeed it can. I've made good progress during the past few days, but almost ten hours in one place ... '

He got up abruptly and made for the door, but stopped when Lesley said, 'You must have a hot drink – tea – coffee – cocoa. And there's no way I'm going to let you leave on a night like this. So, don't be silly. Come back.'

He sighed deeply before returning to his chair.

'As you wish. But you must understand, I will leave very early tomorrow morning. Most likely long before you're awake.'

'That's entirely up to you,' Lesley replied tersely. 'Turn on the television again if you wish. I won't be a moment.'

When she returned carrying a tray on which stood two cups of cocoa and a plate of digestive biscuits, he did not appear to have moved, but still sat staring at the blank screen. She placed the tray on a small table, then, quite unable to resist the wave of pity and tenderness that flooded her being, knelt down and took one of his hands in hers.

'If ... if ... you've done something wrong, I don't mind. No matter what it might be. And I don't insist you tell me what it is. But ... but don't leave. I had not realised how lonely I am, or the great mistake I made by shutting myself away when Geoffrey died. Please ... please stay.'

Gradually she saw the strain – the fear – drain from his face, and he was leaning forward, his free hand on the back of her head; then their lips met and for a brief while a fierce flame consumed the loneliness, the coroding absorption with self, and both were transported to that plane where happiness is a white horse galloping towards a limitless horizon.

Suddenly Lesley was pushed back and he – Harry – the eternal youth – who had come out of a mist-shrouded past, stood up and shook his head.

'No ... no ... You don't understand. This must not – cannot be. It's not what I've done, but what I am. If I stay, you'll be damned. I can't explain any more.'

Lesley could only understand that she was being rejected; disappointment blended with anger and she shouted:

'Go ... go. Spend the night in the barn, if that's what you want. And try to forget I made such a fool of myself.'

For a moment his hand rested on her head, then he was gone. Lesley heard him pass the window, splashing through a puddle, most likely getting drenched, for the rain was still pelting down. She only just resisted the urge to open the door and call him back. Presently she began to cry.

*

Lesley sat by her bedroom window and averted her gaze from the old barn and looked out over the countryside. The rain had long since died away and the sky had been swept clean by a strong wind, permitting the moon to bathe the scene with silver light.

In a few hours he – Harry – would depart, then maybe she could begin to regain a measure of peace, not to mention self-respect. She tried to analyse this unreasonable obsession with a young man she had only known for a few hours and finally decided it must be the result of three months' isolation; once she was back living a normal life, he would be forgotten. Or become an embarrassing memory, an anecdote that could be related when time had tinted the entire episode with the bright hues of humour.

Now, she derived certain comfort from the moonlit scene; the trees that bowed their heads to the prevailing wind, the tall summer grass that shimmered gently under the benign sky, and the distant hills that surely belonged to a fantasy tale, told to three enthralled children, around a nursery fire. Then Lesley turned her attention to the lane which bordered the front garden and wended its way between neat hedgerows, until swallowed by a yawning ravine that marked the position of two facing chalk cliffs, surmounted by gold-flecked gorse bushes.

To the right – a girl was walking slowly along the lane. Attired in a blue dress, dark hair framing a pale oval face, she looked young, forlorn and – Lesley struggled for the correct description – out of place. The wind seemed unable to disturb her hair, while at the same time there was the distinct impression a strong gust would blow her over. She trudged onwards, head lowered, and – yes – she could be crying, or maybe merely sobbing; at any rate she was most certainly unhappy. Lesley considered the possibility of going down and enquiring as to why a young girl came to be wandering along a lonely country lane at that time of night. But a strange reluctance to even get up, let alone leave the house and approach the young wanderer, did not allow her to move, so she sat perfectly still, her forehead pressed against the window-pane.

The girl reached the front gate, stopped, turned slowly and looked up at the window. A study in still life. Lesley felt a thrill of apprehension when she saw the bright eyes that surely were watching her with sad reproach, and the slender hands that came out, palms uppermost, revealing dark lines across the wrists, that could have been scars, only they appeared to glisten.

Then the gate opened, sending out a little groan of protest, reminding Lesley that she had not oiled the hinges, as she had so many times intended. The girl moved on to the narrow path, advanced a few steps, then turned and walked towards the barn. The door was half open, it being all but impossible to close due to a missing hinge, and the slim form slid through the gap with astonishing ease and disappeared from sight.

Apprehension melted before a wave of hot anger. He had refused to stay in the house, had preferred the discomfort of a damp and draughty old barn, so that he might be reunited with this girl. Deep down Lesley knew this assumption lacked credibility, but at that time she was incapable of rational thought, aware only of an irresponsible need to pour out scorn on the author of her anguish.

She leapt to her feet, raced across the room, out on to the

landing, stumbled down the stairs, then, gasping, tears pouring from her eyes, flung open the front door and emerged into the moonlit night.

The barn was a place where gloom fought an even battle with thin spears of moonlight that were permitted entry through holes in the sagging roof. Shadows haunted corners and might well hide someone who did not wish to be seen, straw and broken crates littered the floor; an old iron saucepan had been stabbed by the branches of some plant that had sprouted from the cracked concrete, and its corpse was slowly rotting.

An indistinct shape rose up from a position close to the left hand wall and that soft, well-remembered voice asked:

'Is there anything wrong?'

Lesley heard herself shout: 'A girl ... a creature came in here. She's to go this instant. Do you hear me? I won't ... I won't be put upon.'

The sound of her voice died away and she stood trembling, near to total collapse, as Harry came forward until his face became a faint blur in the meagre light. For a while he did not speak, then: 'A girl you say! With dark hair and a white – white face, no doubt. And could she have been crying? Or merely sobbing and looking at you with reproach, that can so easily turn to hate? If so, you have keener eyes than some, beautiful lady.'

Anger slowly receded, leaving a void that only fear could fill, but she still must rant, reproach – pretend.

'You obviously know her. It's wrong of you to – to entertain someone out here, without telling me. I suppose you are travelling together.'

He smiled gently. 'I lead – she follows. I should have left last night.'

'Who is she?'

Instead of answering he laid a hand on her arm and gently propelled her out of the barn. The wind had died and not a sound disturbed the velvet silence, creating the impression that the entire world slept, save for two people who were isolated in a pocket of time.

'Who is she?' Lesley asked again.

His hair had been transformed into a golden halo when he

leaned against the barn wall and looked up at the sky.

'She was a bore that did something stupid when rebuked. Now, she's a menace. A creature of the night who stalks her prey. One day I may find the courage to stand and face the inevitable. When that time comes I will at last know how and why.'

He expelled his breath as a deep sigh, then reaching out pulled Lesley towards him. He kissed with the greed of a starving man, before saying:

'If she is watching grief will be replaced by rage, but I'll leave at once, so you will not be pestered. Soon the sun will rise and there'll be an entire day to build up a lead. Strange how distance acquired on wheels does not count.'

Lesley knew there was no way she could stop him leaving and now she did not want to. She stared fearfully at the barn doorway and thought she saw a dim shape standing way back in the shadows.

'Your haversack is in the kitchen,' she said.

*

The rising sun had sent its first shafts of light over the eastern horizon when Lesley watched Harry walk down the lane, his shoulder now bowed slightly under the weight of the pack. He did not look back, even though he knew she was standing by her bedroom window, for had he not told her to do so?

The slim, frail figure of a girl came out of the barn, glided rather than walked to the gate, then turned into the lane, and began to follow the young man who had been responsible for her doing something 'stupid'.

For a while Lesley could see both figures quite clearly; the pursuer and the pursued; the living and that which could well pass for the dead; until a bend in the lane hid them from sight.

Presently Lesley whispered: 'Had he remained – it might have been me. Dear God, it might have been me.'

IX

The Switch-Back

The Ray Heywood Story has been told so many times in some form or another, it is now one of those supernatural legends that bear comparison with the Marie Celeste or the Flying Dutchman. Of course the factual foundation on which the legend stands is very frail indeed and I am certain there is no more than one person alive today (now that my beloved wife has passed over) who is in a position to relate the true story.

That one person is me.

So I place not so flexible fingers to typewriter keys, while offering up a prayer that my brain is still capable of marshalling facts, rebuilding the memory of a world that we young blades found after surviving the most terrible war in history, and temporarily raising the dead from their graves to bear testimony to what I am about to relate.

But I must wander a little further back into the mists of time. Ray Heywood was my platoon sergeant. May I stress that the relationship which exists between platoon sergeant and platoon commander, despite the mighty gulf that separates non from commissioned officers, is a close one. Once the battalion goes into action, even more so, for something under an ounce of lead could remove a second lieutenant from the scene and elevate the sergeant to his place.

Heywood was one of those fortunate beings who are blessed not only with a magnificent body, handsome face and able brain, but also with that mysterious extra we call charm, which usually meant that at least ninety-five percent of his fellow beings were prepared to lean over backwards to please him.

He had a mass of golden curls and large blue eyes that always seemed alight with a good-natured, slightly mischievous twinkle. When anyone displeased him, that light slowly died and was replaced by a baleful glare. Then strong men trembled. But I never knew him to raise his voice or place any man on a charge.

Me he managed with respectful firmness. In fact looking back I now realise that most of his soft voice 'suggestions' were only saved from being interpreted as 'orders' by a few well-placed sirs. Frankly I was extremely grateful for any suggestions or orders he cared to issue, for they all paid off, and I am pretty certain that without him, I would have dropped any number of clangers, that could have resulted in the loss of men's lives.

Then VE day came, to be followed three months later by VJ day, and all of us came to realise that we had come through alive and intact, and there was no reason to suppose we would not remain that way until the old man with the scythe came to pay us a personal visit. Frankly I couldn't believe my luck and continued to regard each new day as an unmerited bonus for a very long time. Ray Heywood entertained no such qualms.

Even when the mortar bombs were whistling down on us in front of Caen, I heard him declare that the one with his number on it, would never be made. 'I will never be killed by bullet or shell,' he told me with all seriousness. 'I will outlive this war.'

'How can you be certain?' I asked.

He shrugged. 'One just knows these things. At least I do.'

In March 1946 the battalion, after a rip-roaring party, was disbanded and its component parts went their various ways, in the majority of cases, never to meet again.

But former platoon sergeant Heywood gave former lieutenant Mansfield a job.

I had always assumed that his family were well-heeled, for he often spoke about an uncle who appeared to own vast estates in the north of England, but I was quite unprepared to discover what a big shot he was himself. He made no bones about offering his one time superior officer a job; in fact his letter emphasised – tactfully – our changed relationship.

Dear Philip,

I hope you don't mind my using your first name, but Mr Mansfield sounds too formal and is apt to remind us both of times, every sensible person wants to forget. I bumped into Frenshaw the other day, who not only gave me your address, but the news that you are at rather a loose end these days.

I wonder – would you care to join my lot up here? Did I ever tell you that my family more or less own Heywood Motors? Anyway your one time square basher has been clobbered with the job of managing director. Why? Heavens above knows, unless it be that I own more voting shares than the rest of the mob.

Anyway, how would you like to be my PR man? Not a bad old number, selling the company image to the press, throwing the odd cocktail party – should be up your street, and we won't fall out about salary.

If agreeable ring the above number any time after six. We can then arrange for you to spend some time at the family pile and get to know everyone.

Hope to hear from you soon. Ray.

As being 'at rather a loose end' meant being jobless and near broke, it did not take me long to swallow whatever driblet of pride I still retained and ring Ray Heywood at the number indicated on his heavily embossed notepaper. I was greatly impressed by hearing what had to be the butler announce, 'Heywood Residence', then after I had given my name and stated my need to speak to Mr Raymond Heywood, was rather flattened by: 'I will ascertain if Mr Heywood is at home.'

The ensuing silence was interposed by clicks and harsh breathing sounds, terminated by that respectful, but arrogant voice, saying, 'You are through now, sir.'

Ray Heywood's voice throbbed with charm, if I may be permitted such an expression, while it also radiated the same gentle authority, that in all probability marked the change in Charles II after he had remounted the throne of his ancestors.

'How marvellous of you to call, my dear old sir. I have been hoping so much that you would. And of course ... But I'm not allowing you to get a word in edgeways. Be on CO's orders. Please say your piece. Are you taking up my offer? Coming down this week-end?'

I said: 'I would most certainly like to discuss the matter with you.'

'Absolutely splendid. You must allow me to lay on transport. Expect a vehicle around fourteen hundred hours on Friday. Your place is just off the Bayswater Road, isn't it? Great. I really am looking forward to seeing you again. Bye now.'

And he hung up. My contribution to the conversation had been eleven words.

An ancient, but stately Rolls collected me on time the following Friday and I sat dead centre on the back seat, where lulled by the gentle purr of the engine, I soon fell asleep. I was awakened by a gentle nudge and a gust of cold air. The chauffeur had the off-side door open and was leaning in.

'The County Hotel, sir. Mr Heywood has arranged for dinner to be served for you here, sir.'

I just managed to stifle a: 'Good God!' and replace it with, 'Right. I see. And what about you?'

He gave me the suspicion of a smile. 'I am provided for, sir.'

'Dinner' proved to be whatever I chose from an extensive menu and I decided that if my late platoon sergeant could afford to send a ruddy great car two hundred miles to fetch me, a thumping great bill for dinner, would not do him any great harm. So I went the whole hog. Gin and tonic, starters, grilled fillet steak, served with asparagus, button mushrooms and baked potatoes; all washed down by a bottle of Roederer 28. Rum-baba and liqueurs followed.

By the time I again entered the car the world in general had assumed a rosy hue and I was not all that steady on my feet. Needless to say I had sunk into a deep sleep before we had progressed another mile.

When I next surfaced the hands of my watch pointed to a quarter to nine and the car stood before an imposing flight of steps that marked the front entrance to a strange house.

Heywood Manor was not an old house; in fact it was very new and hideous to behold. Imagine a Hollywood producer's idea of a Tudor Castle built of red brick, with a few Plantagenet bastions thrown in for good measure. Then add the flight of black marble steps that terminated in a colonnaded porch.

If the exterior was eye-catching, the interior can only be described as mind-boggling. A hall lined with white pine panelling; an immense cast-iron brazier, seemingly packed solid with artificial, electric-illuminated logs, suits of oxidized-brass armour; while man-made fibre mats littered the highly polished floor, waiting to up-end the unwary visitor.

Ray received me in what was supposed to be an early Elizabethan study, shook me firmly by the hand, then pulled a flute-backed chair towards a huge dog-ironed fireplace where real logs spluttered cheerfully.

'Scotch was always your poison, dear old sir, as I remember. Help yourself from the small table on your left. Don't be put off by this awful house. My Grandfather's idea and we his descendants have been shouldering the blame ever since. By the way – I do hope the County gave you an at least passable dinner.'

'Fine,' I replied, then raised a hand when he displayed distinct signs of continuing a one-sided conversation. 'May I please ask you one or two questions?'

The slow, well-remembered charming smile lit his face. 'Which is a nice way of telling me I talk too much. Fire away – anything at all.'

'Please tell me – why on earth did you enlist as a ranker in a not very distinguished infantry regiment and content yourself with the rank of sergeant? Frankly in your shoes I'd have dodged the services altogether and remained at home to run the family business. Yours was surely a reserved occupation?'

He half filled a whisky glass and added a splash of soda, which reminded me that I had never seen him drink anything stronger than shandy-gaff when he was in the battalion, then chuckled.

'Frankly running a bloody great show like Heywood Motors, didn't appeal to me. Still doesn't. I suspect there's a touch of Lawrence of Arabia in me; I get a kick out of being ordered around. The war enabled me, at least for a time, to indulge this kinky trait, until some bloody company commander decided I was equipped to shoulder responsibility. I let them edge me up to sergeant, but I refused to go any further. Apart from anything else accepting a commission in wartime is a dodgy business. It's a well-known fact that the sniper always goes for the chap with a pip on his shoulder.'

'You pulled me out of one or two messes,' I pointed out.

He smiled again. 'Well, to be honest, there was a kind of helplessness about you that sort of twanged me heart strings. In fact the thought of you stranded to fend for yourself in Civvy Street, rather haunted me. That's why I took the trouble to find out where you were and what you were doing.'

'Not very flattering,' I objected.

'But, dear old sir, you have a gift beyond price. You bring out the best in everyone. It becomes a pleasure to help you. But you must be worn out. Let me show you to your room. There you can freshen up, then – if it so pleases you – join the family in the large drawing-room. Not in the least frightening, I do assure you. Just a wee bit pathetic.'

He jumped up – there seemed to be more nervous energy than I remembered – placed a hand on my shoulder and gently propelled me out of the room and across the atrocious hall and up a flight of stairs. My room was actually equipped with a four-poster bed that could be shut in when thick tapestry curtains were closed; and several electric lamps had been made to look like guttering candles in green enamel candle sticks. At least the bathroom which was situated to the left of the fraudulent Tudor fireplace, did not pretend to be other than it was, a fact that Ray was not slow to stress.

'Grandfather never took a bath; didn't believe in them, so all bathrooms are fairly recent extras. But, take your time. If you want anything – ring for it. The kitchens are manned practically round the clock and can cater for most tastes. The three main meals – breakfast 8.30, lunch 13.30 and dinner 18.30 are served in the dining-room. If for any reason you're late for any of 'em, not to worry. OK?'

I nodded, then managed to conjure up a 'Yes.'

'Fine. See you in the large drawing-room – second door on the left, as you leave the staircase – when you're good and ready.'

I took him at his word and soaked in the bath for at least half an hour, while pondering on the peacetime edition of Ray Heywood. The charm was still there, if more flamboyant than formerly, but the man seemed to be harder, more artificial, showing signs of strain. I could understand that running a vast business would most likely result in a personality change.

But the question slid across my brain as I chased an errant

bar of soap under pink-tinted water; had I ever known Ray Heywood? Charm is nothing more than a pleasant veil that could well be hiding a far from pleasant character and I had so admired the sergeant, I was fully prepared to accept him on face value. Come to think of it – we were all acting a role during the war. Mainly that of a coward pretending to be brave.

I dressed and went downstairs.

The large drawing-room lived up to its name, creating the impression that a small electric car would not have been out of place to convey the visitor from one wall to another. However the fifteen people present had arranged their chairs in a neat half circle, thus permitting Ray Heywood an unimpeded view of each face from his position a little to the front, where he reclined in an item of furniture that bore a passing resemblance to a throne.

He did not get up, but waved to me when I entered the room.

'There you are, dear old sir! Look here, one of you – Anne, you're the youngest, drag a chair into line.' An extremely pretty girl with a mass of blonde hair did as she was bid, but before I could be seated, Ray again raised his voice. 'This is Philip Mansfield, who used to be my platoon commander. Now he's going to do a really first class job as my PR man. It's damned silly my introducing you to this lot. You'll never remember their names. Anne of course you won't forget and Uncle George who has a glass growing out of his right hand, sort of sticks in the memory, but the rest will make themselves known when needful. Have you settled in?'

I nodded more than necessary. 'Indeed yes. Very nice.'

'Great. If you want a drink just raise the right hand. A being will glide out of the shadows and minister to your needs.'

And by turning my head I saw that there was a man attired in a white tunic and black trousers, standing by a cocktail bar, who presumably was keeping a watching brief for any raised hands. The consideration for creature comfort was so elaborate in this house as to be ridiculous.

A small man with snow-white hair and bright blue eyes, which were magnified by rimless glasses, cleared his throat before speaking.

'We have a perfectly adequate PR department, R.H. Frankly I'm rather at a loss to see where Mr Mansfield is going to fit in.'

'Philip, my dear Charles, will be my personal representative,' Ray said quietly. 'He will be answerable only to me.'

Charles – at least three of them now could be identified – created a bleak smile. 'Are we to understand Mr Mansfield's task will be to publicise your image? Glorify Raymond Heywood?'

Ray laughed gently and I could swear his eyes glittered with malicious amusement. 'Good heavens no! As you should know I dread publicity as does the snowflake the rising sun. But it so happens that I have a few ideas of my own that I would like to toss around, and prefer not to put them through the normal channel.'

Charles tilted his head and addressed the ceiling. 'As does the snowflake the rising sun. I must remember that one.'

'Herewith I give you the copyright,' Ray said gravely. 'You may sell it for what it will fetch.' He turned his head and directed a sardonic smile at a thin young man with a large nose. 'Rodney, I understand that you have been criticizing my practice of testing Saturn on the Switch-Back.'

Rodney – were they all Heywoods? – assumed an angry expression.

'It's a damned silly thing for the chairman and managing director to do. Particularly the way you do it. Weatherby says you took Saturn up to one hundred and eighty-three yesterday. You know the Switch-Back needs resurfacing. I've nothing against you killing yourself, but the Saturn is an expensive piece of machinery and I'd hate to see it go up in flames.'

Ray Heywood nodded with apparent approval. 'I do respect good honest hate. Fear not for the expensive piece of machinery. It is well insured. So is your chairman and managing director. Apart from which the engine talks to me. I will know if it's been monkeyed with.'

Rodney growled something that sounded like, 'Bloody mad,' and Anne Heywood laid a hand on my arm.

'I expect you're wondering what this is all about.'

I nodded, aware that several other voices had started what promised to be a first class row and Ray was sitting silent, his face lit by the well remembered charming smile.

Anne spoke softly in my left ear. 'Let's leave them to it and take a seat at the cocktail bar and have a well deserved drink.'

'And excellent idea.'

We left the gesticulating, arguing half circle and clambering up on to tall stools, ordered gin and tonics, which the man in the white tunic served, before taking up a position some six feet away, to continue his watch for raised hands.

Anne began to explain the situation. 'That lot can be loosely described as family. Uncles, cousins and what-have-you. I'm Ray's second cousin, my father who was his first, got himself and my mother, killed in an air raid. I hope that's clear. The point is all of us own shares in Heywood Motors, some more than others, but Ray has controlling interest. Is that right? His grandfather left him over fifty-one percent of all voting shares, which means whatever he says goes. Now, Rodney, Uncle Charles and quite a few of the others, hate him like poison.'

I said, 'I can hardly believe that. A less hatable man you will never meet.'

She nodded. 'I know what you mean. That famous charm. But when money and power are involved, charm does not always work. Also, I think that Cousin Ray gets a kick out of making some people hate him. He torments Rodney until the poor boy is glassy-eyed with shame and rage. And he does it – I know this sounds mad – so charmingly, Uncle Charles said it took him twenty minutes to realise he was being insulted.'

'Why are they sitting in a half circle?' I asked.

'Ah! I wondered when you'd ask. This is a kind of unofficial board meeting. There's one about once a week. Ray lets them blow off steam, then tells them what he intends to do. Real board meetings are very much cut and dried affairs.'

'What about this business of driving a car at breakneck speed on the – what was it? – Switch-Back?'

She widened her eyes and gripped my arm. 'You know – that place is real scary. It's just beyond Marston Wood. A real racing circuit. Grandfather Heywood built it. Both sides curve up into a fairly steep slope and way at the top, trees have grown and seem to be reaching down to grab the cars as they go past.'

'Is it much used?' I asked.

'You've heard Ray uses it to burn up the concrete with his favourite car – the Saturn. Otherwise a local racing club often ask permission to practise on it.'

It was at this point the meeting (if it could be so called) broke up and Ray made his way towards us. He raised Anne's hand to his lips and did not release it afterwards. She blushed slightly and looked up at him from under long eyelashes.

'I should imagine that my charming cousin has been putting you in the picture. Couldn't have a better instructor. She has a woman's love of gossip, married to an observant eye.' He released Anne's hand and nodded to the barman. 'Double on the rocks, Marvin. Come on you two, don't let me drink alone.'

Anne shook her head. 'Will you excuse me, Ray? I feel worn out and would love an early night.'

He did not look at her. 'As you please. Sleep well and may sexy dreams attend you.'

I think she would have stayed had he made a point of it, but as he remained motionless, she backed away, gave me an almost inaudible good night, then turned and ran towards the door. Ray spoke again.

'Would you love an early night as well?'

I gave him a tactless reply. 'As a humble employee, I can't afford to.'

His head jerked round and I stared into glacial-blue eyes. 'Don't you dare say that again. You're here because I need a friend at my back. A pack of hungry wolves are planning – are always planning damn them – to pull me down – and blast my soul – I just can't help baiting them.'

'Who ran Heywood Motors during the war?' I asked, in an effort to divert him on to a less dramatic track.

'Oh, the family headed by a couple of experts appointed by the War Office. We were making aeroplane engines, you understand. Now we're back on peacetime production, and what is more making a bid to lead the field, our potential is limitless. I'm in the hot seat. Everyone thinks they need me, but few want me.'

'I'm sure that's not true,' I said. 'There's bound to be friction in a family like yours, particularly when big business is involved. Greed and envy play hell with finer feelings. But I cannot believe everyone actively dislikes you.'

He began to laugh softly. 'Good old sir! You only knew the

sergeant who was enjoying a more than slightly dangerous holiday. Now I'm engaged in an only minutely less lethal war. And on occasion I'm forced to imitate the tiger. But you look worn out. Go to bed. Tomorrow, as Scarlett O'Hara so aptly remarked, is another day. See you at breakfast.'

He drained the glass which had been placed before him, slammed it down on the bar, then turned and walked quickly from the room.

*

The entire family were seated round the breakfast table next morning, that is to say after they had served themselves from the long sideboard, where I found three kinds of oven-warm bread, coffee, tea and chocolate, devilled kidneys, bacon, eggs and thin slices of liver; while two attentive footmen stood by to help the indecisive make a selection.

Ray sat at the top of the table, looking handsome, self-confident and in an exceptionally good mood. The same could not be said for the majority of those who slumped in straight-backed, well-padded chairs and toyed with the excellent food. Uncle Charles (surprising how that soubriquet seemed to suit him) gave me something akin to a glare when our glances met, Rodney looked as if he had had a rough night, while a fat man with a bald head, sat with closed eyes, beating out a rapid tattoo with a spoon on the table. Fortunately Anne was seated on my left and quickly identified this impromptu musician.

'That's my second cousin, once removed – I think that's right – Morris Heywood-Makepiece. He's director in charge of design and knows he's a genius. I should imagine he's having creative pains right now. If you really want to cause some excitement, tap him on the shoulder and ask him to pass the salt.'

'I wouldn't dare. Who is that oldish-young man with thinning hair, on Mr Heywood-Makepiece's left?'

She made a gurgling sound. 'What an apt description. He is oldish young, isn't he? That's Morris's son. He believes God speaks through his father's mouth.'

'Philip.' Ray Heywood's voice made me look up. 'I've a treat in store for you after breakfast. Meet me in the hall at nine-thirty. OK?'

'Right,' I said.

'I know what the treat is,' Anne whispered, 'and in your place I'd find an excuse to dodge it. He's going to drive you round the Switch-Back at something like a hundred and fifty miles an hour.'

I may have exclaimed: 'Good God!'

'Mind you,' Anne added, 'he's a great driver. I only went with him once and watching him is really weird. He does seem to become part of the car and there's a kind of mad grin on his face. I was terrified, but somehow knew there was no way that car would crash with him at the wheel.'

'I would appear to be in for an experience,' I murmured.

Anne nodded. 'I'd say yes to that. Take my tip and don't look at the speedometer or Ray. Either watch the road in front or close your eyes. Then maybe you'll hear the engine talking. I did. Sometimes it purred like a contented cat, at others it seemed to be angry, but only in the way a woman is angry with a lover who takes her for granted.'

I frowned and gave her an enquiring glance. 'You're not having me on?'

Her blonde hair danced like wind-tormented corn when she shook her head. 'No. I suppose it must have been the result of an over-excited imagination, but it seemed real enough at the time. Well, I guess you'd better go and get ready. Put on a thick pullover. There always seems to be a hell of a wind blowing over the Switch-Back.'

I took her advice and joined Ray in the hall some half an hour later wearing a polo-jersey and a thick sports jacket. He nodded his approval.

'Take care of the outer man and the inner will take care of himself. Let's get started. It's quite a walk through the woods and ... But of course you don't know what's in store. Or do you?'

'A ride in your super motor car,' I suggested.

'Of course you were sitting next to Anne, who appears to have taken a shine to you. Woman, thy name is frailty. Yes, I'm going to take you for a spin in Saturn, if, that is to say, you can trust yourself to the care of a maniac.'

'You have driven me in a jeep enough times,' I pointed out.

'Ah! A jeep! A pussy cat. Riding a lion is a different matter. At least there's no land mines on the Switch-Back.'

We were walking through a sweet-smelling pine forest, with needles crunching beneath our feet, while from some distance off came the sound of a strange cry that must have been made by some bird, or maybe an animal, but in my disturbed state, I could have sworn it was my name being called by someone in deep distress. Ray did not appear to have heard it, for presently he said:

'I doubt if Saturn will ever be put on the market. I keep adding, improving, until she's more of a racing car than a family saloon. No respectable *paterfamilias* could possibly be turned loose with such a monster. Do you know she'll edge a hundred and ninety if pressed. She doesn't like it and gives me hell, but she'll do it – maybe more.'

I looked at him with growing unease, but having decided to take whatever came my way, there seemed little point in expressing alarm. We crested an incline and began to walk down towards a fairly wide ditch that was spanned by a stout wooden bridge.

'Once we've crossed the dyke,' Ray explained, 'and surmounted that slope, we'll see the Switch-Back – or some part of it. I suppose only an eccentric billionaire like my grandfather could have afforded or wished to build such an oddity. It's not really a race track, not being wide enough, although a local club does practise on it. No, the old boy, like me, was infected by the speed bug and loved nothing better than to tear round doing his ton – that being the best he could manage in his day.'

We crossed the bridge that had a bronze plaque fixed to the left-hand rail, which had the inscription etched in black enamel: IN MEMORY OF ANTHONY RAYMOND HEYWOOD. 1859-1937 ... and Ray stopped and polished the surface with the sleeve of his jacket.

'Himself,' he said with a wry grin. 'I suppose he was a ruthless old bastard, but he was very decent to me. Called me young Navarre. Made sure I had control of the entire caboodle once I came of age, which was a year after his death in 1938. Come on – feast your eyes on the Switch-Back.'

We climbed up the furthermost slope, then descended a few yards and stopped. Yes, I know that many thousands of sensation seekers have made that journey since and looked down on that narrow stream of concrete that runs like a strip of grey ribbon along the floor of a natural valley; curving gently round into a perfect oval, but I doubt if anyone has seen it in quite the way I did on that autumn morning.

The wind chased a cloud across the sun – and a shadow that bore some resemblance to an old man with long hair, went scurrying along the Switch-Back. I thought: death looking for a victim, and hoped to hell it wouldn't be me. But that had to be pure imagination, as was the impression that the tarmac had – when viewed from a certain angle – a sinister glow. But Ray continued to guide me down the slope until we came to a flight of steps that curved down into the hillside and terminated in a vast underground and brilliantly lit room. A man attired in green overalls came out of a glass-sided cubicle and actually knuckled his forehead.

'Morning, Mr Heywood – Sir.'

Ray waved a hand between us. 'Tim Binns, who thinks he's the best mechanic in Britain – Philip Mansfield.'

I was given a grimy hand to shake and a gap-toothed grin, but not a knuckled forehead. Then he turned to Ray and asked: 'You'll be taking Saturn out this morning, Mr Heywood?'

'Yes, Tim. How is she?'

'Purring as sweet as you please. I'll not deny she's a bit frisky. Maybe try to bolt for open spaces, the second you put your foot down, but you'll know how to handle that.'

Ray murmured something that sounded like, 'Bless her,' then ordered in a normal tone of voice, 'Right, take her nightie off,' which resulted in us being led to what looked like a long, canvas-covered hump. Tim bent down and inserted his forefinger in a large ring and ran it up and over the hump, causing a zip-fastener to part, gradually revealing that unholy monstrosity – the Saturn.

The original designer (Mr Heywood-Makepiece?) may have had a super-de-luxe family saloon in mind, but it had long since passed into the realms of the fantastic. Low-slung, streamlined, certainly fitted with a wide passenger seat at the back, a transparent plastic roof, which created the impression that the entire structure might be distantly related to a jet plane. The paintwork was bright-red, that reflected and elongated my own image; rotund, jet-black tyres, the radiator edged with chrome: Saturn (who seemed to have had a sex change) suggested latent power, a downright wicked disposition and utter contempt for anyone who rode in her – with one possible exception.

'Get in,' Ray ordered. 'This is our fun period. A long work day follows.'

If there had been a choice I would have forgone the fun and started straight in on the work, but seemingly I slid on to the front passenger seat without will or effort on my part, blacked out for a few seconds, to be awakened by a terrible roar that might have come from the throats of at least six hungry tigers.

Ray Heywood sat some three feet to my right, his hands resting on a leather bound steering wheel, while he revved the engine and shouted into a small microphone that reared up from the instrument panel

'Tim, she's talking loud and clear. Not too happy about that new oil, but will take it. Stand clear – I'm going out.'

The gear lever slid into place and I became aware that we were moving slowly forward; a patch of daylight grew gradually larger; blue, green and red lights gleamed from the instrument panel – and Ray was still talking.

'You've done a fine job, Tim. She's rearing to go and hinting at all sorts of good things. Don't think she's cottoned there's a passenger aboard. May play up when she does. Right, about to greet the glad morn.'

The car gathered speed. The patch of daylight became a rectangle, then we were out on the Switch-Back; emerged from a tunnel that had been driven obliquely into the hillside. Ray allowed the engine to tick over and pointed to the scene that reared up all around us.

'Isn't that something?'

The Switch-Back curved up to a curtain of trees and bushes on the left and tall grass on the right, looking not unlike an immense gully that would have been half filled with water, were it not for the grid covered storm drains, set at regular intervals dead centre of the track and adding – in my opinion –

to the hazard of driving at very high speeds. I said so.

'If one of those grids works loose, you would really take off.'

Ray shrugged. 'So would I if a log or a tree blew down from the top. Tim drives along the track each morning looking for trouble. Anyway I always do a slow lap before opening up. So not to worry. Here we go ... '

We glided forward and the engine roared briefly until he shifted into second and top gear; then a low, sated purr that reminded one of a large and dangerous cat that is for the time being regarding its keepers with condescending favour. The 'slow lap' was done at around 45 miles per hour and I noticed that in places leaves had collected over some storm drains, but Ray did not bother to report the fact over the two way radio. Then we were back at the starting point and his voice rose to a higher pitch.

'OK, Tim – we're going for the stars.'

After a pause Tim's laconic voice replied. 'Right, sir – make sure you don't reach 'em.'

My God! Suddenly I was pushed back into my seat, the engine replaced its contented purr by a fast rising shrill scream; a roaring wind pounded on roof and windscreen; an invisible giant whose one wish was to fling us up ... up ... up and over the rim and into the forest, so that those who control the universe could truly say: 'They do not exist.'

For that was the great truth that came to me as the needle crept round the illuminated dial: Man and all his works have no place in the annals of nature. Life is life is life is life and was never intended to be planned, trimmed, have roads driven across it, flown over, delved under or even thought about. Creative dreamers often subconsciously realise this and bring to flower the seeds of self-destruction, whereas men like Ray shout their defiance to the stars.

I tore my gaze from the track that raced towards us, gave the speedometer one quick glance and noted that the needle was edging past 130 – then looked upon the face of Ray Heywood. It was transformed by a maniac's grin. Clenched teeth bared, eyes gleaming and all but bulging from their sockets, the face dead white, save for the forehead where inflated veins stood out like blue-black streaks of blood on a field of snow. Then he spoke from behind clenched teeth.

'She ... has ... promised ... me ... one ... one day ... one ... nine ... three ... '

Terror clamped an icy hand over my heart. Ray Heywood was in love with speed and the car which created it, and now that the speed was approaching one hundred and fifty miles per hour, he had become a living extension of the engine. He spoke again in that eerie harsh whisper, while the car quivered and the engine's scream rose to a higher pitch.

'No ... more ... than ... one ... nine ... three ... not ... safe ... '

So, even while under the influence of this terrible obsession, his inborn commonsense still retained a vestige of control. It told him that to drive this car beyond one hundred and ninety three would be more than just dangerous. So far as I was concerned we had been courting danger from the very moment the needle passed the 60 mile per hour mark.

Suddenly the engine cut out. All sound ceased, except for the wind which continued to buffet roof and windscreen, neither did the speed perceptively decrease, until we had glided round a curve. I shot a glance at Ray. The maniac grin had gone and was now replaced by an expression of intense annoyance.

'Damn and bloody hell! A length of wire overheated and burnt out. I could feel it go. Well, we should be able to coast back into the pits, then Tim can take over.' He looked at me and grinned. 'Sorry, old man. Bad luck for your first spin round the Switch-Back. Never mind we'll try again in a day or so.'

'If you can spare the time,' I said, silently resolving that nothing on earth would get me into that hellish machine again.

'I'll always find time for Saturn,' he replied. 'But I do appreciate she's not everyone's cup of tea. Nevertheless, my dear fellow, you've had an experience that is granted to few.' He swung the car round into the entrance. 'Remember, fear is a major emotion that has been much under-rated. Like pain it warns the body of danger, but unlike pain it can be controlled and directed into one particular channel.' He applied both foot and hand brake, then opened the side door. 'But here comes Tim looking sorry for himself.' He placed a reassuring hand on the mechanic's shoulder. 'Not to worry, Tim, Wire burnt out. Gremlins at work. Or maybe Saturn did it herself.

Perhaps dear old sir didn't suit her ladyship. You know what she's like.'

Tim helped his employer clamber from the car. I was left to manage the best I could.

'Don't you fret, Mr Heywood. I'll work on her all day and night if need be. I don't understand it. I replaced all wiring last week.'

Ray touched his nose with a pointed forefinger. 'You must listen to me, Tim. Her ladyship was put out. Now she's sulking, so you'd better put off replacing the wiring for at least twenty-four hours. Now I must push off. I want to show Mr Mansfield the watch tower, before going back to the house. Take it easy, Tim. Don't let the factory bods put on you.'

The man grinned while watching his employer through narrowed eyes. 'No fear of that, Mr Heywood.'

We walked back along the tunnel, then strolled up the track until we came to a flight of concrete steps that led to a tall wooden tower, which reared above the tallest trees. By the time we had stepped out on to a sunken path that ran through the pine forest, I was panting like a worn-out steam engine. Ray pointed to a staircase that spiralled up through the frame and finally gave access to the tower itself, that must have been at least a hundred and fifty feet above.

'I'll not ask you to climb up there, but take my word for it – from the tower you have a view of the entire Switch-Back.'

'Worth the climb, I'm sure,' I asserted without total conviction.

'And of course the surrounding countryside,' he added. 'One day, when the weather is fine, you must try it.'

I followed him out of the wood and back to the house, not at all happy with this new facet of his character. Once again I found myself comparing the sergeant with the tycoon (which I assumed he was) and not being able to match the two. Although now I came to think of it, a tycoon hiding himself in the ranks, could be interpreted as an unreasonable act, Lawrence of Arabia not withstanding.

But during the rest of the day he displayed a shrewdness and complete mastery of his business, that I could not equate with the near madman who talked to a motor car. He guided me round the vast factory and explained the intricacies of the assembly line in a language that even I could understand, and I noticed that the factory floor staff greeted his arrival with enthusiasm, and all seemed most anxious to catch his eye. The famous charm still worked with the other ranks.

I sat in on a board meeting, comprised mainly of the family group I had met the night before. But now there was a great difference. Ray Heywood became the dictator, the tyrant, whose voice took on a staccato bark and permitted no opposition to his will. The platoon sergeant in a bad mood, with a bleak look in his eye that made strong men tremble.

Then we were on our way back to dinner and I became aware that the genial host-employer, drove the Aston-Martin at a moderate speed, observed all the rules of the road and displayed no signs of communing with the engine. Instead he talked of a subject very dear to an employee's heart.

'We haven't had time to discuss your salary and perks. I was thinking of £5,000 a year, you live in the house, have full use of a company car, which means free petrol, oil and maintenance. How does that suit you?'

'Very generous,' I replied with deep sincerity. 'I can only hope I will justify your generosity.'

He spoke without removing his eyes from the road. 'In one way or another you will. Every penny. I do assure you.'

'Nothing will please me better,' I replied. 'But when do I start? Today I have been little more than a paid guest.'

The ghost of a chuckle – his eyes mocked me from the rear mirror. 'Nevertheless you have started. Your mere presence in this car is a form of employment. Sitting beside me in the dining-room and eating a dinner, has to be classified as a prodigious labour. Following me round the factory this morning, then sitting in on a board meeting, merited a fat bonus.'

'You would not care to explain all that?'

'In a short while there'll be no need. In the meanwhile concentrate on Uncle Charles and Rodney. The others growl, occasionally snap, but are comparatively harmless. Or perhaps not. One day you may have to decide who are the guilty.'

'If you feel this way about your own family,' I demanded, 'why bait them?'

'Because angry men, like drunkards, reveal more than they intend.'

He did not speak again until we were ascending the steps to the hall. Then he murmured:

'They may kill Caesar, but never still his ghost.'

The Heywoods dined in style and quantity. All the men wore dinner jackets and the women some kind of evening gown; but even Anne was not certain who everyone was. I counted forty-five people seated round the long table, all of whom seemed to be whispering or listening to, earth-shaking secrets, except for Ray, who addressed mundane remarks to me in a low voice and frowned at anyone who looked in our direction. Presently a belated light of understanding struck me. I leaned forward until our heads were only a few inches apart and spoke in a low voice.

'You want them to think I'm more important than I am. Your personal assistant, for example. Sharer of secrets.'

'Or successor,' he added. 'The dark horse who has arrived from nowhere and sits on Caesar's right hand.'

'And so takes whatever is in store for Caesar,' I murmured.

'What! Cut off the arm and leave the head still functioning! No, you are merely speeding up the action. Fear not, dear old sir, you are not of the stuff from which ghosts are made.'

Irritation made me raise my voice. 'I refuse to believe that anyone wishes to harm you physically. You're more likely to kill yourself in that car.'

It was uncanny. All conversation died along the table, all faces were turned in our direction, eyes seemed to glitter with anticipation, but only Uncle Charles spoke.

'Quite right. If you have any influence with the wretched fellow, make him blow that dreadful contraption up. It will never be a commercial proposition and will sooner or later reach for the sky.'

'That car will never kill me,' Ray said slowly and loudly, as though intending to etch his words on every brain present. 'Unless she's interfered with. Do you understand? If I die in Saturn, it will be because someone has got past Tim and buggered about with the most foolproof car in the world.'

Uncle Charles lowered his head in actual or pretended embarrassment, and I thought – if they want to get rid of him, there will be no need for murder – and Ray creased his face into a smile and went on in a quieter tone of voice:

'Not that I am expecting anyone to be so foolhardy, particularly anyone at this table.' The smile broadened. 'And I do not expect to be taken seriously after downing half a bottle of old claret.'

Anne who was seated on my left, whispered, 'The retainers don't give a damn. But don't let it worry you, nothing is for real in this house. Outside – maybe.'

I turned my head and looked down into her blue eyes. 'Explain that. Who are the retainers? Why is nothing for real in this house?'

She shook her head. 'I don't know. Wine wisdom. I take it in with every glass. Wait a minute while I grab a few strands of reality from a mountain of phantasy. You and I must be real, because we respond to each other. Ray must be real because without him this entire structure would fall to pieces. But the others ... ? I wouldn't be too sure. I mean – take another glass of wine, close your eyes and wait for the roaring darkness to quieten down, then blink three times – and there's only shadows sitting at this table. Plus the retainers.'

'Again I ask ... ?'

'Thin men who dine off the crumbs dropped from a rich man's table. Jobbers, service men, beggars in dinner jackets. They expect a thousand pound tip and considerably more for special services rendered. But such creatures could not swear to their own reality, let alone those who employ them.'

'You are straying beyond the frontiers of credibility,' I protested.

'Good wine is no judge of reality. Neither am I.'

Ray leaned over and laid a none too steady arm on my arm.

'Is my beautiful, second cousin soused? Pickled? Looking at the world through a glass of red wine?'

Anne giggled and whispered in my ear. 'If tonight were tomorrow night – then he wouldn't be here.'

'Not exist?' I asked.

She shook her head very slowly. 'Oh, yes. Ray will always exist – in one form or another.'

*

If a tipsy Anne meant what I think she meant – then she was wrong. Ray gave me a guided tour round two subsidiary factories the following day, ate his dinner that night and so far as I knew slept peacefully in his own bed.

But his confidence that the Saturn would never kill him, proved to be entirely misplaced. Having, the next morning, reached a speed that Tim maintained was somewhere over one hundred and ninety miles per hour, it suddenly swerved, turned over several times, then exploded into roaring flames. The remains of my one time platoon sergeant, which for some reason I was asked to identify, were most horrible to look at and impossible to equate with a former, handsome and healthy body.

The entire family, retainers, servants and hangers-on, all, expressed and displayed signs of deep grief, and one might have supposed that the deceased had never been regarded with other than respect and affection during his lifetime. The inquest, presided over by an urbane coroner, who Anne informed me was a distant connection of the family, passed smoothly, while witness after witness, testified or suggested, that Ray had died trying to ensure that Heywood Motors turned out the best and safest cars in the world.

I was prepared to pack my bags and depart immediately after the cremation, but the reading of Ray's will, or rather a codicil that had been signed the day before his death, brought about a change of mind.

Having insured against death duties, he left fifty-two percent of voting shares, divided between Anne, Tim and myself. Anne also inherited the house and half a million. Tim was requested to remain at his present post and maintain both the Switch-Back and the Saturn. I thought that he had been relieved of the latter duty, which surely made nonsense of the first. But when I spoke to him on the subject, he shook his head.

'Mr Ray wanted me to remain here for a purpose, and remain here I will. That business of me owning those voting shares don't mean a thing. I'll make you my proxy and you can use it to vote anyway you please.'

'But what on earth will you do with yourself all day?' I asked. 'There's no Saturn for you to maintain now.'

'There's other cars the factory like to try out here and I usually give 'em the once over, after the mechanics have done their worst. Then there's Model T which the racing club is hoping to perform wonders with, one day. My time will be well-occupied.'

Mine certainly was. I had not the slightest idea how to run a great company, and although with Tim's proxy and Anne's backing, I could have dominated the board if I so wished, there was little point when I did not know what to dominate it for. Uncle Charles offered to buy my shares for a respectable sum and why I hesitated is still a matter for serious conjecture, because my one and only ambition was to salt away enough money, so I need never face that foul evil called work again. Maybe I entertained some hope that the offer would be increased if I hesitated, or an even better one would come from another quarter.

Then one evening I received a telephone call from Tim.

He spoke in a low, rather tremulous voice. 'Could you come down to the Switch-Back early tomorrow morning, sir?'

I said, 'What do you call early?'

'Just after six. When it gets lightish.'

'If it's important I do so – OK. Care to tell me what it's all about?'

I could hear his breathing and it sounded quick and shallow, like that of a man who is under some intense excitement. Then he said, 'Not now, if you don't mind. Just be here early tomorrow and I'll explain then.'

He had used an internal phone, so there was no dialling tone when he hung up, just complete silence. But I slammed the receiver down, for suddenly there was a feeling that if I held it to my ear for one second longer, another voice would have spoken.

I did not sleep well that night.

*

A cold wind blew through the pine wood and over the Switch-Back when I arrived a few minutes after six next morning, and slowly descended the curving steps to that vast, brightly lit underground space. Tim was waiting in his little, glass-sided office.

'Cup of coffee ready, sir. Get it down, because we're going up to the watch tower and it'll be mighty cold up there.'

I half emptied the mug he gave me. 'Not me. I've no head for heights.'

He shook his head slowly. 'I don't think you understand. Mr Heywood is back on the Switch-Back. Driving the old Saturn – doing all of a hundred and ninety.'

I stared at him goggle-eyed for some little while, before saying: 'Don't talk such utter rot, man.'

He went on as though I had not spoken. 'Started two days ago. I saw Mr Ray in the Saturn, crouched over the wheel – that funny look on his face – and Lord Almighty – it was all so real. And Mr Mansfield, you've got to come up into the tower where you can see the entire track, and see for yourself.'

I was frightened – terrified – and therefore angry. I shouted, 'Being down in this place for years on end has cracked you, man. The Saturn finished up as a heap of twisted metal and Mr Ray – two handfuls of ash.'

When he next spoke it was with a voice that a parent might use to a backward child. 'That I well know, sir. And I also know I've seen Mr Heywood twice, driving the Saturn along the Switch-Back. Just one lap. Then he disappears – car and all. And you – and maybe Miss Anne – must see him too. Or I'll really go crazy, for this is not the kind of thing a man can keep to himself.'

I clasped shaking hands to my forehead. 'I don't want anything to do with this ridiculous business. I came here because Ray asked me to and I knew that whatever the job was he'd do all the thinking, because he always had. Then I found myself being used as a front man in a particularly vicious family war. Now … '

'Mr Ray wants to tell you something very important, sir,' Tim said gently. 'I think he's tried to reach you in other ways, but only him driving Saturn full out will work. So you come along with me, sir, for he'll soon be doing that one fast lap.'

I shook my head violently. 'No, I can't. If what you say is true, then that's one more reason. I haven't the strength to look upon a ghost.'

Anne came into the office and kissed Tim gently on one cheek, then smiled at me. 'Yes you have, Philip. You'll be surprised. When Tim told me – only you and me – I was terrified and felt just like you. Then I knew that if I didn't come and see for myself, I'd be passing up an unique experience. And that's life isn't it? Experience. Taken often and in small doses.'

'But someone you have known ... '

'Ray was of the stuff from which ghosts are made. He knew it, so did I and you must have sensed it. And a friend in life, is surely not less a friend in death. So, come along and try to enjoy your unique experience.'

She took me by the hand while Tim slipped the strap of a pair of binoculars over his head. 'You have a way with words, Miss Anne. Always had. There's no doubt that you're the man of the family, now Mr Ray's gone.'

'But not departed,' she said, tightening her grip on my hand. 'Let's hurry. We've got that awful ladder thing to climb yet.'

I remembered and started to protest. 'But I've no head for heights and ... '

'Neither have I,' Anne confessed cheerfully, 'but you'll be surprised how curiosity overcomes fear.'

Again she was wrong. My fear was too great to be overcome by anything, while my curiosity was absolutely nil. I cannot believe there ever has been a more frightened man on this planet, than the one who started to climb that awful spiral staircase, which in due course – after much prodding and encouragement from Anne – arrived up and out on to an open-sided observation cabin. Fortunately it had a waist high wooden wall on all sides and a gabled, shingled roof, which gave it at least the illusion of security, even if the entire structure did sway in the wind.

Tim placed what I am certain was meant to be a reassuring hand on my hand and shouted: 'See the entire Switch-Back ... a large oval curved out of the lower slopes. But we've only got a downward view, but when Saturn takes the curves, she – Ray – will mount the slope ... then you have a brief view through the side window.'

I nodded, being very conscious that I was beset by three fears. That the wind might blow me over the low wall; the climb down again; the spectral appearance of Ray and his car. I believe there was the thought that if the latter proved too much for me, I could always close my eyes.

I may have adopted this excellent idea, for suddenly I was looking down on what seemed to be a toy car with a transparent roof, that raced along the track, presumably without sound, although that may have been smothered by the wind, knowing that Tim was attempting to thrust a pair of binoculars into my hands. Time was wasted while I fumbled to get the damned things adjusted to my eyes, then finding the car (which I was not all that keen to do); the rear wheels of which kept sliding into my line of vision, then out again: eventually I had the entire thing captured in a moving frame, albeit only for a short while.

Taking the curve, so that he was half way up the slope, and I could see him so plainly he might have been only a few feet away, crouched over the steering wheel, then he turned ... He did indeed ... turned his face in my direction ... and there was the maniac's grin, but it could well have been a dead man's grimace. And oh my God! I knew he was looking at me.

Then I jerked the binoculars from my eyes and I believe there was the muffled sound of a crash, but Tim insisted on shouting in my ear: 'Did you see him? Did you see him?'

I was incapable of making a coherent reply and presently Anne and Tim somehow got me down to ground level.

*

A sense of duty is a dreadful burden.

More cruel, distasteful and stupid actions are committed in the name of duty, than any sensible man would deem possible. I was reared on a mental diet of Lord Nelson, Florence Nightingale, Captain Oates and that stupid little wretch who stood on a burning deck, and hence have a very strong sense of duty. After my hair-raising experience in the watch tower, it gave me no peace.

It reasoned that Ray had given me a job when I most needed one, had left me what amounted to a lot of money, and had trusted me. Now it would seem – if Tim was to be believed – he wanted to contact me and would continue to drive that ghost car over one lap on the Switch-Back, until I did something about it.

Anne expressed an opinion that reinforced that put forward

by my sense of duty. 'If I had to guess, I'd say Ray is trying to tell you, or someone, that the accident was no accident. Also, who did the dirty on him. Maybe not, but you or someone should try to find out. If he really wants to contact you, I mean.'

I sighed deeply. 'So do I. I was rather hoping you would talk me out of it.'

'I would like to, but I don't think I really should.'

I thought deeply for a few minutes before coming to a decision. 'There's no way anyone is going to get me up in that tower again, apart from which it is far too high for a good look at the driver. Not that I am all that keen to have a close view of him, but if some kind of contact is to be made, he's got to be – well – near.'

Anne nodded. 'True. But how will you go about it? Stand on the track?'

I shuddered. 'God forbid. No, I was thinking that perhaps Tim could find me a viewpoint just above and facing down the track. Then I'll have ... ' I could not continue for I suddenly realised exactly what I would have – a full view of that ghastly face, every detail revealed as it drew nearer, complete with its dead man's grimace.

Anne sensed my horror and squeezed my hand. 'Seeing is not all that bad. Touching is so much worse. We'll go down this afternoon and see Tim.'

Tim nodded when I explained what was needed. 'Easy enough to give you a little bay on the straight run to the first curve. Even so you'll only have the Saturn in view for about ten seconds. Best sighting will be when he passes you. For two seconds you'll only be about six feet apart. Miss Anne, if you're going along, how about taking a movie camera with you.'

'Absolutely not,' I interrupted. 'I want no ghoulish record of this awful business. If that is Ray out there, I want him to let me know who and how, then sheer off. Then I will spend the rest of my life trying to forget.'

'You're right, of course,' Tim agreed. 'And I don't suppose anything would have shown up on the film. I understand that ghosts don't as a rule. Anyway I will get some blokes busy building the bay. I don't suppose it'll be ready in time for tomorrow morning. May have to wait until the day after.'

'Make it as quick as you can,' I replied. 'I'd like to get this business over in the shortest possible time.'

'It's not entirely in my hands,' Tim replied. 'I can't guarantee Mr Ray will run every morning. He missed yesterday for example, but was there this morning. I'll ring you when everything's ready.'

*

Somehow the story got out. Looking back I realise it was nigh impossible to keep such a phenomenon a secret. The woods were open to the public and any number of people could have been looking down on the Switch-Back, when Ray did his post-death lap. Including someone from the big house.

Uncle Charles approached me that evening and asked a direct question.

'What's all this about Ray haunting the Switch-Back?'

I swallowed – how the hell do you know? – just in time, shrugged and said: 'So – it's started already! Bound to happen. What is he supposed to do? Walk down the centre of the track, looking for his car?'

Charles looked at me through narrowed eyes. 'No. Drive the Saturn one lap, then disappear. Early in the morning.'

'Well, I've been down on the Switch-Back for the past two mornings and damned if I saw him. Oh, come on, surely you don't believe in ghosts.'

He said, 'No, of course not. But I can't help wondering why you were out there at sunrise. Not a pretty view at this time of year.'

'Maybe I was looking for a ghost that never appeared. Strange, no matter how much one may jeer at such a story, there's always a faint hope that it might be true.'

He nodded. 'That's a fact. Then you'd say it's not worth my while getting up for an early trudge through those woods?'

'Most certainly not.'

He laid a hand on my shoulder. 'Then I'll stay in bed and leave ghost hunting to more enterprising types like you.'

There was a supercilious grin on his face when he turned away and walked quickly down the corridor. I wasted no time in telephoning Tim.

'Have you started to build that bay yet?'

'No. Getting the men ... '

I spoke quickly. 'Don't. There isn't time. The story about Ray haunting the Switch-Back is already making the rounds. Charles Heywood was thinking of going out there. In two days the place will be cluttered up with sightseers.'

His voice was unnecessarily loud when he spoke.

'What do you suggest, sir? Call the entire thing off?'

I sighed deeply. 'I'd love to, but I can't. It's as though Ray is beside me, trying to make contact. Is there another car you can lay hands on that will better one hundred and ninety miles an hour?'

'Yes. The model T. It's a racing car that belongs to the Brightfield Racing Club. I've got it here under wraps. Why?'

I hesitated, because of what I proposed to do, could result in either loss of life or sanity, but the spine-chilling idea was deeply embedded in my brain and refused to be dislodged. I cleared my throat.

'There's only one quick solution. Go out on the Switch-Back and match him speed for speed – so we're driving side by side.'

The ensuing silence was eventually broken by Tim's rasping voice. 'Good God, man! Have you ever driven at near two hundred miles an hour? A moment's inattention – such as being distracted by something coming up on your off-side – and you'll follow Mr Heywood's lead – go up and over. One ghost car is enough.'

I shouted: 'Do you suppose I want to go out there? My bowels heave at the very thought. But I've go to. Do you understand? Bloody well got to.'

A few seconds later he spoke in a calmer voice. 'You'd better come out here so we can talk this over. And bring Miss Anne with you. At least she'll be dead against this.'

'And so am I. But I'm still going to do it.'

*

To this day I remember very little of my third journey to the Switch-Back, due I suppose to my brain refusing to consider the suicidal action I was proposing to take. I really only came back to full awareness when Anne guided me into Tim's office.

He spoke to Anne. 'Have you talked him out of it?'

'How could I? He hasn't said a word to me since we left the house.'

He turned to me. 'Look, sir, I'm old enough to be your father, so I'll speak plainly. You have much to be thankful for. You came through the worst war in history unscathed, are blessed with the three treasures that should guarantee happiness, health, wealth and youth. Now you're planning to put the lot into the melting pot. If Mr Ray were here he'd say the same.'

'But is he saying the same now? It seems to me that he is leaving me no option but to go out there and match his speed. As I see it, that must be the only way he can tell me – in one way or another – who was responsible for that crash.'

Tim thought for a long time before replying. 'If someone tinkered with that car without me knowing, then only God knows how they did it. I checked everything from tyres up before Mr Ray went out. The track itself was dry. Surely the truth is he asked too much from Saturn. She was never intended to do more than a hundred and twenty. It was his added improvements that made the extra speed possible.'

'Then why is Ray haunting the track? Before he died he kept hinting that someone was after him and for my money, that some one succeeded. If I've got to take a bit of a risk to find out who the bastard is, then I'd be all kinds of yellow rat if I didn't take it.'

'God protect a grateful man,' Tim murmured.

'Philip,' Anne said quietly, 'don't imagine that you owe Ray anything. He was using you, as he used everyone. You were brought here to frighten the family. With your arrival came rumours of a take-over bid, a merger. Only Ray himself really knew what he intended to do.'

Tim creased his forehead into a frown. 'I liked and admired him more than any other person I have ever known. But frankly, looking back, I think he was a bit mad.'

'Shall we take a look at this car?' I suggested. 'The one you call Model T.'

Tim sighed and led the way out of the office and across the expanse of concrete to a wide bay where a racing car stood. It had four immense tyres, a slender, but long radiator, a wide cockpit and a chassis that tapered off into the likeness of a fish's tail. Tim walked round this mechanical marvel, then looked at me with a wolfish grin. He spoke with the voice of an aggressive stranger:

'This baby has at least twelve tigers packed in under her cowling, that most reluctantly obey a driver who knows what he's doing and has years of experience to back him up. If a greenhorn attempts to do more than sixty – they slaughter him. Now, how much experience have you got in driving a contraption like this?'

I considered the question for a few minutes.

'About two years. Two prewar years of course and I never clocked anything like two hundred. Around one twenty, but that was on a crowded track and I was always scared stupid. I should add my father was Sir James Mansfield and he was the best teacher ever.'

Tim looked at me with renewed interest. 'Ah! That makes a difference. The son of Britain's one time speed king should have an even chance. I would suggest you and I go out for a trial run. No dramatic speed, not with me aboard, but just to get you used to the car and her funny little ways, to say nothing of the track itself.'

'I suppose there's no chance ... ?' I began.

'He only makes one lap on the day he appears. So far as I can judge he comes into being – going full out – anything from five minutes to seven and five minutes past. I suppose there must be a reason for the fluctuation in time, but I can't imagine what it can be.'

'What do I do?' Anne asked.

'There's a small army walkie-talkie by the entrance, and I've rigged up another in the car. Both are tuned in for mutual broadcast and reception, but I'd like to try them out when the car is in motion. You can man the one at this end.'

I put a driving helmet on, then climbed in behind the steering wheel and started the engine. It had been a long time since I had driven a racing car and despite my brave words, the prospect of pushing this roaring monster up to a hundred and ninety odd miles an hour, made my blood run cold. I did not even think of what would be alongside should this bizarre experiment be successful.

Tim settled into the seat beside me, wearing a helmet

equipped with earphones; then the Model T roared up the slope towards that patch of daylight, and I felt like a man astride a horse that would throw him whenever it so wished. Once out on the track I felt a little more confident, for there was a seemingly unending stream of grey concrete ahead, with gently curving slopes on either side, and here were no walls to extravagate the build-up of speed. Tim shouted a warning:

'There's no need to risk your life twice or mine once. Just keep her down to a civilized speed and get the feel of the car and track.'

I did three laps at an average sixty-five and was beginning to enjoy myself when Tim nudged my elbow.

'That's enough,' he shouted. 'Take her in. I've got to work on this radio. Nothing is getting through.'

I completed the next lap before gliding into the entrance, remembering that hair-raising ride in the Saturn with Ray; the day he said, 'I'll always find time for the Saturn,' and 'OK, Tim, we're going for the stars,' yet denying that he would ever do that.

I braked to a halt well within the vast underground room and switched off the engine, then slid from behind the steering wheel and joined Tim who had made a much faster exit. We both waited for Anne who was staggering under the weight of a portable walkie-talkie.

'Fine old mess-up,' she complained. 'I've been out there twisting knobs and yelling my head off and not one intelligent word did I get out of the thing.'

'I did ask you to leave the knobs alone,' Tim protested gently. 'No wonder I couldn't get reception.'

'But your voice was so faint and I thought that a slight adjustment would put it right, but all I got was that sound of frying eggs.'

I interrupted what threatened to become a pointless argument.

'Anne, put the set down on the car bonnet. I've some experience of these things and can usually get them to work.'

This was pure showing off, for although I had been sent on a RT course, I had forgotten almost everything I had been taught. However, I turned one knob from left to right, was rewarded by a roar of static, dimly aware that Tim was adjusting the car model in a like manner. Suddenly we all heard a voice that seemed to be trying to make itself audible over the static, or perhaps it would be more accurate to say through it. Extremely faint, even though at times I got the impression it was shouting, we gradually deciphered what seemed to be a series of numbers.

'I make it out to be zero ... seven ... zero ... five,' Tim said.

'Nine,' Anne corrected. 'I'd swear the last number is nine.'

'Must be a private code,' I suggested.

Tim shook his head. 'But it's on our wave length and co-ordinate numbers. Listen to him. Seems to be doing his nut. Adjust your set one degree to the left.'

Scarcely had I obeyed this instruction than both sets sent out a veritable bedlam of sound; static roared like a vast crowd of enraged football supporters – and through it came the distinct tone of Ray's voice.

'Philip ... tomorrow ... zero ... seven ... zero ... five.'

My name and the four numbers were repeated three times, before that well remembered voice and the static faded away, to be replaced by complete silence. Tim depressed the on-off switch several times.

'I'd say,' he said quietly, 'all the valves have blown.'

'What did it mean?' Anne whispered.

'Ray will put in an appearance at five minutes past seven tomorrow morning,' I replied with praiseworthy calmness. 'But why he couldn't have given us a straightforward message, is beyond me. Name some names, for example.'

'I'm not up on ghosts,' Tim confessed, 'but my sister who is a regular sitter in the Hoxley Circle, told me that communication is very difficult and a spirit is very lucky if he or she gets a few words over. And they make sense.'

'But I have still to risk my neck tomorrow morning,' I protested. 'But at least we now know exactly when he will come into being.'

'Take a bit of working out,' Tim said thoughtfully. 'You've got to remember he – I don't know how to put this – starts at a hundred and ninety odd miles an hour. You must be doing that, or faster, to draw level. So ... '

'Can you do your sums later?' Anne asked. 'Philip, if you must do this, at least take Tim with you.'

'The answer to that one, is no,' Tim stated firmly. 'As I said before, I respected and liked Mr Heywood when he was alive, but I've no intention of getting a close-up view of him now he's dead, particularly in a car driven by someone who must be unbalanced to even consider such a project anyway. Sorry to speak so plainly, sir, but that's the truth.'

'Then you drive the car,' Anne insisted.

I raised a protesting hand. 'Hold it. This is strictly a two man show. Tim and me. Anne, I don't even want you anywhere near the track. Where will you be, Tim?'

'Up in the watch tower. From there I can give you the tip over the radio, the moment he comes into sight.'

'You can't stop me watching,' Anne stated. 'I'll be up in the watch tower with Tim and God help him if he tries to stop me. I'll maintain an icy calm, even if you're spread all over the track.'

I kissed her gently. 'Don't worry. Nothing will happen. Ray always looked after me, particularly when I was technically in the driving seat. Now that I will be in fact, should fully arouse his protective instinct.'

'Yes, if what comes into being out there is Ray Heywood as we knew him.'

I shrugged. 'None of us are as we were at the last meeting.'

*

I did not go down to dinner that night, not being in a mood to dine among those who were fast coming to the conclusion I was nothing more than a sheep well worth shearing. Even now I can only surmise what Ray's plans for me had been, if indeed my role was to be other than that of morale booster, but the fact remains that once he was dead, his former associates soon lost whatever apprehension my initial appearance had caused.

Surprisingly I slept well that night, although next morning I felt tired, drained of energy and a great disinclination to face the ordeal which awaited me. As I walked through the woods, this grew into something not far short of a waking nightmare; my imagination presenting a trailer of the main event, in which I drove the car at a suicidal speed, while a thing that had little in common with the Ray Heywood that I had known, leered at me through the side window.

Tim remarked on my appearance the moment I set foot in his office. 'You look dreadful. Why not call the entire thing off? That will make Miss Anne happy.'

'No way,' I said brusquely. 'Where is she?'

'Up in the watch tower, sitting on a walkie-talkie. I insisted. Down here she would have created a scene, which is the last thing you want. Now, there's not all that time to spare, so sit you down and I'll explain the layout as I see it.'

I sank into a chair and accepted a cup of steaming coffee which he pushed across the table.

'Mr Ray giving us the exact time he's due to appear will be a great help. If – that is to say – that is what he intended those list of numbers to mean. We know he comes into being immediately outside the entrance to that tunnel at around one hundred and ninety miles per hour. The Switch-Back is just under three miles long, so the entire lap will take something under a minute. Ample time to get killed in, but not a great deal to successfully drive a car full out, while trying to hold a conversation with a man who has been dead for over a week. Do you get my point?'

'Clearly,' I said.

'So, you must draw level with him in the quickest possible time, which means – and hear this – allowing one minute to build up speed, another two point seventy-five to reach the entrance – and by the grace of God and me risking my neck in testing these bloody and possibly quite wrong calculations – you'll be driving side by side from the very beginning.'

'You've been testing the car out there on the Switch-Back?' I asked. 'Despite all you said?'

He nodded. 'There can only be a spoonful of sanity between us. But please understand this. No more after this morning. This must be the one and only trip. Find out what Mr Ray wants – or give up.'

'You have my promise. But tell me this – how will I communicate?'

He removed the empty coffee cup. 'If I get you out there on time, doing the right speed, then my job's done. Spooky intercourse is yours. Right – let's get you ready.'

I know very little about what makes men act as they do, why the habitual coward suddenly masters his fear, but I do know that as Tim helped me to put on padded jacket and trousers, rubber boots and finally the gleaming helmet, I no longer cared what happened to me out there on the Switch-Back. But I was most anxious to meet whatever fate that was reserved for me, and – so to speak – get it over.

Once I was behind the steering wheel, Tim plugged in two leads to a built-in radio and explained how it worked.

'The microphone is fitted to the lower part of your helmet, so all you have to do is speak. The earphones are all but covering your ears – so just listen. By six-fifty I'll be up in the watch tower with Miss Anne. When – whenever anything appears, I'll notify you and give location. Right?'

I adjusted the goggles and gave him an idiotic grin.

'Right.'

I knew he never really expected to see me alive again, and if it had been possible for me to give the matter any coherent thought, I would not have expected him to see me alive again. Yet, I could not wait to get out on the Switch-Back. The car roared along the tunnel and I really believe that if I had closed my eyes, some instinct would have steered it towards that patch of grey light. A glance at the illuminated clock told me the time was six-fifty-three, which meant I had twelve minutes to do a practice lap, then gradually build up speed so as to be doing around one ninety at the right place and the right time.

The Model T glided out of the tunnel and on to the track; became a vigorous animal hungry for speed; snarled impatiently when I changed gear, then leapt forward when my left foot touched the accelerator. Tim's voice admonished me.

'No need to go mad. Keep her down to under forty until I give the word. I may say it's bloody cold up here and Anne sends you her love.'

That distorted, but still familiar voice, was oddly comforting, creating the illusion that I was no longer alone and whatever horror came to me, would be shared by two companions. I completed one circuit of the track, had passed the entrance, before Tim spoke again.

'Take her up into the eighties. Gradually – there's plenty of time.'

I again glanced at the clock. The hands now pointed to two minutes past seven. Three minutes to the moment of truth – if we had translated Ray's figures correctly. The car seemed to rejoice when the speedometer needle began to creep round the dial, for the engine raised its voice to a triumphant scream, the tyres hummed a gay, if a tuneless song, that changed into a shriek of rapture when we (the car and I) mounted the slope to swing round a curve.

'Up to a hundred and beyond,' Tim's voice filled my head. 'Ease her up ... faster ... faster ... you're doing fine. Two minutes to zero. When you reach one-two-zero – hold it.'

My body merged into the quivering car, my hands became an extension of the steering wheel, and under, in front and over me was a terrible, but exhilarating power that might kill, but would never destroy.

Tim's voice again. 'It's now or never. If now – then go full out. Ram your foot down ... that's it ... Be prepared to cut slightly ... '

I dare not remove my gaze from the track in front, for the car had become a shrieking monster that seemed to be only just resisting an urge to overturn; and what was the point of Tim shouting: 'Not so high – keep on the lower slope,' when the power was in charge – not I?

'You're on the home track ... entrance coming up ... look out for HIM ... too fast ... five seconds too fast ... '

The tunnel entrance flashed by and I had started the essential lap, when Tim's voice all but blew my ear drums in.

'He's right behind you ... left hand down, cut speed ... *He's Right Behind You.*'

The earphones went dead and I became aware of movement just beyond the off-side window; a gradual merging into view of a bright-red bonnet: and – Oh God! I did not want to turn my head to the right, for only He and possibly Tim knew what speed I was making, and no man would wish to see what was crouched over the steering wheel. But I could not resist fearful temptation; a momentarily change of view point; and I saw him ... I did ... I did ...

Face, dead white, looking at me, wearing the maniac's grin, teeth bared, eyes bulging, deep lines carved round the mouth and nose. A facsimile of a mask created by death? The ghost of a corpse? Ray Heywood himself occupying a do-it-yourself body? One theory is as good as another, but that brief glimpse was enough to make the hair stand up on the back of my neck – what followed will haunt me for the rest of my days.

Static crackled in the earphones and through it came Ray's voice; speaking slowly, conveying a hint of mockery:

'What you lack in brains, Philip, you make up in guts.'

I had read somewhere that no one has yet held a conversation with a ghost. I had assumed that was because the ghost for some reason always remained silent; it had not occurred to me that the live one – the seer – might be incapable of speech. I think my vocal cords were frozen by fear, the rest of me being engaged in keeping the car on a straight line and negotiating curves. That voice went on.

'Did you imagine that someone had tinkered with Saturn and sent me up and over? I told you that was impossible. She would have told me. No, I fooled them all. I sent myself up and over.'

I must have drawn slightly ahead, for suddenly I saw his face looking at me from the rear mirror. I might have screamed had any kind of vocal action been possible. The voice became a harsh whisper.

'Lonely in life – lonely in death. Badly need friend in life – even more badly needed in death. Besides – you mustn't hurt the family. Mad in life – sane in death.'

We were rushing towards the final curve and the face in the mirror was even more hideous to behold; now a blank white mask lit by ice-cold eyes.

'Philip – it is so easy. When you mount the curve – keep going up – leap towards the stars. I will help you. Help ... '

The bright red bonnet drew level again and I knew he was looking at me from behind his steering wheel; head turned to the left, that terrible cold glare bridging the distance between us. I mounted the slope as we began to race round the curve, dimly aware that the tunnel entrance lay a mere half a mile ahead, so the spectral lap must soon come to an end.

But the red mudguards were coming nearer and I automatically swerved to the left, went a little higher up the slope, and when I jerked my head right, tried to send him a look of silent appeal, those eyes were dead – dead as those of a fish on a fishmonger's slab.

The tyres screamed and the car shuddered and I must have

been seconds away from that death he wished for me, when Tim's voice exploded in the earphones: 'Right hand down – steer into him.'

Possibly it was the sound of that familiar voice that saved me, although what it said should have been a deciding factor, but I am certain had that brief instruction been uttered by anyone else, I would have been incapable of following it.

The red car with its transparent roof was crowding mine and I almost imagined I could hear teeth-jarring grinding of metal, when with a mighty effort of will, I turned the steering wheel to the right; sent the car hurtling down to the track below, there to spin round several times as I frantically applied the brakes. The fact I did not turn over must be classified as a minor miracle, but so far as I was concerned, the moment it shuddered to a stop, black oblivion took me into its kindly embrace and I temporarily lost interest in ghost cars and whatever drove them.

*

I took Anne's hand in mine and Tim stared intently at the Model T that stood a few feet beyond the glass walls of his office.

'Ray must have been suffering from some kind of persecution complex,' I said. 'He most probably did believe that certain members of the family were plotting his death, but would do it in such a way they would never be implicated. By beating them to it, after making a public statement to the effect that if he died on the Switch-Back it would be because someone had interfered with the Saturn – it was intended to bring dire suspicion down on those who were guilty by intent.'

'But no one assumed that his death was other than an accident,' Anne pointed out.

'One person did. Me. The not very bright platoon commander who could always be controlled. Advised. Instructed. My role was that of prosecutor. Stoker of the fires of suspicion. And it would have worked too, had he not started to haunt the Switch-Back.'

Tim turned his head and looked at me with a certain grudging respect. 'Why did he do that?'

I smiled grimly. 'It would appear that death cures all ills.

Mad in life – sane in death. He said so. Freeze the ego that has just formed an irrevocable purpose. Get me out on the Switch-Back and kill me before I could harm a single member of the family. Such is the fruit of sanity. But I can understand why he wanted a friend. He will be very lonely for a very, very long time.'

'You mean we haven't seen the last of him?' Tim asked.

I smiled again and ignored Anne's shudder.

'I should imagine that many people will see the ghost of Ray Heywood in all sorts of places.'

*

Time has proved me right. My suggestion that the Switch-Back be destroyed, was disregarded, so stories – true or otherwise – of Ray driving the Saturn at unbelievable speeds, usually at sunset or sunrise, abound. But he is not confined to the Switch-Back. Report has him terrifying local residents as he races silently along country lanes, or, causing a nasty accident on the M1 motorway.

He has also been seen on foot. At least three independent witnesses have told hair-raising accounts of meeting him in the pine forest, presumably on his way to the Switch-Back; all testified to the dreadful grin that appeared to be etched on his face.

I was amused to see that the television people have taken an active interest in the affair and actually planted a camera in the watch-tower – now built of reinforced concrete – where a commentator waffled away for half an hour, relating the more lurid tales, promising to break off when – and if – Ray appeared in his mechanical apparition. Regretfully my one-time platoon sergeant and friend did not oblige.

However, I can but hope that this account will reach a sufficiently large audience to kill those scurrilous tales that have grown up round the name of Ray Heywood over the years. The worst being, in my opinion, the one allegedly based on confidential information (whatever that might mean), that he committed suicide because of unspecified crimes that were about to be brought home to him. It was a bad government that first decided a dead man could not be libelled or slandered.

I will close on one more interesting point. I went to see Tim just before his death last year and it was he who brought up the matter of Ray Heywood and the stories which had caused us so much distress. Presently, to keep the conversation alive, more than anything else, I said:

'To this day I haven't understood how I came to drive a great racing car at near two hundred miles per hour. Particularly when one remembers what was coming up on my near side.'

Tim chuckled. 'You never reached anything like two hundred. In fact I'd be surprised if you clocked much over a hundred. And when I told you over the air that Ray was just behind you, he seemed to deliberately slow down so as to draw you both back to something under eighty.'

'Then he tried to kill me.'

Tim shook his head. 'I don't think so – not now. The purpose of the exercise was to panic you and me. He wanted you to kill him – again. When you swerved into the Saturn it turned over and burst into flames – before disappearing. One could say you killed a ghost.'

'Then what the hell is it that goes roaring down the Switch-Back and other places? Are all these stories the result of over-heated imagination?'

Tim grinned impishly. 'Not necessarily. What everyone now sees is a ghost of a ghost.'